FIND ME
on the ice

PRU SCHUYLER

For anyone who has ever been forced to question their own thoughts and mind because of some abusive, narcissistic asshole.

You are incredible, and I'm so proud of you.

PLAYLIST

"Mr. Forgettable" by David Kushner

"If You're Gonna Lie" by Fletcher

"Bells in Santa Fe" by Halsey

"Burn" by David Kushner

"Surrender" by Natalie Taylor

"If I Could" by Brynn Cartelli

"Talking Body (The Young Professionals Remix)" by
Tove Lo

"Long Sleeves" by Gracie Abrams

"stuck in my head" by BLÜ EYES

"One Foot in Front of the Other" by Griff

"Liberated" by Britton

"Hurricane" by Halsey

"Can We Kiss Forever?" by Kina, featuring Adriana Proenza

"I Lost Myself" by MUNN

"Lie About You" by OSTON

"It'll Be Okay" by Rachel Grae

"I Need You to Hate Me (Piano Version)" by JC Stewart

"Always Almost" by Rosie Darling

"Afraid of the Dark" by EZI

"Lay by Me" by Ruben

"The Look" by Ali Gatie, featuring Kehlani

"On the Go" by Bebe Rexha, featuring Pink Sweat$ and Lunay

"Different" by Maggie Lindemann

"Dancing with Your Ghost" by Sasha Alex Sloan

"In the End (Mellen Gi Remix)" by Tommee Profitt, featuring Fleurie and Mellen Gi

"Here's Your Perfect" by Jamie Miller

TRIGGER WARNINGS

Domestic violence (not between main characters)

Physical assault

Physical abuse

Graphic violence

Graphic sexual scenes

Depictions of non-sexual child abuse

Murder (not of a main character)

NIKKI

R*eality is a devil. No one can outrun it. It always catches up to you.*

"Nikki? Nikki?" a young man calls from behind the counter, scanning the small crowd waiting for their orders.

My eyes read his name tag—*Jeff*. I wonder what Jeff's life is like. Does he have a family? A girlfriend? A boyfriend? Does he ski? Does he secretly have an obsession with serial killers? Does he—

"Nikki?" he calls out once more before my brain finally registers the name.

You would think that after all this time, I would be better at responding to that name, but here I am, looking like an idiot as I approach the counter. Grabbing the pizza from Jeff, I offer a smile that I'm sure shows my embarrassment.

But he brushes me off without a glance or a word, grabbing the next order to hand out. Everyone else might be offended or upset to be forgotten so easily, but not me, never me. A ghost is what I became all those years ago and a ghost I will remain.

Hiding in the background is a skill that I acquired after three years of practice. And I walk out of the pizza parlor with the same permanent sinking feeling that lives in my gut, one that will stay with me until the day I die. Or the day *he* does.

Because every face has *his* eyes. Every shadow has *his* profile, *his* figure. Every laugh is an echo of the past. Every scream is my voice, and every minute of my future is stolen.

One day, no matter how hard I resist, death will come, and he won't come knocking. He will come with rage and fury that would make the Devil jealous, and when he sees fit, he will kill me and bottle up my screams as a keepsake.

My feet carry me out of the building in precise steps, one after the other. Taking a deep breath, I turn toward my shop, Nikki's Coffee. My free hand slips into my pocket and grabs my keys, fiddling until it wraps around the one I need.

As I approach the door, my phone starts ringing, and I slide the key into the top dead bolt and unlock it, ignoring the sound going off in my pocket. I repeat the same steps on the next two dead bolts and let myself inside. My phone quiets at the same time the door seals shut.

Silence envelops me, calm, reassuring, *deafening* silence. Most people can't stand it. They have to sleep with a TV on, a radio on. They have to have some form of buzzing around them to drown out their thoughts. It gives them a sense of comfort. But *this* is my comfort.

Silence is my friend. It protects me.

I walk toward the restrooms and unlock the door to my loft, pulling out my phone. Chloe's name pops up next to Missed Call.

Chloe is my best friend, my little trust fund baby, who moonlights as my hero. I got out of Oregon as fast as I possibly could. I drove to what I thought would be the quietest town I could get to at that day and time. I watched her enter her house alone and thought she might be able to point me to the homeless shelter or at least give me a place to crash for the night.

But when I showed up on her doorstep, quite literally, bruised black and blue, she didn't bat an eye, and she immediately took me under her wing. She seemed to sense my fear and desperation, and she saved me. She is the sole reason for me being where I am right now, both physically and mentally.

She didn't hesitate; she ushered me inside and refused to let me leave until I opened up to her. Trust me, I tried to leave. I was terrified that I couldn't trust her, that she might know him. That she would believe him because of who he was. But she didn't, and she didn't care who he was or the power and position he still held. She risked everything to help a stranger she owed nothing to. She became a stranger I would owe everything to. She gave me a chance at life again.

After I enter my loft, I lock the door, which takes longer than you might imagine. I start at the top with the chain lock, moving downward to two dead bolts, a swing bar, then a custom barrel bolt—ten inches in length— and last but not least, the open bar barricade. Which is a fancy term for a two-by-four, held in place by two metal brackets.

Ding. My phone rings in my pocket. It is Chloe's text, which always follows a missed call.

She is a bit older than me. She's twenty-nine, and I'm twenty-two. Our relationship bounces between a mother and daughter to sisters to best friends, depending on the situation. At times, it can be confusing, but I swallow the discomfort because I owe her *everything.* This coffee shop might have my fake name on the door, but it has her real one on the lease.

The same goes for my car, my phone, my debit cards. I don't exist. I am merely an extension of Chloe Dupont.

It was her idea for the coffee shop. She wanted a business adventure of her own, outside of what her family does, and I was the perfect built-in worker.

The Duponts are filthy rich. They own Zonama, the largest online retailer. I'm not talking millions. I'm talking billions. They influence the entire economy with their platform. It's equal parts impressive and intimidating.

Why they had picked Duluth to headquarter in surprised me. Why not pick, like, California or a major US city? But Chloe said that her dad wanted to keep it in a smaller town, and no one questioned his decision. Apparently, he had spent a lot of time here when he was younger and wanted to move back.

I've only met her parents one time. They were nice and incredibly down-to-earth despite the empire they had built and the wealth they had both been born into.

Ding. The follow-up reminder that, two minutes ago, I got a text.

Chloe: Hi! Did you eat tonight?

I type out a quick response.

Me: I just got home with pizza! :)

Chloe: Good. Get some rest. I'll see you in the morning! XO

Without sending a response, I lock my phone and set it on my kitchen counter. No other texts or calls will come through tonight. Unless they're from Chloe. I know that for a fact. Because there is only one contact saved in my phone—hers.

I pour myself a glass of water, quickly scarf down three slices of my pizza, and then store the rest in my fridge for later.

My bed is calling to me like a siren. With my mug of water, I swipe my phone from the counter, and in less than five steps, I'm at the edge of my bed, pulling the comforter back and climbing in.

I don't think the loft was ever intended to be used for a living space, but Chloe had a vision when she saw the place and turned her vision into a reality.

Her brother, Derek, is a surgeon. He works constantly, but he still managed to find time to do the majority of the physical labor while Chloe decorated the small studio apartment with the softest hues in pale and earth tones. Red, orange, yellow, green, blue, purple— she picked every color of the rainbow. And somehow, it still looks put together and simple.

She was also the one who insisted I dye my hair the pale pink it is right now. My natural color is comparable to the brown hues of dark chocolate. And I had never done a color outside of going a little lighter or darker brown, outside of my one slipup. So, going pale pink is something Trey would never expect, so different from my usual routine.

It took much longer than I'd expected to get from my dark brown to this shade of pink. And I vividly remember the anxiety and bone-deep fear that coursed through me as Chloe's hairdresser dyed my hair. The fear that he had instilled in me if I broke any of his rules.

I'd made the mistake of shaking things up when I was still with him, opting for a red hue in my hair.

I paid the price for that mistake. I learned two lessons that day: Trey Roark didn't want to love me; he wanted to own me, shape me, and mold me into whatever he desired. And I learned to never make the same mistake twice.

My fingers danced over the doorknob before twisting it, and I walked into the entrance of his home. Nerves coursed through me.

What if he hates it?

I'd decided to add some red highlights and a reddish glaze over my hair. Along with the color shift, I let the hairstylist cut a few more inches off than she normally did. Instead of hitting below my breasts, my new hair stopped right at my collarbone.

"Hey, babe. I have a little surprise to show you," I sang through the house.

Trey was probably still holed up in his office. He often spent long hours there.

I was right.

Five feet down the hall, the office door opened with a fierce force. An angry Trey strolled through, eyes on his feet. "This day could not get any fucking worse."

Hoping he liked the change, I cleared my throat, attempting to grab his attention. But when he looked up, my heart cracked, broke. And so did any shred of Trey I'd thought I knew.

7

He looked at me with disgust, like the mere sight of me caused him physical pain.

When he spoke, his voice was furious, ragged. "What have you done to yourself? I just told you how horrible my day was, and you thought this *would make it better? Stupid. I like your hair brown, and you know that. Are you intentionally trying to piss me off?"*

I fiddled with the healthy ends of my hair, my heart beginning to race faster and faster with every step he took toward me. "I-I thought a change would b-be fun."

My breaths were coming in and out in short bursts. Trey wouldn't physically hurt me. Sure, he'd said things some might find mean, cruel even. He was an emotional guy who always said things he didn't mean and always made up for it later.

I heard it before I felt it. The smack of flesh on flesh. My cheek caught on fire.

He had slapped me. Hard.

His scowl deepened. I still couldn't believe he had just hit—

Another smack. My other cheek burned hotter, and a stream of warm liquid ran down my face.

"I don't like your hair like this. You look like a cheap whore."
Smack. Burning hotter than the last.

"Why would you try to make my day worse? I liked your hair before. My girlfriend will not look like a slut with this fake red."

A harder smack. My lip split.

"You will not stray from what I like. Next week, you will get this fixed. And I do not want to see a strand of your hair resembling what it is now."

Smack. Harder. Smack.

8

I remained frozen in place, unable to move. Both out of shock and out of fear.

I anticipated the next blow, but it didn't come. But he wasn't done yet.

His hands closed over my throat, and in the blink of an eye, he slammed me into the wall behind me, squeezing harder by the second.

He leaned his forehead against mine as he said, "Baby, you know I didn't want to do that, right?" His grasp softened until he was just pinning me against the wall with barely any force. "I'm sorry. I shouldn't have snapped. I've just had a really bad day. You know I love you."

As fast as it had all seemed to happen, it ended. And when his office door closed, the pain settled in. I immediately questioned if what had just happened was a figment of my imagination, if it was just a bad daydream.

My shaky hands found my tender face, and it was soaked. My fingers drifted to my throat, and when I swallowed, there was pain that burned like fire. With my lips quivering, I walked out of his house in silence. I listened for the slightest creak of a board or turn of a knob.

But thankfully, silence remained.

And by the following Friday, my hair was dark brown once again, courtesy of Trey making the appointment himself. I was also gifted flowers and a new diamond bracelet that I found on his kitchen counter when I let myself in that evening. Along with a note that read, I'm so sorry, honeybee. I didn't mean to go as far as I did. I never want to hurt you. I love you. I hope you can see that. It will never happen again.

That was one of the many lies he told.

Because it did happen again. It happened when he hit me so hard that I went unconscious, when he kicked me so hard that it broke some of my ribs, when he grabbed my hair so hard that it ripped skin from my scalp, when he threw me down the stairs and I ended up in the hospital from the terrible "accident."

Lie. Lie. Lie. Endless lies.

Which was why I had to get out, escape. And there was only one way he would let me leave.

His own words were, "You are mine. Always mine. No one else will love you or touch you. Till death do us part."

So, I died in every sense that mattered.

My parents buried an empty coffin, but they didn't know that. They thought I was inside, starting to rot away. They mourned me, as did Trey in his own sick, twisted way. My friends cried and then eventually moved on with their lives—I assume at least.

Everyone in my life thought I had died, everyone but me. No loose ends. That was the only way it would work. And it did. It worked.

But I can't take a chance. One slipup, and he'll find me. I know for a fact that if I had stayed or if he ever found out that I was alive, he would kill me.

FIND ME ON THE ICE

The day they buried my coffin, Nikki Satinn was born, and Morgan Dove died.

And that is the way it will stay.

CAM

"Fuck," my voice rasps into Stephanie's ear as I thrust harder, her knuckles turning white as she wraps the sheets tighter around her hands.

"Ahh!" she cries out hysterically as another orgasm tears through her.

And I give her every inch she craves, faster and faster, harder and harder. Until I feel her clench around me once again. I grab her hips tighter, pulling her against me, and with one strategic thrust, she shouts, her screams muffled in the bed as she unravels around me.

Feeling my balls starting to tighten, I thrust rough and hard inside of her. She moans deliriously. With a few more smacks against her ass, I pull out and come all over her reddened ass.

I quickly grab a towel and clean myself up and throw on boxers and joggers while she comes down from her high.

She rolls over and stares at me. "Why do you always wear a shirt when we fuck?"

Tossing a towel to her to clean herself up, I answer, "Because I like to."

She can see my dick, ass, legs, and arms. But no one sees my back, especially not anyone as unimportant as Stephanie.

I like Stephanie. She's ... nice. But I don't want anything more from Stephanie than this. Which has been clear to her since day one.

As she cleans up and gets dressed, I try to stop the inevitable question by saying, "There're snacks in the kitchen if you want anything before you leave. I'm taking a shower."

The bed frame creaks as she moves to the edge of the bed. "Cam, I can wait for you. Can we grab some food?" she asks pathetically. It's almost cute.

Twisting the knob on the bathroom door, I roll my eyes to the comment I was trying to avoid. It's awkward *every time.*

They usually get the routine down by the second hookup. But Stephanie asks me the same thing; it never fails.

Don't get me wrong; she's sweet, and she has that whole *damsel in distress* thing going on. But I have no feelings for her at all—nothing against her.

She wants everything that I won't give. Which is probably why when I text her to come over, she does, hoping this will finally be the time I ask her out or something.

I'm not leading her on at all. I set the rules from the get-go. Sex, sex, and only sex. No sleepovers. No breakfast after. No showers together. Nothing that would give her the idea I want anything other than sex. But I think she still somehow found her way there anyway. Which is why this is the last time I'll invite her over. It's better to cut it off now before she catches any real feelings.

"Thanks, but you know that's not how this works. I've got plans. Can you make sure to lock the door on your way out?"

Turning my head, I see the look of defeat in her furrowed brow.

One that I hate I caused, but a necessary one regardless. I don't want to hurt her any more than I want her to develop feelings for me.

"Okay," she sighs.

I shut the door, leaving her to see herself out, with a slight sting in my chest for the pain I know I caused her.

I turn the water on as hot as it will go. My muscles are so sore from last night's practice, and fucking Stephanie for an hour didn't help. But I couldn't get my brain to shut off. I needed an outlet before practice tonight so I wouldn't take someone's head off.

Which was when I texted Stephanie to come over. I should have cut her off a while ago—she's always been a little *too* attached—but I was desperate.

And when I'm up late at night and I need to expel some energy in order to sleep, I know I can text her and have her in my bed within fifteen minutes.

I quickly wash my hair. Grabbing my sponge and soap, I lather up my body and rinse, loving the feeling of the hot water run down my body. The slam of a door sounds through my house not five minutes later. Shutting the water off, I wrap the towel around my waist and step in front of the mirror, looking at my own foggy reflection.

Quickly, I swipe my hand over the mirror, clearing the view.

Wet strands of my dark brown hair stick to my forehead. My dark blue eyes look empty, like no thought or emotion exists behind them. I often look in the mirror and feel like I'm looking at someone else entirely. Like a version of myself, but never really me.

I don't know how to explain it. The person in my mind and the person in the mirror don't match. A complete disconnect some days. But unfortunately, one version cannot forget the other, no matter how hard I might try. I catch glimpses of the me I keep locked away in my head sometimes. When I do, uncontrollable dread and pain tear through my body.

When I turn, one of the long scars on my back catches my eye.

That feeling, the one I do my best to push away, is already latched on to me before I can shake it, its teeth sinking deep into my neck, sucking out my sanity.

My heart's on the floor, tingles shoot across my shoulders, and a sour taste forms in my mouth before my father's voice echoes in my ears as the flashback slams into me.

"Piece of shit. Worthless. Just like your slut of a mother. Are you going to be good, or do you need the cuffs tonight?" He demanded a response.

Placing my hands in my lap, I stayed quiet and prepared for the first slash of pain.

"You earned these. Actions have consequences. What are the consequences of a missed shot?" he asked me.

I stayed quiet—I'd learned that the hard way. Without hesitation, the whip cracked in the air and sliced into my back. Liquid poured down my back, but I didn't yell, didn't scream. I took my consequences, every single one of them, until he reached four lashes. One for a poor pass, one for a penalty, one for a missed shot, one for a missed game winner. Sometimes, there were bonus ones thrown in when he felt I was lazy or had an attitude.

But as long as I kept taking them from my dad, he wouldn't lay a finger on his beloved wife—my mom.

"My son will be the best, the absolute best, and nothing less."

My ringtone pulls me out of my nightmare of a memory.

"Fuck!" I scream for what feels like hours, hating that I remember his voice so clearly after all these years later.

Utterly enraged that he still holds this power over me, I smack my hand on the countertop. It worsens when we lose games or when I make a mistake in practice. The feeling of impending agony that would await me still chills me to my bones.

My father was and is the most repulsive human I have ever known. He abused and manipulated my mother and me for years and years. Until the pain killed her and left me wishing it had done the same for me. But he was a hero to everyone else in town—Deputy and Coach Costello.

He had to have the perfect image—a beautiful, doting wife and a son who was the best hockey player in town. After all, he had been the best in his day.

If there is one thing I learned from him, it's how to play hockey. He was unofficially my coach for my whole childhood and officially my coach for all of high school. The love and absolute hate I have for the game is overwhelming some days. Sometimes, I can't seem to find the difference.

Picking up the ringing phone, I see *Kos* on the screen. My thumb swipes to answer.

"What's up?" I say, trying to keep the shakiness out of my voice as I wipe the running tears from my cheeks.

Alec says, "I'm here. Hurry up."

"I'll be right out," I tell him before hanging up.

I usually ride with Brett to practice, but he had physical therapy today, and he is just going to meet us there. I've lived with Brett since I joined the team three years ago. Neither of us had family here and figured it would be the easiest and most sensible decision with how much time we'd be spending together on the ice anyway. And he wanted someone to split rent with him.

The redness in my face has dissipated when I meet my stare in the mirror again. I hastily throw on boxers, joggers, and a shirt along with some tennis shoes before heading downstairs with my duffel bag.

When I get downstairs and reach the front door, I see Alec parked against the curb. I hurry outside and slide into the front seat, knowing time is running out before we're late. I barely have the door shut when Alec speeds off.

"About time," he says as he pulls out of the parking lot and flashes me a sincere smile. He opens his glove box and grabs something. "Here." He tosses me a bottle of eye drops.

"Still red?" I ask, uncapping the bottle.

"A little. Are you good?" he asks, glancing over at me for a moment with concern in his eyes.

Concern, not pity, which is an important distinction. One that made telling Alec about my past okay. He never pitied me. He respected the pain and torture I had gone through, but he's never looked at me any differently.

"Yeah, just an episode," I confess.

Ones I wish would stop happening. But I don't know that they will ever fully go away.

Alec nods and turns the hype music up.

We arrive at the arena a few minutes later, and I'm itching to get on the ice. I love hockey more than I ever thought possible when I was younger. It's my constant, and it always has been. On the bad days, on the good days, when I need an outlet, hockey is always there. It has been the only thing in my life I can truly rely on.

Alec parks, and we walk inside and head to the locker room to gear up. My body moves through the motions of changing into gear from the thousands of times I have done it before.

Gliding onto the ice feels like flying. It's one of the best feelings in the world. Skating next to Alec, I survey the team. We are looking good this year, and I'm excited for the first game next weekend.

Brett nods at me as I fall into the shooting drill, slapping my stick on the ice. Brett passes it to me, and my focus narrows on the goalie and the net. Working the puck side to side, I purposefully favor my right side, hoping MacArthur falls for it. He does, leaning just the way I want him.

I shoot the puck, and MacArthur dives for it, but the puck flies into the net with force.

"Nice shot," he calls out to me as he passes the puck and readies himself for the player going next behind me.

FIND ME ON THE ICE

This practice is drill and skill heavy, focusing on puck handling and one-on-one, one-on-two, two-on-three, et cetera.

I'm facing Kos and a rookie, Rich Kremmer. The rookie I'm not worried about, but Kos is fucking fast. Dribbling the puck, I pass the rookie with ease, leaving Alec. I'm illegally checked from behind, and I fly forward *hard*, but I manage to maintain my balance.

It's like a light switch is flicked in my head. I might still be on edge from earlier, but I forget about the puck and spin to find the rookie with a smug smirk on his face.

Digging into the ice, I charge up to him and shove my face in his, smiling.

"Do that again, and I'll break your fucking arm, Greenie," I hiss through my teeth.

Kos skates up and pushes us apart and gives me one look to tell me to cool the fuck off.

The rookie doesn't get the same treatment.

Kos grabs him by his collar and yanks him up to his full height. "You pull that shit again on anyone on this team, and I'll do it my-damn-self. No bullshit on the ice, do you understand me?"

He nervously nods, and Kos releases him.

"Twenty suicides," Coach orders us.

I'm going to kill this kid.

"You're a team. You get praised as a team and punished as a team. Kremmer, you pull that again, and your ass is done."

21

I wonder if I could piss Greenie off enough to do it again. I laugh to myself as we line up. At least I'll be able to sleep better tonight, knowing I'll be fucking exhausted.

The rest of practice goes by fairly fast. Only a few drills followed the suicides. On the ride home, Brett and I just talk shit about the rookie. But as annoying as he is, he's a great defenseman, and we were lucky to get him. But he needs to get his act together if he wants to be a Nighthawk.

My phone vibrates as we walk inside, and I see a text appear from Kos.

> *Kos: Fireflies grand opening tomorrow night? Please, dear God, you'd better come. We need a night out. It's been too long.*

Mila is opening a new location right here in New York City. I know it's going to do well here—better than in Duluth for sure. I assume that it isn't a coincidence that her next location is opening here. I imagine Laura convinced her of its potential success.

I could use a night out, honestly. Something other than practice, sex, and flashbacks would be a nice change of pace.

When we get inside our condo, we go to our separate rooms in silence, completely drained from practice.

> *Me: I'm in. Send me the address and time. I'll bring Brett.*

I don't know how Alec does it, balancing hockey with Laura and Jack. Laura runs our marketing department, so that definitely allows them to have more time together. She has been handling all of the social media lately, and she has been going wherever we go, Jack included.

Alec is a really good dad. I find myself envying him sometimes because of their relationship. But I'm terrified to have kids. I have no clue how he handled finding out about Jack like he did, no warning or preparation. But I guess everyone isn't my father and they aren't scared to turn into him.

I climb into bed, naked, like usual. But sleep won't find me soon—if it even does tonight. So, I let my mind drift, fantasizing about what tomorrow could be, who I could bring home for the night.

My phone vibrates.

> *Kos: Before I forget, masquerade is the theme tomorrow, masks required, so don't forget to pick one up. You literally won't be let in, and then I'll be pissed. Make sure Brett has one too.*

I send him a thumbs-up and set my phone down. I start counting the spackled dots on the ceiling until my eyes slowly close, and I fall asleep with ease for the first time in a while. Maybe I should thank the rookie after all.

3

NIKKI

Stepping onto Chloe's private jet, I tighten the hoodie over my head and face. And I question ever becoming her friend. This is crazy. How in the hell did I let her convince me to fly to New York for a spur-of-the-moment friendscapade? The only reason I gave in is because I can cover my face and head in between destinations, and I will not be leaving my hotel room, except to go to Fireflies for the masquerade-themed opening night. This is, like, rule number one of what not to do if you are trying to stay hidden. But Chloe fricken Dupont managed to break that rule with her charming self.

As we settle into seats, she smiles, her dirty-blonde curls flowing effortlessly down her shoulders.

"Breathe. It will be okay, I promise. We have a ride straight from the plane to our hotel, and I even arranged ter at the back of the hotel for more privacy.

y to relax. I have all of the bases covered."

I haven't relaxed since the day I died. It is almost too easy to feel comfortable with this. But I deserve this. I deserve to feel free for one night, to let loose and be myself again. I deserve to dance the night away with no care or concerns in the world.

Pushing my anxiety and fear away as best I can, I take Chloe's hand and lightly squeeze it.

"Okay, I'll relax and try to have fun." I laugh when she smiles. "But only for tonight. Tomorrow, I am right back to paranoid Nikki Satinn."

At some point, between the flight and Chloe showing me outfit inspo ideas based on the clothes she packed, I doze off. Only to be awakened by the wheels touching down in New York.

"Here, babe. Here, put this on." Chloe hands me a white masquerade mask that is completely covered in gorgeous white feathers. Some of the tips of the feathers are painted gold.

It's stunning. I know exactly why she picked it. It's reminiscent of a dove. She knows the meaning behind it, which brings tears to my eyes.

Dove. My fingers brush over the inside of my wrist, the only piece of my past that I've kept—the tattoo of a dove, my real last name.

"Chlo." I smile at her as I caress the feathers of the mask. "Thank you."

I keep the images at bay that try to surface, but a stab to my gut slips through at the thought of my mother. I miss my parents so much.

Slipping the mask band over my head, I adjust it until the mask is sitting on the bridge of my nose. Then, I throw the hood of my hoodie up, covering my hair and head. Chloe leads the way off the plane and into the car waiting for us. The driver gives me an odd look that I do my best to ignore. I'm guessing it's not every day that someone gets in with a mask and a hoodie on. Before we left home, Chloe explained that Bill, her driver, would take care of the bags and get them to the hotel for us as well as do anything else we might need.

She shoves her phone in her purse before saying, "I hope you don't mind, but I brought us outfits for tonight. I know you always insist on doing shit yourself. But that's dumb."

She laughs when I shoot her a glare. She has done enough for me in this lifetime tenfold.

"Nik, come on. You deserve to be spoiled, and I have the means to do it. And when I saw this dress, it would have been physically impossible for me to leave the store without it. I think it might have killed me. You were meant to wear it, I swear, especially with that mask."

It's hard to be mad at her for doing nice things for me. It's just hard to explain. Nice gestures don't always feel selfless or kind. It's a fine line between happiness and suffocation. If my ex did a nice thing for me, it meant the

27

opposite was inevitable. So, it's difficult for me to take Chloe's kindness at face value. He rewired my brain when we were together, convincing me every thought I had was wrong, every feeling I had was crazy. He continued until I was a shell of myself, and now, every day is a struggle for me to decipher what is a genuine thought of my own and what has been manipulated by him.

I'm nodding before I realize it, forcing my brain to think happy thoughts—that Chloe did it for me because she loves me, no ulterior motive.

"Thank you. I mean it, Chlo. Thank you." My voice is small and weak, but it's my own.

She throws her arms around me, doing her best to avoid the mask. "I love you, Nik, always."

"I love you too," I whisper to her, squeezing her a little harder, not wanting to let go.

I crave contact in any form. A hug, a high five, any skin-to-skin contact I can get feels like taking a deep breath after being underwater for too long.

Don't even get me started on my sex life. There is none, not a one-night stand, nothing since I became Nikki. It's embarrassing what turns me on these days. I swear a guy can shake my hand, and my clothes practically disintegrate. At this point, eye contact for longer than a second gets me wet. Which means tonight might be the first time in a long time that a guy touches me more than from the pass of a coffee cup. And I am so fucking excited. I need to wear a mask more often. I can be anyone tonight. I can be fearless, sexy, and *free*.

"Stop fussing. You look like a damn goddess. I'm almost mad at you for it." Chloe slaps my hand away to stop me from fidgeting with my hair as we move closer and closer to the entrance of Fireflies.

I audibly gasped when Chloe showed me the dress that she had picked out for me. The gold satin material flows down my body like it was made just for me. It crisscrosses across the back from right above my butt and all the way to the thin straps that run over my shoulders. I opted out of the jewelry she had offered me because they would potentially fall out of my ears or break, and they were probably worth more than my life.

Most of the scars on my body are on full show tonight, not hidden by this small dress. Not many people notice them. Most of them are small enough that they are missed at first glance. The tiny ones scattered up and down my arms are from when he shoved me and I fell into the glass coffee table, including the longer scar that runs right beneath my jaw. A much larger milky-white ridge runs from my mid-forearm to my pinkie from when he threw his large pocketknife at me because I'd spoken out of turn. There are plenty of scars that cannot be seen because of my dress and because a lot of them show no physical mark.

A flash of luscious brown hair flits past my vision as the girl a few feet ahead of us in line is spun by who I imagine is her boyfriend. As she turns, feelings of déjà vu hit me. I know this girl somehow. When she laughs and says something to her friend, it hits me. Laura Young. I wonder if she would recognize me at all. We never had personal conversations outside of the ones that usually arose during short interactions. It's impossible not to notice the group that is with her. All the guys are easily over six feet, and all of them look like they are straight off of a magazine cover. With masks covering a portion of their faces, a sexy, mysterious aura surrounds them.

My brain quickly puts the pieces together. The one who was spinning Laura must be her fiancé, Alec. Charlotte is with them, too, and has one of the towering men wrapped around her petite frame. She is wearing this stunning navy-blue dress that clings to her every curve. And then they disappear into the darkened club, bright flashing lights outlining their bodies before the door shuts behind them.

After a few more minutes, we are next to enter. The bouncer checks our IDs.

Thank you, Chloe, for the best fake only a lot of money can buy.

"Have fun." The bouncer smiles at Chloe and me as we enter.

Lights strobe and flash all around us as our ears adjust to the loud music. The dance floor is a rainbow of different-colored masks. This Fireflies is almost identical to the one back home—circular bar in the center of the room, touch-reactive flooring, the whole works. I went one time with Chloe, but my anxiety was too much. I had a panic attack in the restroom and told her I would never go back there.

Without meaning to, Chloe and I wander near Laura's group. Spinning to face Chloe, I'm about to ask if she wants to get a drink when I'm bumped forward.

"I'm so sorry!" Laura's words slur together as she catches herself on my arms. Her eyes connect with mine for a brief second. Laura's head tilts a bit to the side, like she recognizes my eyes, but can't place them.

I don't blame her. At work, I am usually in laid-back clothes with minimal makeup on. And I don't usually have a mask that covers half of my face. She continues to stare at me, no shame in the fact that if I didn't know her, she would be locked down in a stare-off with a stranger.

Something compels her to look at my wrist, and I know what she's looking for—the dove. I'm surprised she remembered it. I never go out of my way to point it out, fearing that, from that one tiny tattoo, he will somehow find me. When her gaze latches on to it, I swear her eyes actually light up like a light bulb. She shrieks and throws her arms around me, clearly recognizing me. A wave of alcohol burns my nose.

How in the hell is she already this drunk? They just got inside.

I laugh to myself.

"Nikki! Hi. It's Laura. I don't know if you remember me. I used to go into your coffee shop with Jack all the time when I lived in Duluth." Her words slur slightly.

Laughing in my mind, I smile as I feel Chloe's arm brush against mine. She's being the overprotective friend that she is, which instantly spreads warmth through my entire chest.

"Of course I remember you, Laura!" I do my best to shout over the music. "I couldn't forget you or Jack's cute little face if I tried."

I laugh, and she cheeses. A flush sweeps over my body out of nowhere, and the gentlest tingle dances across the back of my neck.

Laura pulls my focus back to her. "Oh good! I was worried. I thought I was the only one. Oh my God, I love your hair."

She laughs, and I question if she wanted to say all of that out loud.

"Thank you. I did that," Chloe interrupts and smiles.

My hair has been pink the entire time I have known Laura, but I don't know what else to do but smile. In my element, I could talk her ear off for hours, but not here, wearing a gorgeous dress in a club.

A deep voice cuts through the music. "Lu!" Alec, her fiancé, seems to part the crowd of people as he approaches.

And he is not alone.

I look away, putting my attention back on Laura, who is already wrapping her arms around Alec's waist. He lifts her chin up and kisses her as if no one else were in the room. That tingling sensation burns the back of my neck again right before I find the breathtaking source. Pools of the deepest blue are locked dead on me, studying me, memorizing me. His face is hidden by a mask of golden feathers, the tips painted white. My seemingly perfect match for tonight.

The few people between us seem to slowly fall away as he makes his way over, his eyes staying glued on me. I'm unable to look away. Like the second he looked into my eyes, we froze, never to melt again.

When I begin to think this is where I will stay forever, Laura greets him, pulling me out of my stupor. "Cam, this is—"

"Ahh, hold on!" I cut her off as a wave of confidence washes over me, and she turns to me, looking almost offended. I lean into her ear. "Laura, do one thing for me. Super please, don't tell him my name," I say.

If I'm going to live tonight how I said I would, then let's keep this going. I am not Morgan. I am not Nikki. I have no name, no rules, no boundaries. As long as this mask is on, I am free to just be. Although I don't know if *free* is the right word because I do something that I would never do, not as Morgan and definitely not as Nikki. I am possessed—that's the only explanation.

Pushing my shoulders down, I walk up to this blue-eyed sex god, getting a full look at him for the first time. Black button-up, rolled cuffs, with black tattoos wrapping around his left forearm and scattered tattoos on his right. A tattoo of a raven stands out among the rest, and I remember it. He came to my coffee shop before. I remember thinking how strange the tattoo was. The raven is missing an eye and a chunk of the feathers on its head. And all around the bird is smoke, like it's emerging through it. It's quite eerily beautiful. Slim-fitting black jeans outline his muscled legs.

He must be one of the hockey players.

Blue Eyes licks his lips before glancing at my parted ones. The air between us is thick, something I've never felt before, especially with a stranger. I think if we touched, we might electrocute this entire room. Although it could be from the fact that by his mere eye contact, I'm ready to go fuck him in the restroom.

He stays completely still, stalking my every move, every breath, every blink, until I'm on my tiptoes in these heels, my hands on his chest, my lips pressed against his ear, and a voice I recognize as my own says, "Dance with me."

My heart thrashes in my chest, running off of the high of my confidence.

What the fuck has gotten into me? I laugh to myself. I just walked up to the hottest man I've ever seen in my entire life and told him to dance with me, seemingly fearless.

Firm, rough hands fly to my waist, and Blue Eyes shifts his head, bending down slightly. His warm lips graze my jaw, moving up, and then he flicks his tongue against my earlobe. Then, the deepest, smoothest voice I've ever heard falls from his full lips. "Don't start something you can't finish, Little Dove."

Little Dove.

Squeezing my thighs together, I try to come up with something to say, something to knock him off his high horse. He has no idea what I can and can't fucking handle.

But I can't get a single word out before his hands slide lower on my back, bordering on the top of my ass, and he says, "Go find a good, nice boy to dance with, Little Dove. This is not the path you want to take."

A growl of anger forms in my throat, but it doesn't reach him because of the booming music. His hands start to slide off of me, which irritates me even more.

A good, nice boy. A good, nice boy!

There are two things in this world that piss me off more than anything else. One, being told what to do. And two, being underestimated.

I unclench my hands from his shirt, not knowing that I was squeezing so tight that my knuckles turned white. And I do something that he is definitely not expecting.

Sliding my hands around his stubbly jaw, I bring his lips down hard onto mine. He remains still for only a second, and then, like a volcano, he erupts. His callous hands grab my waist, squeezing so hard that my back arches, pushing my chest into him. Our breaths are fast, uneven. His tongue parts my lips, tasting me, savoring me. I gasp as he bites down on my lip, and a small moan rumbles from my mouth into his. I kiss him like it's the last kiss I'll ever have, like my last breath will be taken between his lips.

His fingertips dig into me, and I can feel my panties dampen. He wants this. He wants me. And now, I'm going to give him exactly what he said he wanted. Sliding my hands down his chest, my lips still melded with his, I push off of him, watching the hooded almost-black eyes look at me in a way no one ever has. Like I'm claimed. Like I'm his. Normally, that would terrify me, remind me of Trey. But this look is so much different. Blue Eyes is looking at me with passion. Trey looked at me with hate. He never wanted to love me. He wanted to own me and abuse me.

I smirk. "See you later, Blue Eyes. I'd better go find me a good, nice boy to dance with."

Spinning, I grab Chloe's hand before meeting her wide eyes, her jaw on the floor.

She pinches herself. "Holy shit, that wasn't a dream. We are totally doing this every weekend."

I scoff, "No, absolutely not."

CAM

L*ittle Dove, Little Dove.*

Thank God she walked away because after that kiss, I don't think I would have been able to push her away again.

Clichés are stupid. Fairy tales don't exist. But when she kissed me, I felt an *actual* spark between our lips. I'm going to chalk it up to static electricity.

I usually don't send women away from me unless I want the chase. Which is fun in its own way.

As she walks away from me, I want nothing more than for her to turn around. But it's better for her if she doesn't. Nothing good would come from her being with me.

Good-bye, Little Dove.

"When's the wedding?" Kos asks as he approaches me with Laura on his arm.

"Fuck off, Kos," I growl, hating how affected she left me.

He and Laura disappear into the crowd as they try to morph into one person. And soon, I'm alone—my favorite place to be.

I scan the crowd. The place is packed. Eerily, it's almost set up the same as the one back in Duluth.

When I first met Laura, I'll admit that I thought we were going to be something special. We clicked right away, and we had fun. But we are so much better off as friends. I saw a girl burdened by so much pain. It's weird, you know? Like attracts like. Laura has had a lot of loss in her life, but we aren't as alike as I once initially believed.

She's experienced pain and loss, but she's never begged death to take her because dying would be the only release.

The pull I once felt toward Laura is long gone. I love seeing her and Alec together. I truly think they are meant to be together. I haven't felt drawn to someone since Laura.

But the pull I feel to Little Dove is much different from the one I had with Laura. It's almost primal. To others, those doe eyes look innocent, like a girl who has never seen trauma or pain. But that couldn't be further from the truth.

I saw her scars, ones many people probably miss. But not me. I'm much too familiar with what scar tissue looks like. It almost glistens in the flashing lights, looking slightly translucent. It's absolutely beautiful.

There had to be at least twenty to thirty small scars on her forearms, rough and jagged. Mismatched, different thicknesses. I don't think it was from a blade of her own. They were all the same shade, meaning they had happened a very long time ago and they happened all at once.

Who is this girl?

My eyes haven't moved off the pink-haired golden goddess since I found her a moment ago. She and her blonde friend are heading toward the bar a mere ten feet away, and I track them the entire time until they reach it.

My body drifts toward her of its own accord, being drawn to her like a magnet. She crosses her arms and leans against the counter, causing the thin gold material to rise up the backs of her thighs, stopping right below her ass.

She looks like she was molded by the most delicate hands, made to be the most beautiful creation in the world. Part of me thinks she knows it too.

This little brat shifts all her weight to her right foot, and her hips adjust, lifting the dress even higher, teasing the hell out of me. And she knows *exactly* what she's doing.

I slam my heel into the ground to stop myself from walking over there and showing her exactly what teasing gets her.

I want to smack her ass until my hand stings and her cheeks redden. And then I would run my fingers between her legs, and I know I would find her soaking wet for me.

It has been a long, long time since I had such a visceral physical reaction to a woman. Or ever really. Which is surprising, even to myself, considering how many women I've slept with since signing with the Nighthawks. And, well, long before that.

Slamming my eyes shut, I grab my hardened dick through my slacks and adjust myself so I'm not riding the zipper so hard. I blow out a slow, steady breath as I open my eyes.

My pants are immediately too tight again when my gaze adjusts to the flashing lights and locks with the eyes shining behind a white-and-gold mask. Little Dove licks her lips before sucking the bottom one into her mouth before spinning back around to the bar.

As much as I try to resist, I take a step toward her, then another and another. When I'm almost in reach of her silky skin, her friend drags her away. She watches me the entire time, smiling, until the crowd fills our vision.

Good.

I hope she stays out of sight, far away from me. Because she and I are not ingredients for a fairy tale.

We're a recipe for a fucking disaster. And I've never wanted to be ruined so badly in my life.

Running my hand down my face, I sigh and spin around, looking for the group.

They aren't hard to find. This group of guys, all six foot or taller and built like Captain America, tends to stand out in any crowd.

I walk over to them, instantly regretting not getting a drink or taking ten shots at the bar.

"You good?" Reed asks, leaning away from Charlotte and toward me.

I nod once. "Yeah, I'm good."

So fucking far from good. But I know whatever feelings are coursing through me are probably better left untouched and unexplored.

The song comes to an end, and thankfully, my group needs another drink, and we head to the bar. Kos buys us two rounds of shots, which I quickly down, hoping to get Little Dove off of my mind.

But my eyes can't stop scanning for her, looking for her, and it's starting to piss me off. I don't even know this girl.

Why the hell am I obsessing over her five seconds after we met?

I order two more shots for the group. They can handle it—well, everyone, except Laura probably. She's the world's biggest lightweight.

Slamming the shot glass down, I turn around and lean back against the bar on my elbows, again looking

41

for that pink hair in the bland sea of everyone else. Immediately, I find her, spotting swishing gold fabric. I have a direct line of sight to her, which doesn't help me not to stare.

It looks like Little Dove is a woman of her word. She did exactly what she'd said she would. She found a good, nice boy. A *boring* and inexperienced boy.

I watch them, swaying, grinding, reacting to the music. She hasn't caught me watching yet, so I enjoy my view unabashedly. Her body is free, weightless, moving with no care in the world. It's breathtaking. She's breathtaking.

I can't help but chuckle at Mr. Nice Guy's moves. He's not the worst dance partner in the world, but he's got to be a close second. I know she isn't enjoying herself—at least not in the way I could make her.

He isn't changing his rhythm, isn't teasing her in any way. Not running his fingertips over her bare skin, blowing hot breath into her ear while whispering how amazing she feels against him.

And she is well aware of his shortcomings. Her back is barely arched, not craving his touch against her ass. She isn't flushed, no red speckles on her chest or neck.

I wonder how red she would turn if I whispered into her ear how perfect her ass was, how good it felt to have her pressed against me. I wonder how she'd react if I slid my hand under the side of that dress and grabbed her breast in the middle of the dance floor.

Would she be too embarrassed and run? Would she look at me with hooded eyes and bite that plump bottom lip? Would she let me show everyone in this room that she was off-limits to anyone but me? Would she beg for more?

Fuck, I shouldn't have worn jeans tonight. But I never get this hard without even touching someone. Let alone just thinking about her and watching her while she dances with someone else.

But if I had worn anything less constricting, then every person in this room would have had a perfectly clear idea of exactly what Little Dove was doing to me.

I can't help the smirk that breaks free, forming on my lips, as I watch him grab her hips a hair too low, awkwardly low. My body is vibrating, needing to go to her.

Don't do it. Don't do it. Don't do it.

I almost gain my willpower back, but then she rolls her eyes at Mr. Nice Guy's attempt at a hip roll. And her irritated gaze lands directly on me.

Even in the dark room with sporadic lights, her eyes drop to my straining zipper, and her lips fall slightly apart.

My restraint snaps, and I'm stalking over there almost pathetically fast.

Unfortunately for Mr. Nice Guy, the clock has run out on his ability to touch Little Dove.

Grabbing his shoulder, a bit tighter than needed, I pull him hard, backward and off of her. He trips, and I let him fall to the ground right as my hand steadies a stumbling Little Dove.

"I've got you," I coarsely whisper into her ear.

Mr. Nice Guy shouts something, but with one sharp look from me, his lips seem to magically seal shut.

Sliding behind her, I run my left fingertips across the crisscross back and settle them on her hip, squeezing gently but sharp enough to shock her. She gasps.

"I couldn't stand by and just watch *that*. Watch you settle for the feelings he was giving you. You should be bathed in pleasure, Little Dove, worshipped," I moan into her ear, feeling her tight ass push back against me.

She rests her head against my chest, turning her head to the right, and I lean down, giving her my ear. "And you think that's supposed to be you?"

I groan, "I have no doubt in my mind that I could make you feel things you never have before."

Lightly, I trail my right fingers across the top of her shoulder, working toward her collarbone. Her chest is heaving, and I wonder if anyone has ever paid this much attention to the little things about her body. I continue to trace my fingers across her bare skin.

By the way she reacts to my simple touch, I know the answer to that.

The scars on her arms and shoulders dance in the flashing lights. They are all relatively small, except for the one on her neck. I lightly sweep my fingers up the side of her neck, paying extra attention to the stark white scar a couple of inches long, right below her jaw.

What happened here, Little Dove?

I run my thumb over her bottom lip as she looks straight up, the back of her head falling back on my chest, and stares into my eyes. I push my thumb into her mouth, resisting the urge to wrap my other hand around her throat. Her tongue immediately flicks against my thumb, sending a jolt straight to my cock.

This image—her staring up at me with my thumb in her mouth—gives me way too many ideas that I want to thoroughly explore.

"Fuck," I moan into her ear, watching her pupils blow as lust overtakes her. "Stay with me tonight, Little Dove, and I promise I'll show you what real pleasure is. *Over* and *over* again."

She sucks hard on my thumb at my words, and my eyes roll into my head. Mentally, I take a picture of this moment, of the moment I see her say *yes* in her mind. Her eyes relax, and the suction in her mouth loosens. A moment of perfection.

An explosion of, "Fuck," fills the room as piercing white light floods our vision, ruining this perfect scene in front of me.

Little Dove leans forward, but I secure her in place with my left hand so she doesn't lose her balance.

"Shit, I gotta find Chloe!" Little Dove shouts, and the sudden bone-chilling fear in her voice scares the living hell out of me.

She is panting, and I can't tell if it's from my touch or the fear that has taken over her. She hastily searches the room with her gaze, scanning every person so precisely and carefully. Only looking at them when they aren't looking at her. That small detail doesn't go unnoticed by me.

I pull her tighter against me, afraid that if I let her go, I'll never see her again. I just got a taste of who Little Dove is, and I'm not ready to give that up. I need more.

Suddenly, her posture is straighter as she finds her friend. Who is heading right toward us, almost jogging.

"Hey, we gotta go, love. Paps are on their way here. I got a tip." Her friend's eyes are wide as hell as she grabs Little Dove's hand.

A voice blasts through the speakers as the light goes back off. "We are so sorry for that, everyone. Technical difficulty. Next round is on the house!"

The crowd erupts in cheers and deafens me to Little Dove's conversation with her friend.

What was her name? Chassis? No, Chloe—that's right.

My ears finally settle with a slight ring, and I hear Chloe say, "We have to leave *now* if we are going to get out before they're parked around the whole building."

Little Dove nods frantically as she steps away from me and toward her.

"W-wait. How can I see you again?" I desperately ask her, gently grabbing her wrist.

She smiles, reminiscing about the small time we had together, but her eyes are somewhere else entirely. Slightly too wide, strained, scared. I want to kill whatever is making her feel this way.

She whips her phone out and shouts over the music, "What's your number?"

I give it to her in one breath and watch her walk away—or practically be dragged away by her friend.

The second she's out of sight, my phone rings, and I answer, "Little Dove?"

"Now, you have my number too. Call me when you miss me, Blue Eyes."

5

NIKKI

Fuck. Fuck. Fuck. Fuck. Fuck. Fuck. Fuck. Damn, that was hot. Fuck.

"I shouldn't have given him my number," I shout at Chloe. "Why did I do that? That was so stupid!"

We need to get out of here. Chloe is dragging me through the crowd. We rush out the front door right as the car pulls up in front of us, and we jump inside.

The second our door shuts, Bill, our driver, slams on the gas, and flashes of light go off in the rearview mirror.

That was way too close.

My heart is about to burst out of my damn chest. I cannot believe that just happened. Well, actually, I can't believe *a lot* of things just happened.

One, that I almost had my face captured by the paparazzi with my inconveniently famous best friend. Two, that I danced with that guy, Cam, like *that*. I have never been turned on so much in my life. Never been so willing to hand over control.

I was about to rip my clothes off on the dance floor before the paps showed up. Getting so caught up in the present was thrilling, freeing, exactly what I wanted, what I needed. But I can't live like that forever—or even for another second.

Nikki. Nikki. Nikki. Nikki. Nikki.

My name is Nikki Satinn.

Nikki Satinn. Nikki Satinn.

I repeat the name over and over in my head. To remind myself why I'm here in the first place, why nights like this are too risky, especially with someone as publicly known as Chloe. Why nights with a guy like Cam are dumb and irresponsible. And that a night is all it can ever be.

One picture, one snap of a moment, and Trey will find me. Being a cop has its perks. Trey might think I'm dead. But if someone he knows or someone I knew sees a photo of me and tells him, he will stop at nothing to find me. And all of those job perks will allow him to do just that.

Three years, I have been hiding in the shadows. I can't let myself have nights like this because it makes me want more. But more is dangerous.

Part of me wants to take a gun and lodge a bullet between his eyes. I don't think I would be able to pull the trigger in the end, to take someone's life. But I guess people don't know what they are capable of until they are staring death in the face.

Anger boils up inside of me. Pure rage for the power Trey still holds to ruin one of the best nights of my life without even knowing it.

"Fuck!" I slap my hand on the headrest in front of me.

Chloe's hand immediately falls onto my arm. "Hey, are you okay?"

My brows crease, and my eyes fly open as I whip my head to her. "Am I okay, Chlo?! I'm about to lose my mind. But I'm pretty sure we've already passed that!"

Gasping, I do my best to slow my heart rate, my breathing. Just the thought of him potentially finding me has me almost spiraling into a panic attack.

Five things. Name five things I can touch—a coping skill I found online for panic attacks and anxiety.

My gasps are loud enough to grab the attention of Bill.

As my fingers wrap around the headrest in front of me, I whisper, "One."

Kicking my shoes off, I grab one of them. "Two."

I push myself to count five things, to focus on each one, not giving myself a spare second to continue getting lost in my own head.

Chloe shoves her purse in my lap, and I reach inside and grab the first thing my hand touches—sunglasses.

"Three."

I hold the bag up. "Four."

Wrapping my fingers around the charcoal strap across my chest, I say, "Five."

My breathing starts to slow, and I inhale long and hard, sucking air in until it burns and then slowly exhaling. I continue to do this until my breathing is normal and my head is clear.

Needing to feel something cold, I lean my head against the window and close my eyes for the remainder of the ride. And when the car rolls to a stop at our hotel, I'm so emotionally and physically drained that I just want to sleep until we head home.

"You want to stay in here a bit longer?" Chloe asks as she rests her hand on top of mine, squeezing gently.

"No, I want to go shower and crawl in bed," I say.

She nods, and we walk in silence into the hotel, then our room—or I should say, luxurious suite. Because Chloe Dupont does it no other way.

"Come here," Chloe says when the door behind us clicks shut.

Her arms are stretched out wide, waiting for my hug. And I throw myself into them as the lump in my throat breaks free, and sobs heave from my chest.

"It's okay, Nikki. It'll be okay," she says softly as she rubs my back.

My voice is uneven and shaky as I say, "I'm so exhausted, Chloe. I don't want to do this anymore. I'm sick and tired of living in the shadows because of him. If

Trey didn't still fucking own me, I would have enjoyed the night and probably fucked Cam. But, no, I don't get to meet people. I don't get happily ever afters. I get fucking nightmares."

"I'm sorry," she says, her voice thick with sorrow.

"I just want to shower and go to sleep. I'm sure I'll feel better in the morning and just forget about this night." I sigh, forcing any residual feelings from the night away.

Without meeting her eyes, I turn and walk into the bathroom with a newfound heaviness. I wasn't even sure the weight I always felt could get heavier. I start the shower, strip, and step into the burning hot water, letting it wash the sweat and stickiness from dancing and the feeling of hope down the drain.

I wash my hair fast, just wanting to feel the comfort of a warm blanket, and step out of the shower, wrapping a towel around myself.

Steam fogs up the oversize mirror as I approach the double sink. Removing the towel from my body, I wipe the mirror off until I'm faced with my own reflection.

Who am I? Do I have any hopes and desires besides staying safe? The truth is that I can't afford the thoughts of dreams and wishes because they will make me reckless.

My empty stare travels over my body, spending extra time on the abundance of small scars up and down my arms and the tops of my shoulders. My heart catches on fire as my gaze locks on to the thick white scar on my neck.

He has taken everything from me—my sense of safety, my family, my life. He takes and takes and never stops. He takes the peace out of my dreams when I sleep. He takes the air out of my lungs when I think of him.

Anger surges inside of me as a memory surfaces in my mind, one I wish I could forget completely. But one that reminds me exactly of who Trey is.

I quietly set Trey's dinner plate in front of him, careful to avoid his gaze.

"Thank you, baby. It smells amazing," Trey said with a smile on his lips.

I made his favorite tonight—steak with mushrooms and mashed potatoes—hoping the mood he had come home in would be better before we went to bed tonight.

"Thank you," I said as I settled into my seat at the table next to him.

Placing the fork and knife in my hand, I waited for him to take his first bite. As he cut the steak with ease and placed the slice into his mouth, he hesitated before biting down.

He glanced my way, and a second later, disgust turned his lips down.

I set my silverware down before whispering, "I-is something w-wrong with the s-steak?"

He sighed loudly before slamming his fist on the table. "It's salty, Morgan! It's fucking salty! How hard would it be to make it right? Give me yours."

Without looking up from my lap, I slid my plate over to him.

He cut a chunk out of mine and shoved it into his mouth, chewing aggressively.

He chuckled and scoffed before saying, "Of course yours is perfect."

"I-I'm sorry, Trey. I really didn't mean to," I whispered to him, afraid of what was to come.

Sometimes, Trey's anger was instant—a slap across the face, a punch to the stomach, a grab and yank of my hair until patches ripped out. Sometimes, his anger stirred and came later—that version was always much worse.

This was one of those times.

"I'm eating yours. You eat mine, all of it, and don't leave a speck of food on that plate. Then, clean this up." With that, he stood from the table with my plate in his hand and walked to his office.

My body quivered as I force myself to eat every last bite on the plate, knowing there was no more salt on this steak than there was on mine.

After I finished, I washed the plate and utensils by hand, dried them, and put them away as quietly as I possibly could.

After I wiped down the dining table, I headed upstairs, hoping to be in bed as fast as I could. I knew sleeping wouldn't stop the inevitable, but I could surely hope it did.

I crawled under the sheets seconds before his voice tore through the silence in the house.

"MORGAN!" Trey screamed.

I could hear the slight change in his tone that only existed when he'd been drinking. It didn't happen often, but when it did, it meant that I'd better keep my head down, my mouth shut, and my mind disconnected from my body. Because the nights he drank were the nights I hoped he would finally kill me. Because dying would be so much better than whatever he had planned.

I hurried, remaking the bed and flattening the sheet that I'd wrinkled. I tried to calm my already-sporadic breathing as I exited the bedroom and met him in the dining room.

I could feel his stare as I approached him, attempting to keep a little distance between us. But that seemed to anger him even more.

I yelped as his hand fisted my hair, and he dragged me from where I stood to our seats.

"What is this, Morgan? You missed a spot! For fuck's sake! All I ask is that you eat your food and then clean up. You can't even seem to do that!" He jerked my head up to his and bent my head back, forcing me to look at him. "Oh, you have nothing to say?"

Tears flooded my eyes as the pain seared my scalp. "I'm sorry! I'm sorry!"

He laughed. "I'm sorry too, Honeybee."

Over time, Trey had become more unpredictable, more malicious, and even more menacing.

"Trey, please d-don't. I'll be better. I won't miss anything next time. Please." I begged him to stop.

"*Tsk, tsk, tsk. You know the best way to train a dog is by physical punishment. By doing this, I know you will never make that mistake again. Words can't be trusted, but actions can. I'm doing this for you, Honeybee. Remember, I'm trying to help you be better.*"

"*Trey, please, please,*" I pleaded. I cried out as he dragged me by my scalp to the living room. "*Please, I'll do anything. Anything!*"

"*Desperation is a pathetic look on you,*" he snarled as he ripped my head up to him, our eyes meeting.

In the blink of an eye, his fist slammed into my ribs. I screamed and cried. He pulled up higher on my head, forcing my back to arch and my rib cage to open.

The next blow did much more damage than the last. The burning sensation attacked my side before the sound of my ribs breaking reached my ears.

He looked almost shocked, like he hadn't expected to do that, or surprised that it'd seemed to happen so easily.

He breathed heavily in my face. Droplets of his spit mixed with tears on my cheeks. "*Stop crying.*"

"*No. You can beat me, break me, but you can't make me stop crying.*" Something inside me compelled me to push back, to fight him, if only for a second. I regretted it immediately.

"*You're wrong.*" He smiled.

He lifted me up off of the ground by his fist in my hair. I felt my flesh tear away from my scalp. I crashed to the ground hard and fast. But it wasn't the ground I found—at least, not at first.

With an explosion of glass, my body and head slammed into our glass coffee table, shattering it into a million pieces. I felt the shards sticking out of me everywhere. When I breathed too deeply, my ribs made me wince, and the shards dug in deeper.

I couldn't move without agonizing pain lighting up every inch of my back, my shoulders, my arms, and my neck.

"When you stop crying, I'll help you up. You can stay there until then. I'll come back in ten minutes."

I settled into the excruciating position, holding still, as the shards of glass sank deep into my skin. I forced short breaths of air into my lungs, trying to ignore the sharp sting in my ribs. I couldn't move my head. I couldn't look anywhere, except to the ceiling.

I lay there for ten horrifically long minutes, until he returned, until he helped me up, my face dry and my body soaked in my own blood. He cleaned me up, carefully and gently extracting each and every shard of glass. Thankfully, none were too big or had done more than apparent surface damage. He left me alone to bathe, and I fell more and more numb and drifted further inside of my own head.

When I walked out of our master bath, he brought me wine and Dove chocolates. He doted on me, massaged my feet, treated me as he should. I knew that as soon as this kindness wore off, the real Trey would resurface. But I didn't plan on being here when it did.

6

CAM

"Fuck!" My body flails in bed as reality yanks me from my nightmare.

I'm burning up. Sweat drenches me head to toe, soaking into the sheets beneath me. My ragged breaths are fast, mirroring the beats of my heart. I push my hand through my damp hair, pushing the saturated curls off of my forehead.

I'm sick of these nightmares, the same ones that have haunted me my whole life, but more so when the anniversary of my mom's death approaches. If my dad wasn't already rotting away in prison, I would return the favor of what he did to my mom.

When I was younger, after practice one day, the boys and I had decided to grab a bite to eat. The longer I could stay out of my house, the better. The inevitable would always come— my dad's so-called punishments— as it did almost every time I went home after practice or a game. I took his lashings as I always did so that my mom wouldn't have to. If he got all of his anger out on me, there would be none left for her.

She was never supposed to be the one who died from his wrath.

But I was at dinner with my team later than I should have been, and she was the one who paid for it.

When I had gotten inside, I felt it all around me. The wrongness in the air. I knew instantly that something was wrong. I began searching the house, and I found my parents in their bedroom upstairs. He was on top of her, pinning her to the ground with his hands around her neck.

When he saw me, he fucking smiled. I punched him, kicked him, jabbed at his eyes. I tried to hurt him in any way I could.

It distracted him enough to at least give her a few moments to catch her breath. He started punching me in my stomach, ribs, and sides. I thought I could take it, that if I could hang on a bit more, he would get tired, and then I might get the upper hand.

But when he kicked my leg inward, right below my knee, it snapped so easily under his strength. And I couldn't stand anymore. I couldn't get to him to stop him. No matter how hard I screamed, no matter how much I tried to get up, I couldn't save her.

I'd failed her.

When I was twelve, my dad murdered my mom in front of me.

I wish it had been me that night instead of her.

Glancing at my phone, I'm thankful I at least woke up at a decent hour—seven fifteen a.m. I don't have to be at the rink until about ten a.m.

My eyes immediately scan the message from Brett that he sent four minutes ago.

> *Brett: You up yet? I want to run to the mall before practice. That little one by the rink.*

If I don't go, I would probably just sit here on social media for the next hour.

> *Me: Just woke up. I'll be out in a few.*

A second later, his response comes through.

> *Brett: Cool.*

Locking my phone, I throw it next to me on my solid black comforter and head for my bathroom, itching to be under the water and clean the sweat off my skin. Sweat usually doesn't bother me a whole lot; however, waking up in sweat from my nightmares feels an awful lot different from when I sweat at practice because I'm exhausted on the ice.

nis feels heavy, dirty. I turn the water on as hot as go and pull the valve to start the shower. I kick my boxers off and step into the scalding water.

A sigh much louder than intended slips past my lips. I'm sick of dealing with this every fucking night. My shoulders and neck can't get any stiffer. I want to be able to close my eyes at night, just relax, and get a good night's sleep. But I haven't had one in years.

I lather my sponge with soap that has hints of green apple, amber, and musk. As I run the sponge over every inch on my body, my heart begins to calm, and my breathing slows back to normal.

Shutting the water off, I shake my head, trying to get most of the water out before I step out of the shower.

I wrap a soft white towel around my waist, catching right below my hip bones, and walk to my closet. I snatch a pair of SAXX boxers, black joggers, my go-to Nighthawks hoodie, and socks. I slip on the boxers and joggers. Then, I slide my arms through my black-and-white Nighthawks hoodie and shiver as my body cools off after the shower.

My phone dings, and I shake my comforter until it falls out.

Brett: Hurry up, dude.

I slip my phone in my pocket and rush to finish getting myself and everything ready.

Popping the cap on my deodorant, I swipe some on quickly before grabbing my practice bag, putting on my tennis shoes, and heading to the living room.

As I open my bedroom door, he greets me, "What's up? You ready?"

"Yeah," I say, feeling numb from the overexertion of emotion from my nightmares.

"You ready for tomorrow?" He smiles as we walk out of our front door.

Competitiveness floods my body when I think about tomorrow night's game. "We are going to win, no doubt at all."

Tomorrow, we are traveling to Minneapolis, Minnesota, to play the Mystics. They beat us last season. But that was a crazy time for Kos. He had just found Laura again and discovered he had a son. It wasn't only his fault that we lost. But it hurt us a lot that his head was out of the game. So, this time, we aren't getting off that ice without a win.

I smile with the energy of tomorrow already dancing across my skin. Hockey is the only place where I feel right, like me.

"I feel good. I bet Kos is fucking thrilled to be going back," he says.

"That's for sure. He's out for revenge."

After a quick stop into Dick's Sporting Goods for a new pair of joggers for Brett, we head to practice, which goes by faster than I would like.

Coach calls us in, and we hustle over to him for his end-of-practice speech.

"Our plane is leaving at eight o'clock. All of your asses had better be in your seats by seven forty, or when we get back, I will make you skate suicides until you puke. Am I clear?" he asks.

"Yes, sir," we answer collectively.

"Get out of here. Tomorrow, we will whoop the Mystics' ass."

"Kos," I call out so he knows I'm free to take the puck as we fly down the ice.

No defenders are between us and the goalie as Kos, Brett, and I skate into our zone. Brett and I swing wide as Kos brings the puck down the center. Brett drives toward the goal, and Kos passes the puck to me. As Brett wraps around the goal, Kos slaps his stick on the ice on the opposite side of the net as Brett.

I can see the play before it happens. As Brett crosses the threshold of the side of the net, Kos confuses the goalie, calling for the puck. The goalie favors Kos's side, and I slap the puck into Brett's stick. At lightning speed, he wraps it right around the corner of the pole and right into the net.

The buzzer sounds, and the arena erupts in cheers as we tie the game one to one. We fly into Brett, chanting words of praise and happiness. The energy is contagious.

It's the third period with fifty-two seconds left as we skate up to the center for the next face-off. We need to score now and hold them until the final buzzer.

Kos faces off with their center, and the puck is kicked out in the madness, right into Reed's stick. Everyone falls into place as he passes the puck to Kos, and he again races toward our zone. As Kos passes it to Brett, it's intercepted by one of the Mystics, and we immediately go on defense. Their player passes it to one of their wings right outside of our zone.

The crowd shouts, "Twenty seconds!"

Their wing pulls back and slaps the puck hard. But instead of the puck flying, the blade slides across the ice, snapping off of his stick.

Brett takes off for the puck as the Mystics' wing flies to their bench to change out. I trail him and spot a Mystic charging Brett. I dig into the ice with everything I have. I need to get to this player before he gets to Brett.

Almost there. Almost there.

I plow into the Mystics' player and knock him on the ice right as Brett grabs the puck and takes off to the goal.

He dribbles, pulls back, and fires. The puck slams into the net, and the shouting and cheering from the crowd is deafening. The buzzer fills the speakers, and the time runs out. We all race toward Brett and then to our goalie, Matt. We can never win a game without him, so we always celebrate with him the second it's over.

"Woo!" we all scream and chant as we jump into each other.

This is the feeling I chase every time I hit the ice. This is the only feeling that is good in my life. Pure, absolute joy.

After the game, we all head into the locker room to shower and change. Walking out, I pull my phone out and ignore all of the social media notifications. Sometimes, I wish I had someone to call after the game to talk about it with.

My thumb seems to find her number with ease. The pink-haired Little Dove that has crossed my mind daily since we met. I could call and see what she's up to, how she's been. But I'm interrupted.

"Cam, wait up," Kos hollers to me as I walk out of the arena with a smile on my face.

I lock my phone and slip it into the pocket of my Nighthawks hoodie. I turn on my heel and wait for him to catch up as the crowd parts around us. The Minnesota fans don't seem to want an autograph from us tonight.

As he reaches me and we fall into step together, he says, "Hey, I know it's super last minute, but I thought you might want to join Laura, Jack, and me. We're driving up to Duluth to visit her mom and fly back afterward. Do you want to come with us? I thought you might enjoy the change of pace on our day off."

I had plans, important ones. Get on the plane tonight, go home, and try to sleep. But I suppose I can make a change for ol' Kos. "Well, now, I have to call and cancel the party I was going to throw tonight. But, yeah, I'm in."

He scoffs, "Shut the fuck up. I know damn well you avoid the masses after games unless it's going to End Zone with us. You definitely aren't planning a party. If you were, Reed would have been advertising that anywhere and everywhere, and Charlotte would have told Laura. And I haven't heard a word from anyone."

A smile tugs at my lips. "Well, I guess I have no excuse then."

"You're in? We're leaving right now. Laura got the rental car before the game," Kos says.

I nod. "Yeah, let's go."

NIKKI

Sliding the last pan of cinnamon rolls into the oven, I move my head, humming to the music that's filling the shop from the built-in speakers.

This is the last of my prep before we open at seven a.m. My morning routine is my favorite part of the day.

It's consistent, almost never changing, aside from special bakes when I'm feeling up to it. And I love waking up before the rest of the world. Nothing compares to that silence, to the moment where the earth seems to stand still, the sun barely lights up the sky, and the shadows that haunt my every waking day are still nestled in their beds.

My phone chimes, and I hover my face above the screen as it unlocks.

> *Chloe: I'm running a bit late. I'll be there in about forty. I'm sorry!*

Rolling my eyes, I start filling the display case with the fresh muffins, rolls, scones, and croissants for the day. Chloe is usually late—the number of minutes differing every day, but late nonetheless. But it's hard to be mad for her tardiness when she is not technically on the schedule. It has just become habit that she works when I work. Although her work style consists of talking to the customers and hanging out. Which is fine by me. I always enjoy her company.

After I fill the case up, the cinnamon rolls are ready to come out of the oven. I quickly ice them and load them into the case alongside the others. As my hips sway to the music, memories of being with Cam at Fireflies dance in my head.

No one has ever made me feel so alive, so free, so turned on. He was barely touching me, but I could feel it in every nerve in my body. I could feel every cell stand on edge and anticipate his next move. I would have stayed dancing with him the entire night if it meant I could feel that way forever.

But unfortunately, I don't get to live that life, not now and probably not ever.

The soothing voice of Jamie Miller fills the coffee shop as I close my eyes and sporadically dance to the last few seconds of the song.

BEEP, BEEP, BEEP, BEEP, BEEP.

My phone alarm goes off, which is my cue to open the front door.

As I walk toward the front door of my shop, I smile at the regulars already waiting.

Charlie and Ryan, the cutest couple in the entire world, just got approved to adopt, and I could not be happier for them.

I welcome them inside as I flip the sign on the door to display *Open*. "Good morning, guys."

They smile back at me, and Charlie says, "Good morning, Nikki." He pauses and takes a deep breath in. "I think this is quite literally the smell of heaven."

I roll my eyes at him. He is excessive with the number of compliments he gives to both me and the shop. But I am thankful for them nonetheless.

"Your usual?" I ask him as they follow me to the counter.

"You know it," Ryan says as he pulls out his wallet.

"Ooh, wait, I want one of those!" Charlie points to the warm cinnamon rolls that are covered in white frosting.

"I got you," I reply calmly while I'm beaming on the inside.

When people like what I made, whether a cinnamon roll or a frappé, I feel proud. Proud that something that I made and created is loved. It's affirmation that I'm enough, that I'm in the right place and everything's okay.

I pour two cold brews with half-and-half for Ryan and Charlie, grab a roll and place it in a paper bag, and bring it to the register.

I don't have to tell them the total because they get the same thing every day, aside from the addition of the roll today. But Ryan doesn't ask how much they owe; he just taps his card on the reader. Once approved, I print the receipt and hand it and the bag over to him, the coffees to follow.

"Have a good day, guys!" I genuinely smile at them as they turn to leave.

"You too, Nikki!" Charlie waves his coffee at me.

A twinge of guilt strikes my heart. I love my customers, and I feel like I have gotten to know my regulars very well. But it always makes me feel like a fraud.

People open up to me, tell me about their lives. They're honest, genuine, and passionate. And I lie to their faces every time I see them.

I eventually make myself feel better. Knowing that I don't have any other choice usually makes it easier. I mean, I'm still me behind the hair and the name. I still show them who I am to a degree.

But sometimes, the guilt hits me harder.

The rest of my regulars give me their orders, and I hastily start on them while trying to shut my feelings down.

When I grab a quick drink of my own coffee, the bell above my door rings, letting me know someone has entered.

"Hi, babe. Don't worry; I have arrived," Chloe announces as she makes her way to me and joins me behind the counter.

"You should have seen me. I was panicking like never before." I chuckle as I stir the caramel macchiato.

She grabs a towel and smacks me with it while she tries to stifle her own laugh. "Need help with anything?" she asks as she ties an apron on. Then, she puts her name tag on, which says Jenny—she uses it to deter any questions about who she really is.

"Right now? No, everything's ready for at least the morning. We are getting low on almond milk though if you want to grab a new one from the back."

"Yes, ma'am." She salutes me as she spins and heads to the cooler.

I giggle and hand out the drinks to the remaining customers. "Have a great day, everyone!"

A string of *thank you* and *you too* flows from their lips as they turn to leave with their coffees in hand.

Grabbing the dirty dishes, I quickly bring them to the sink to rinse them out. The hot water stings at first, but it quickly subsides. Right as I grab the first stir stick, the bell chimes again at the front.

As I quickly scrub the stick with my back facing my new guests, I call out, "I'll be right with you guys!"

The mumbles coming from behind me sound vaguely familiar. A shiver runs down my spine, and the back of my neck burns—the same feeling I felt only nights ago. When one particular blue-eyed boy broke down every barrier I had.

Laura's and Jack's voices are almost nostalgic to me. Right as I'm about to turn and greet them face-to-face, Chloe comes out of the back room directly to my left, and her eyes widen as she freezes in place.

She not-so-subtly glances at me. "Want me to get them?"

That confirms my suspicion tenfold. I'll be a big girl and not let some little crush inhibit me from doing my job. Without a word, I shake my head.

I mean, let's be honest here. I had a mask on, it was dark as hell in there, and I left like Cinderella. The amount of actual time we spent together was very minimal. I'm sure he has forgotten me altogether.

I take a deep breath before turning around.

My eyes stay glued to the floor and then on the countertop as they reach the counter to order. I know this defense will only last me another second before I have to look up.

"How have you been?" Laura asks with pure happiness in her voice.

Ugh. This is it. If he's going to remember, it's going to be now.

Slowly, I lift my eyes to meet hers, and I force them to stay there. My perfect smile forms on my lips as I say, "I've been really good. How are you? How has life been

74

treating you?" My words fall from my lips of their own accord.

She can't help the knowing gleam from shining in her eyes. Immediately, she glances at Cam. I know it's him. I can see the raven tattoo in my peripheral vision.

Laura, can you be any less subtle?

She beams as she glances up to Alec, but I don't follow her stare. Instead, my gaze moves to Jack, who I swear has grown a foot since I last saw him.

"Oh my gosh, Jack, you are going to be taller than me soon!"

He smiles and places his hands on the counter.

"What can we get for you?" Chloe asks as she joins me at my side, carefully brushing against my hip to show her support.

"I'll have my usual—salted caramel cold brew. Chocolate milk for Jack. Alec?" Laura asks, and when she glances my way, her eyes reveal everything.

She totally knows that I know that this is the mystery guy from that night. She could have just left him in the damn car, but instead, she invited him into my shop and put him right in front of me.

Hopefully, with his drop-dead gorgeous looks, Blue Eyes comes with no brains.

"I'll just have water, please," Alec says, completely unaware of the real dynamic at play.

Moment of truth.

"And for y-you?" My word stutters as my eyes meet the mystery man.

Holy shit. I didn't think that a mask could truly hide so much of someone's face. I was very, very wrong.

Blue Eyes isn't simply attractive. He doesn't just take my breath away; he takes my fucking *soul*. Another man will never compare to the beauty in his features. His sharp jawline, high cheekbones, and beautiful, large eyes are irritatingly perfect.

Ugh, guys who look like that know it too. They know how to use their looks and wield it like a weapon. And Blue Eyes will be very wrong to underestimate me in any way.

It dawns on me that more than a brief second has passed while our eyes have been locked on to one another.

"I'll take a black coffee, please." Blue Eyes's deep voice causes goose bumps to break out on the tops of my arms.

"You got it." My voice is quieter than I would like.

But I don't think he has really placed me yet. The longing look of familiarity dances between us, but I think he's having a hard time putting his finger on it.

"We'll grab a seat. Cam, get our drinks," Laura orders.

Cam. I wonder if it's short for Cameron or if it's just Cam.

"Aye, aye, captain," he retorts in a mocking tone.

Thank God Chloe is filling the cups for orders because I'm fucking helpless right now.

Cam has me all weird. I'm flustered and overanalyzing everything he does to see if he recognizes me. But so far, he hasn't given me an indicator that he has.

"That will be right up," I tell him as he sets his phone on the counter and places his palms down on either side, wrapping his fingers around the edge of the counter.

He is just watching me, studying me.

I wonder if he does this to everyone. Is it because no one stops him? Because he looks like a golden-tan god?

"If you prefer to have a seat, I can bring them to your table," I offer with a hint of sternness in my voice.

"That would be great actually, thank you." He smiles, grabs his phone, and pushes off of the counter, spinning at his torso, and he heads over to the booth that Laura always sits in.

I exhale the breath I was holding as an ounce of pressure releases from my shoulders.

Spinning to Chloe, I already know what to expect.

"Nikki, it is fucking fate. Please get his number, dear God, for the both of us," she mumbles as I help her finish making the drinks.

Glaring at her, I say, "You know damn well that I cannot do that."

Grabbing two of the drinks, Chloe whispers, "Wrong. You won't."

I grab the black coffee and chocolate milk and lead the way to their table. "Stop it, Chlo."

They all drop whatever conversation they are having as we approach.

A knee hits my thigh, and I bite down on the inside of my cheek in an attempt to stop the blush. Cam's knee is now pressed firmly against my right mid-thigh, and he clears his throat.

But I ignore him, which is harder than I thought it would be. In my peripheral vision, I see him shaking his head ever so slightly. I'm sure he has used this routine on every waitress.

I set the black coffee down, and all I can think about is getting back behind the safety of my counter. I don't fear Cam—quite the opposite actually. But that is far more worthy of my fear.

Jack smiles up at me as I reach across the table on the left side and hand Jack his milk.

"Here you go!" I say in a cheery voice.

"Thank you!" He sings as he grabs it from me.

I quietly clear my throat before saying, "Please let us know if there is anything else we can get for y—"

Suddenly, my arm is in a grasp, and my heart plummets to my gut. But as fast as the fear and anxiety arrived, it dissipates as I realize what's happening.

Cam has my forearm in his grasp, and the most devilish smile appears on his lips. It takes me all but a second to realize what caused this reaction from him, and I suddenly wish I had worn long sleeves today.

Stupid.

He gently tugs me forward, pressing me harder into the table and into his knee so I have no choice but to face him. I look down.

His sultry tone murmurs the pet name he gave me as those blue eyes look up at me through dark lashes. "Little Dove. What a surprise." His thumb strokes over the inked lines of the dove on my skin.

Dangerous shivers course through my body.

"I'm sorry. I think you must have me confused with someone else," I say, ready to yank my arm back out of his touch, but I hesitate for some reason.

He leans forward and sits up, still holding my arm and now tracing circles with his thumb. His gaze shifts, resembling a similar look I saw in his eyes when he had his thumb in my mouth on the dance floor.

He takes a deep breath, and as he exhales, he seems to have drifted closer, somehow sitting up even taller.

I should have backed up long ago. Put more space between us. But I don't think that really would have made a difference. He probably would've just hopped over the table.

Pulling me down until only mere inches separate us, he closes his eyes and takes a deep breath. "Little Dove, Little Dove."

It takes me a moment to realize he just breathed me in. I don't know whether to be turned on or creeped out. Or embarrassed at the fact that Alec, Laura, Chloe, and Jack are watching this.

"It is most definitely *you*."

CAM

It is way too pleasing to watch her squirm with my closeness. What would she do if I pulled her forward and forced her to bend at her waist to get closer to me? Run and hide? Kiss me?

It's ironic really that I can barely read her in a room full of light, but in the dark, I knew every little thing that she wanted, every thought she had. But now? I really don't know.

Maybe I pushed her too far. Maybe I should just stop and let her breathe.

Nah.

Her heart is pounding—I can feel it in her wrist. I bet she is nervous as hell right now. Maybe she thinks she can still convince me it's not her.

But I know it is from the tattoo she has to the way her body swayed side to side as she tried to hurry as she helped us. It might not have been the same dancing I saw her do at Fireflies. But in the time we spent together, I memorized how her body moved beneath the lights. Her having an apron on and a T-shirt didn't change that. The movements sparked that memory in my brain.

I wish everyone else would walk away and give us the room we clearly crave right now. My focus is on Little Dove, ignoring the onlookers.

She is so stunning. What I thought was just a lighter blue in her eyes is so much more. The outer rim is darker, cerulean almost. The color dissipates to the palest of blues closer to her pupil.

Her bright blue eyes and that pretty pink hair remind me of cotton candy, and my weakness has always been my sweet tooth.

"I'm sorry. You must have me confused with someone else. I've got to go. Please let Chloe know if you need anything else." Her words are choppy, no rhyme or rhythm to the flow, and her breathing is unsteady.

If I didn't know any better, I would say that she wasn't comfortable. But the look in her eyes right now says everything her mouth doesn't.

I'm about to open my mouth to say that I'm sorry if I made her uncomfortable, and that if she doesn't want to see me again, then I'll respect that. But the second my lips part, she pulls her arm out of my grasp and speed-walks to the counter. But she doesn't stop there. She goes through a door and out of sight.

Fuck. I blew it.

When I finally glance toward Kos and Laura, they look like sad parents who just watched their son get his heart broken.

Laura sighs and says, "You should go after her, you know."

Leaning my head back against the booth, I stare at the ceiling and say, "Well, you saw how well that just went. I don't think pushing it would really be the best way to go."

Someone clears their throat, and I turn and see Chloe standing at our table, looking at me with regret in her eyes.

"Look, Nikki is going to kill me for this. But she is just scared. She will be the person to push you away before you even have a chance to do that to her. She had an amazing time at Fireflies with you. I-if you want, I can take you back there to see her."

"Yes," I say without hesitation.

I don't know what exactly it is about her. But she is a puzzle I desperately want to solve.

Chloe is beaming, proud at the risk she took. "Well then, right this way." She steps aside to let me join her.

Sliding out of the booth, I have … nerves? Although, I do love a good playful chase, it isn't my usual routine to have to quite *literally* chase the girl. But routine gets boring, and she is anything but.

So, here I am, following Chloe behind the counter and through a door that leads to a hallway. The walls are white, and everything is so incredibly clean and tidy. I sneak a peek into the open rooms that look like they're used for storage as we pass them by. We stop at the last door that is closed.

Chloe knocks on it and announces herself, "Hey, it's me. Can I come in?"

The sign on the door is a white plaque that says *Boss Bitch*. I can't help but smile at that. But I would rather it have her name there, as I still do not know it.

What is up with this girl? She oozes mystery, and I want to fucking solve it.

I hear feet shuffling toward the door, and I take a step out of view from the doorway and wait. I think if she sees me right away, she might just slam the door shut.

The doorknob twists, the door opens, and Little Dove says to Chloe, "Chlo, I just need a minute, okay? I'll be out in a few."

Chloe's wide eyes dart in my direction, and I take a hesitant step into view with my hand rubbing the back of my neck.

"Hi, Little Dove."

She holds her breath and just stares at me with wide eyes. "What are you doing back here?"

Chloe slowly backs away as I inch into the doorway Little Dove.

"I-I wanted to apologize for making you uncomfortable. It wasn't my intention, truly."

She exhales and bites her lip, not in a sexual way, but as if she is teetering on the edge of stepping aside and letting me in or never speaking to me again.

The bell of the front door chimes, and Chloe looks torn between staying where she is or going to greet the customers. Thank God she chooses the latter.

"I'd better go."

"Chlo—" Little Dove tries to stop her, but Chloe glares at her and turns, hustling away.

Tired of waiting, I invite myself in. "May I?"

Her mouth tries to form words, but she just closes it, nods her head, and steps aside.

The room is perfectly put together and, of course, impeccably tidy. A large L-shaped oak desk faces the door. A dusty blue love seat and white accent chair sit on the other side of the room with a coffee table. And that is exactly where I go.

This love seat has got to be the most comfortable piece of furniture I've ever sat on.

She sits on the white chair, still speechless. She licks her lips and finally graces me with her smooth, sultry voice. "You didn't make me uncomfortable, you know."

I hold her eye contact. I would say it's intentional, but I can't take my eyes off of hers. They are so incredibly beautiful, as is the rest of her.

"Then, why did you run away?" I ask matter-of-factly.

She squints her eyes. "I did not run."

I smirk. "You tore your arm from my hand, spun on your heel, and practically ran. Please tell me how that was not running away, Little Dove." I lower my voice on her pet name.

She sucks her cheek in between her teeth, clearly holding some words back. I quietly chuckle.

"Fine, smart-ass. Maybe I ran. So what?" She crosses her arms across her chest.

I swear to God, it takes physical restraint not to look down to where her breasts are being pressed so tightly together, almost spilling out of the top of her shirt.

Mischief dances in her eyes, and she knows exactly what she is doing. So, let's see where this goes.

"If you wanted to get me in a private room, you only needed to ask," I say, slightly lifting my hips up and widening my legs.

"I have no doubt that is true. I'm sure any woman on earth could invite you into a private room, and you would run like a lapdog," she snarks with fire in her eyes.

I shrug. "Not every woman. But I do have a weakness for a certain pink-haired girl that caught my interest a few nights ago. Her? Yes, I would follow her into a private room." I sit up, holding her gaze. "Every time."

She gulps and rolls her eyes.

Fuck, I wonder if she likes to be spanked.

"Well, even if that were me, maybe I don't want anything to do with a certain blue-eyed boy that I hypothetically met at a club a few nights ago, or I would have texted him."

"Hmm, I doubt that." I chuckle, trying to push as many buttons as I can. I like to watch her get flustered and all riled up.

"You don't know me, and you can't know that," she quips.

I lean forward. "I know you liked pressing your ass as tight as it could get against my cock with only that thin dress and my jeans separating us. I know you liked when I stuck my thumb in your mouth. And I *fucking* loved how it felt when your tongue flicked it over and over." I lick my lips and stop myself from going over to her. "You're right. I don't know for sure that you want anything to do with me. But I know, that night, you did. And, God, what I would have given to have you come home with me. The *things* I would have done to you—with your consent, of course, Little Dove."

Her thighs are squeezed together so tightly, and her chest is rising so fast that I think she might be the one to make a move.

But as much as I want to take her across that oak desk right now, I'm occasionally a man of patience. This being one of those times. When I take Little Dove, I want to be in such a state of desire that she is all I can think about, all I crave. And that simply takes time.

"I want to take you out for dinner. Tonight," I tell her, waiting with bated breath for her answer.

She chuckles and puts her forehead against the palm of her hand. "I don't know. I don't think it's a good idea."

Rising off of the love seat, I walk over to her, gently caress the back of her hand that's resting on her forehead, and pull it away.

She hesitantly looks up to me. I can't stop myself from reaching out and touching the smooth skin of her cheek. I cup it, sliding my fingers under her ear and stroking her flushed cheek with my thumb.

"Please," I whisper to her.

I almost have to slap myself for begging her. I have never begged a woman for her time.

She stares at me for what feels like forever, as if a war is waging in her mind. Then, ever so slightly, she nods her head, and a small smile forms on her full lips. "Yes."

"Can I pick you up at your place?" I ask her, still stroking her cheek.

Her eyes quickly widen. "No, but I will meet you there. Speaking of which, where will we go?"

Well, I won't ask for more details on that scared reaction to my question right now, but I definitely will later.

I have only been here a handful of times with Laura and Alec. But I do remember loving the cheese-stuffed ravioli at Elevation. I also remember the crazy-high prices, but I don't really give a shit about that. I want to hear her moan while she eats the most delicious pasta she's ever had.

"How about Elevation?"

Sliding my hand away from her cheek, I drop it to my side. I can't help but notice the tiniest frown form on her lips.

"That is way too expensive. Also, you need a reservation, like, months in advance. How about Culver's?"

"No." I laugh. "How about Elevation? I can get us a table; don't worry."

A perk of being a Nighthawk is that tables magically seem to appear when you want to eat at a sold-out restaurant. Also, I remember them having great security, no paparazzi allowed inside. I don't want to scare her off right away.

"And if I say no, will that change your opinion on where to go?" she asks.

"No, not at all. They have the best pasta, and I want to watch you drool over it."

She sucks in a breath. "What time?"

"Eight."

"I'll be there." She smirks. "Probably."

That mouth is going to get her into trouble. In one swift movement, I cage her in the chair, placing a hand on either side of her head. I push her legs together with mine. "Don't stand me up, Little Dove."

The reaction I expect from her never comes.

She shoves me hard in the chest, all while remaining seated, and I stumble back. And when I meet her eyes again, they are full of fear. All warmth drains from me.

"I-I'm sorry."

I reach out for her hand. But she pulls away, looking embarrassed.

"Don't be. I'm sorry. I shouldn't have shoved you. If you don't want to go to dinner now, I'll completely understand." She drops her gaze to my chest, and her demeanor has completely shifted.

Once again, I'm wondering who in the hell hurt her.

Placing my fingers under her chin, I lift her head, and she meets my eyes.

"Please don't apologize. I won't do anything again before telling you, I promise. I would love to get dinner with you. On one condition," I tease slightly.

"What?" she quietly asks.

I chuckle, not realizing we have gone this long without exchanging this information. "Tell me your name."

She smiles, but her eyes are still pained. "I'm Nikki."

I stick my hand out between us. "Cam."

"It's nice to meet you, Cameron." She smiles, and this time, it reaches her eyes.

"Just Cam," I say lightheartedly.

She nods. "I suppose you'd better get back before they start to worry."

"Yeah, we should probably go," I say.

I offer her my hand. She takes it and stands up, then releases it. Baby steps—that's okay.

We walk in silence out of the back room.

When she is about to turn and walk over to Chloe, I say, "Ask for me when you arrive. I'll have the reservation in my name."

Alec, Laura, and Jack are all leaning against the counter. I acknowledge them once before turning back to Nikki.

She smiles and says, "Eight o'clock—got it. See you tonight, Cameron," she says mockingly.

I shake my head, smiling. Even if it's not my actual name, it sounds damn good, coming from her mouth.

"Thank you," I tell the waiter as he sets two waters down on the table.

My palms are sweating. They are fucking *sweating*. When have I ever been this nervous for a first date?

I check my phone for the millionth time. Seven fifty-five p.m. I made sure to be here twenty minutes early because I wanted to be here first. And I wasn't sure how early she usually got to things, so here I am, sitting here for almost twenty minutes, trying not to pathetically look up every time a waiter brings someone to a table.

This restaurant has the best atmosphere. The lights are dimmed. Red, black, and gold decorate every table and room.

Another waiter walks into the room from the front, and I track him, waiting for him to move out of the way so I can see if it's her. But when he steps aside, it's not Nikki. It's two women, clearly on a date by the way they are looking at each other. If they are not on a date, they should be.

I tap the screen of my phone—7:58 p.m.

The waiter seats the two women and heads back up front, getting ready to torture me with someone else.

I glance at the dozen red roses that I got her, which are sitting on our table.

I grab my water and take a sip. This is really good water. I feel like that's an odd thing to think because water generally tastes the same, but somehow, this is … better?

Thankfully, my brain seems to distract itself because when I check my phone again, it's eight p.m. on the dot. And Nikki still isn't here.

Setting my glass down, I try not to think that she really won't show.

My waiter approaches again. "Sir, can I get you anything while you wait for your company?"

I shake my head. "No, thank you though."

"Are you sure? A few appetizers or some of our best local wine?" he counters.

But he isn't getting another second of my attention. Because Nikki has just entered the room, and suddenly, I'm standing up, holding the roses, and watching her look around the room to find me. And that is a beautiful sight, watching her stunning eyes scan the room for *me*.

Her curves are encased in a black wrap dress, tiny straps holding it up. Her pink hair is in loose waves behind her shoulders and tucked behind her ears. She is in strappy black heels, but I know that I will still tower over her.

She hasn't spotted me yet. But when she finally does and those stunning blue eyes lock with mine, I genuinely forget to breathe. She is the most breathtaking woman I have ever seen.

It's just something I can't place. Something about her that calls to me. She's barely told me anything about herself, but I feel like I know who she is.

The host and Nikki approach the table, and I step out to greet her. The guy who walked her over stares at her a little too long before walking away. For two seconds, I look away from her to glare at him. He meets my eyes, and I tighten my jaw and stand a little taller.

He immediately looks away and goes back to his job.

When I look back at Nikki, who is now two feet from me, her lips are pursed.

"Did you just mean-mug the host?" She giggles. "Be nice."

I smirk and chuckle, but more at the fact that I've been calling him a waiter in my mind this whole time when in fact he is not a waiter; he is a host.

I step toward her and pull her into my arms. With my hand gently resting on the back of her hair, I press my lips and nose on the top of her head.

I breathe her in. "You look fucking beautiful, Little Dove." I press a kiss into her hair before pulling away. "These are for you." I hand her the roses and walk around her and to her chair before I can see her reaction.

I pull her chair out for her and gesture for her to sit. She sits, and I help scoot her into the table before walking around and taking my seat.

This is so weird for me. I've been on countless dates, but they usually have one goal—to go fuck back at my place. Then, they leave, and I try to sleep. Simple, easy. This is so not that.

This feels real. I don't want to fuck her tonight. Hold on. That's not exactly what I mean. I desperately want to tear that fabric off of her, pick her up, and bounce her on my dick. I don't give a fuck if the whole restaurant watches her cry out my name.

But I don't want to rush this. I want to know her, the bad and the good. I don't want the same pointless conversations that I've had before. I want to know the real her.

She clears her throat and takes a quick sip of her water. "Um, to be honest, Cameron, I haven't been on a date in years. I'm so far out of my element. So, I have no idea how this works anymore." She laughs.

I chuckle at her, but I'm astonished at the statement she made. Years? She could get any guy she wanted.

On the note of honesty, I will give her some of my own. "I have been on lots of dates, Nikki, but I haven't been as nervous before as I am on this one. And in full transparency, the dates I'm on usually have one intention. So, this"—I motion between us—"is new territory for me."

"Well, that makes me feel a little better, I suppose." She smiles.

Our waiter approaches and takes our orders, refilling our waters afterward.

"I have an idea. Tell me if you think it's stupid," I say.

She nods.

"We play a game. Say something about yourself, either a truth or a lie, and then I'll guess what it is. We'll take turns."

She thinks on it for a second. "Okay, let's do it. Gentleman goes first." She gestures to me.

I wish I had at least thought of one before I asked her to play the game. "One time, my teammates dumped a bucket of ice water on me while I was in the shower."

She squints at me at my easy statement. But this could totally be a lie. It's not, but it could be.

"Truth," she guesses.

"You're right." I smile. "Your turn."

"Hmm." She taps her fingers on the table. "I've never had a pet."

Never? That seems to be a bit of a stretch. Everyone has had at least a goldfish or a hamster.

"Lie. No way that you've never had a pet."

She is beaming as she says, "Ha! It's true. My parents never had a pet because my mom was always so allergic to everything. And they thought fish were pointless to have, so I never did."

"But why not get one now?" I ask her.

My family had two German shepherds when I was growing up, and I couldn't imagine my childhood without them. Especially when Rocco took a chunk out of my dad's arm while he was hurting me. It would have seemed so lonely without them. But they both passed away when I was eleven.

She shrugs her shoulders. "I don't know. I've always really wanted a German shepherd." Her eyes seem to glaze over as she imagines it. "With their cute little faces and big ears. And they're so smart, and they can be trained so well. If I ever get a dog, it will probably be one of those."

"I actually had two shepherds as a kid. They're my favorite too." I smile at the small similarity we share. "All righty, my turn. I read the Fifty Shades book series."

She bites her lower lip as she studies my face. "Truth."

"Why truth?" I scoff. I can't believe she got it right.

"I don't know. I feel like you might have taken notes from them. You totally did, didn't you?" She smiles, anxiously awaiting my answer.

I can't hold back my smirk as I answer her, "I did, and, yes, I took notes—mental ones, but still."

Her cheeks redden as she thinks of her next statement. "One night, when I was at the library, reading, I fell asleep and didn't wake up until morning."

I can totally picture Nikki's idea of a crazy adventure being staying overnight at the library. "Truth."

"Correct." She claps at my victory.

"I lost my virginity when I was seventeen," I say.

"Lie. No way in hell Cam Costello waited until he was seventeen to have sex," she says with so much conviction.

Leaning into the table, I whisper, "Truth." Then, I tease her because she said my last name. "And someone has been stalking me."

"Shut up. Of course I social-stalked you," she says with so much sarcasm. "Every girl should do that to any and every guy they date."

"Fair enough. Your turn." My stomach grumbles. I hope food gets here soon.

She leans into the table, and this time, I let myself look at her chest, which is pressed up against the table and spilling out of the top of her dress.

"Come here," she whispers, and her tone shoots straight to my dick.

I lean forward and turn my head for her to whisper in my ear.

She exhales, and the warm breath that caresses my ear causes my eyes to roll to the back of my head and my blood to rush to my cock.

"I was reading this super-dirty book one night in the back of the library. And I was so turned on that I couldn't resist sliding my hand up my skirt. I couldn't believe how wet I was from one little scene in a book," she whispers, and I think her voice is the sexiest thing I have ever heard.

Jesus fucking Christ.

At this point, I don't even care if it's true or not. That alone was a gift to my goddamn ears.

I turn my head and pull back just enough to meet her eyes. "Lie."

She purses her lips. "Ugh. Yes, it was a lie, but only partially. I did do that; it just wasn't at the library."

"Truth or lie? I'm hard as fuck under this table right now," I whisper near her mouth, our faces only inches apart.

She glances over my shoulder before looking back at me and saying, "Can I feel to find out?"

Oh my God.

Lifting my hips, I try to find a comfortable position, being this hard in these tight-as-fuck pants.

She quickly sits back in her seat, and I learn why.

Our waiter steps up to our table and sets our food down. "Is there anything else I can get you right now?"

She answers for us politely, "No, thank you."

When she looks back at me, she has such a dangerous look in her eyes. I don't get rock-hard boners from something being whispered in my ear.

What is this girl fucking doing to me?

NIKKI

Take a deep breath, Nikki.

I can't believe that I almost ghosted this date. I know the risks are insane, too high. But don't I deserve at least one night out a year to just *be*? Don't get me wrong; the ever-living fear still beats with every thump of my heart.

But I should be able to have time like this for myself once in a blue moon. And every other day of the year, I will live under my usual rock.

I honestly had no expectations for this date, other than the undeniable sexual tension and little touches. So, I thought that was how this entire night would go.

By the way he's dressed and how incredible he looks, I can't say I would've been too disappointed if the only conversations we had lacked any depth.

When I walked in and saw him, I almost fainted, knowing that *he* was who I was meeting. He looked like he was heading to a cover shoot for *GQ.* He's wearing a black button-down with his cuffs rolled, exposing the black ink on his arms. His shirt is tucked into black slacks that hug every inch of him.

What shocked me the most? His honesty. He could have sat here all night, using every move in his book. But instead, he wants to play a game of truth or lie, and he has come across really genuine. But then again, maybe my judgment isn't very accurate.

I knew my latest one would push him over the edge, and I would be lying if I said that watching him adjust in his seat, knowing he was hard because of me, didn't feel so fucking powerful.

What else is enjoyable? Watching him try to get rid of the waiter as fast as he can.

"I hope you enjoy—"

Cam cuts him off, "Thank you very much. We will let you know if we need anything." He shoots a quick smile his way, and then his attention finds me once again.

The waiter smiles and nods to us, then walks away without another word. I'm glad he didn't take Cam's shortness as being rude to him. He genuinely seemed fine when he left.

I totally judge people by how they treat anyone in the service industry. But I know that this probably isn't Cam's usual predicament when dealing with waitstaff. At least, I hope it's not.

His eyes are darker than I have seen them. And I can feel the desire in his stare dance over every inch of my body that he can see above the table.

But as fun as this back-and-forth is, he is one hundred percent losing my attention to this eggplant Parmesan that was just placed in front of me.

"This looks *incredible*," I say as I pick my fork and knife up, readying myself to dive in.

Taking the first bite, I start to think that the people in love with inanimate objects on that one crazy addiction show maybe aren't that crazy after all. Because this is the most delicious bite of food I have ever tasted.

"Mmm," I close my eyes and moan before I swallow, my eyes rolling to the back of my head.

When my eyes open, Cam is looking at me with the sweetest, most endearing stare.

"What?" I say with the biggest smile on my face.

"Nothing. I just wish you'd look at me the way you do that eggplant Parm." He chuckles.

Why is that the greatest pickup line that I have ever heard?

"Because only food that tastes this good deserves *that* look. Sorry, Cameron," I say sarcastically.

"How do you know I don't taste that good?" He smirks. "You haven't even tried."

The bite I just swallowed catches in my throat at his words. And now, I'm coughing like an idiot, and he is beaming like he won the damn lottery.

"Are you okay over there?" he asks mockingly. "Maybe you need mouth-to-mouth? I will totally volunteer," he says so much louder than I would like. He smiles, then takes a sip of his water.

I almost hate how much fun I am having, how easy and natural this feels. I hate that this is going to have to end. But I will enjoy it until then.

"Do you want to be covered in red sauce in five seconds?" I raise my eyebrows.

"You embarrassed, Little Dove?" Cam asks as he takes another bite of his ravioli.

"Shut up and eat your damn pasta." I motion to his bowl with my fork.

With his eyebrows raised, he points to his mouth that is currently chewing.

"Yeah, well, just keep doing that." I can't help the laugh that breaks my character.

We continue to eat and make smart-ass comments to one another, and before I know it, two hours have passed, our dishes have been cleared, and the restaurant is emptying out.

Cam pays for our meal, which I certainly wasn't waiting around for him to do. But the second the bill was brought, he handed the waiter his Black Card without even looking at the ticket.

This is what I have learned so far about Cam Costello.

His star sign is Cancer, and his birthdate is July 1.

He has so much more to him than what meets the eye. It's in the little things he probably doesn't even realize he's revealing.

When he mentioned his family, I noticed he avoided talking about his dad. And the one time that he did, his fist was clenched on the table—probably an involuntary reaction.

He spoke of his mom with such kindness and respect that I wanted to cry. And when he told me that she had passed away, I reached across the table and held his hand while he continued to share about her. I also noticed he never mentioned how she had died. But that she was cremated and he has her ashes in an urn at his house so that she can always be with him.

He loves hockey more than anything—that is clear as day with how his eyes and face light up at the mention of ice or a puck. I could honestly listen to him talk about hockey all day long, and I barely understood a single thing he described. He lives with one of his teammates and is practically on the ice all day, every day.

His open communication is probably what shocks me the most. But the haunting look that I have caught in his eyes time and time again is a close second. It felt familiar as soon as I saw it.

I want to know what caused it, who caused it. But I also know it's none of my damn business unless he wants to tell me.

The walls around my mind and heart are shifting, crumbling, and being rebuilt, all at once. It's fucking aggravating. I want to just go on a date that is this incredible and pursue it. I want to be able to do whatever the fuck I want. But most of all, I want to be able to tell the truth.

I want to be able to introduce myself with my real name, tell people about my real past, my parents, my life, *me*. But instead, as Cam opens up about his life, I feed him lies, born from twisted truths. And that feels like a sucker punch to the gut.

In the bits of myself that I did reveal, woven perfectly in the untruths, it felt refreshing. It was one of the first real conversations I'd had in a long time. Well, with someone other than Chloe. I love her and am so thankful for her, but I needed this.

On top of learning about some of the big things in his life, I learned little things. His favorite color is blue. His comfort movie is *Thor: Ragnarok*. His favorite TV show right now is *Stranger Things*.

He has a soft spot for kids. He spoke of Laura and Alec's son, Jack, like he was the proudest uncle in the world.

He enjoys reading, although he doesn't get to do it much with his schedule. I would like to see how many hours he spends scrolling on social media. Probably enough time to read a book a week, I bet.

Everything I have learned about him makes me hate that this inevitably has to come to an end. I could talk to him forever. But he also informed me that they will leave tomorrow morning. It's for the best. For him and for me.

I work in the morning. And it's already after ten, and I still have a full face of makeup to clean and to do my routine for bed.

"I should get going soon. I've gotta be up at five tomorrow," I say, trying to hide any sadness in my voice that this is coming to a close.

The second I say that, the energy shifts. All happiness seems to drain from us.

"Yeah. I have to leave early tomorrow with Alec, Laura, and Jack. We have to return the rental and fly back, and then I have practice tomorrow night. I should try to get some sleep," he says, but doesn't make a move to leave.

Which means I get to be the bad guy.

I scoot my chair out and quickly text Chloe to come get me. She only lives about two blocks over, so it shouldn't take her long.

Cam joins me at my side, handing me my roses, which I immediately take a deep inhale of. That is one of the greatest smells on earth. With each step we take towards the door, my like for Cam grows, as well as the desire to never leave this date.

"Thank you for the roses, for dinner, for one of the best nights that I've had in a long time," I say honestly.

He opens the door for me, and I step outside, instantly scanning the surroundings for anything suspicious. All while also looking for Chloe's car, which is nowhere in sight. I quickly check my phone—no new messages. I'm trying not to have a damn anxiety attack at the thought that I'm going to have to walk the two blocks to Chloe's house.

Cam turns, somehow noticing my shift in mood. "Is everything okay?"

I scan the street once more, hoping that I'll spot her Porsche any second. But I don't see her anywhere.

I keep my voice even and calm. "Oh, Chloe is probably just running a few minutes late. Don't worry."

Without a second of hesitation, he says, "I'm going to worry. And there's no way in hell that I'm leaving you out here with no ride home, Little Dove. I'm waiting with you."

I smile up at him as heavy silence falls on us, and questions flutter through my mind. *What happens now? Who should start this conversation? Who should end it?*

I incessantly check my phone over the next minute or so as we wait for Chloe to show up, but she hasn't texted back or called.

Shit. She probably fell asleep. She was supposed to pick me up at nine thirty, and now, it's almost eleven.

"Just let me give you a ride. It's getting chilly, and not to sound like a total dad, but I would blame myself if you

FIND ME ON THE ICE

got sick from this when my car is nice and warm," Cam says with that impeccably smooth tone.

My heart is fucking melting, but I'm much too aware of the reality of our situation to become a puddle at his feet.

"That's sweet, Cameron, but I'm sure she'll be here soon," I say as my chest feels tighter than usual.

He rocks back and forth a few times before saying, "How long are we going to wait out here before you stop being so stubborn and let me drive you?"

I playfully glare at him. "I am not that stubborn."

"I'm sorry, did you not discuss your stubbornness when we were talking about star signs earlier, you little Taurus?" He smirks.

My chest flutters at the details he remembers from that conversation. I'm about to say some smart-ass remark back, but it really is starting to get cold, and Chloe has yet to respond.

"Where'd you park?"

He laughs and points to a black Nissan Altima that Laura has rented while she is here. She was happy to hand the keys over to Cam for this date. Something she usually doesn't support so blatantly, he told me. I guess I'm just special that way.

I step off of the curb, leading the way, and say, "Don't think for one second that you're getting invited inside, by the way." I bite my cheek to control the laugh and smile trying to break free.

He throws his hand on his chest, seemingly pained at my comment. "I'm a virgin, I'll have you know. I'm saving myself for marriage."

This time, the laugh bellows out of me. "Ha! If you're a virgin, then I'm the fucking Pope."

"I'm pretty sure the Pope isn't supposed to say fucking," he says jokingly.

"Yeah, well, you're definitely not a virgin, so I can say whatever I want," I say smugly as he opens the passenger door for me.

I go to sit in the car, but he grabs my waist before I can. He pulls me back against his chest with my ass pressed firmly against him. And, dear mother of God, does my body respond to his touch.

Pressing his warm lips against my ear, he whispers, "Oh, Little Dove, I am the furthest thing there is from a virgin."

He takes a breath. When the hot air hits my skin and his fingers tighten on my waist, my breath quickens as I anticipate his next move or word.

He runs the tip of his tongue up the shell of my ear, and warm shivers run down my neck.

"One day, Nikki, I want to show you the stars, the ones that only exist in the darkness of your closed eyes, that only form because of how good I make you feel."

Hearing my name, even my fake one, coming from his lips feels like being bathed in sunlight.

"With every flick of my tongue"—he sucks on my earlobe—"across every single inch of your skin, I want to watch you completely unravel from my touch."

Pushing back into him, I feel exactly how much he is enjoying this and how much he would enjoy everything he is promising.

He slowly releases my waist without a word and walks around to the driver's door with a smile stretched on his lips.

We each slide into our seats before I say, "As much as I want that and would love that, you live in New York, and I live here, Cameron. Anything romantic or sexual would just end in pain. And I've had enough of that for a lifetime."

I point to go straight, and he puts the car in drive, taking off.

I pause for a moment before smirking and saying, "But it's a nice thought. I will certainly revisit that moment in the future—probably under my sheets at night," I say, blatantly showing my intentions.

Cam rolls his eyes and licks his lips. "Nikki, you cannot friend-zone me and tell me you are going to get yourself off while thinking of me in the same sentence."

I hold my finger up. "Technically, it wasn't the same sentence." I purse my lips, stifling bubbling laughter.

He closes his eyes and shakes his head for a second before glancing at me, waiting for directions.

"Take a left up here. I'm going to my shop."

He glances at the clock on the display. "This late?"

Wondering how much I should reveal, I think that this might be one whole truth that I can give him tonight. "I live in a loft in the back of the building. A one-stop shop for me." I laugh.

He smiles softly and chuckles.

When he pulls onto my street, I can see the shop about two blocks down. My heart sinks, as I know this will end in mere seconds.

Cam pulls up next to my shop and puts the car in park, looking at me sheepishly. "Um, so this is very foreign territory for me, but how serious is that friend zone?"

I smile at him, but it almost immediately turns to a frown. "Cameron, we would never see each other. And our lives look quite different. You being here is like stepping out of your life and coming into mine. But I don't think that transition would be quite so smooth the other way around."

He won't meet my eyes and is staring at the floor with an empty look. The pain that erupts in my chest is so very unexpected. I know he's cute and kind and a lot of other amazing things. But nothing could have prepared me for the locked-up feelings that are breaking free from their cage tonight.

I continue before he can interrupt, "I like my life here. It's quiet, peaceful." I'm going to hate myself for saying this because it is such a dick thing to say. "Even though we have lines we can't cross, I don't want you out of my life completely—"

He cuts me off, looking at me with such ferocious passion in his eyes, "Nikki, please don't use the phrase that we can still be friends—unless friends to you means kissing, cuddling, watching late-night movies, and having sex ... *lots* of sex. I will be your friend, Little Dove, but you will be more to me."

I want to say so much right now. I want to say, *Fuck Trey; let him find me,* and take the risk. I want to let myself have one goddamn good thing in my life for once. I want so much in life that I can't have, and I don't know that I ever will be able to have them.

But instead, I reach across the console, grab his face in my hands, pull him over to me, and kiss his cheek, holding it for longer than I probably should. "Thank you for everything, Cam." I offer the best smile I can, although I know it resembles more of a frown.

His eyes light up for only a second. "You called me Cam."

I have to leave before I do anything reckless. "Good night, Cam. I hope you have a safe flight."

As I close the door, I smile genuinely for the moments we did share. Ones that I will certainly cherish.

10

CAM

Another win for the books. We beat the Elmont Eagles, one of the other New York teams, three to one. Which means we are heading to End Zone next to celebrate the win.

I have never wanted to skip a night out more than tonight. At the very least, I want to bring someone with me—a certain someone who's in Minnesota.

Brett and I make the short drive back to our place, change, and leave immediately for the bar. I slipped on a black hoodie, gray joggers, and a Nighthawks cap, placing it backward on my head.

I meet Brett in the living room, and his face is locked on to his phone.

"Ready?" I ask him as I pull my phone out of my pocket.

"Oh, yeah. I'm more than ready." He smiles, and I have an idea of why he is so excited.

nally got out of a toxic relationship with his ex-girlfriend of two years and is having fun getting over her by bringing home a different girl almost every night.

I follow Brett out and unlock my phone, pulling up my texts, specifically Nikki's. We've been talking almost daily—well, maybe that's a lie. I have talked to her daily since I left. In the middle of the night is usually when the thought of her lingers the most. Typically, I am waking from a nightmare, and I swear I can smell her in the room. Like sweet berries, mixed with vanilla.

I don't know what's wrong with me. I'm usually good at keeping emotions out of all of my relationships of any kind. Aside from my teammates, of course. But I can't shake her. She's like a sickness that's spreading through my body and taking over. Part of me is terrified, and part of me never wants to beat this cold.

In the mornings, I send her a text, often accompanied by a photo of myself in bed with messy hair so she can see what I would look like if she woke up by my side. On practice days, I shoot her a text afterward, either of me sweaty in my gear or in a towel, wet after a shower.

This is the first game I've had since last weekend, since I left her. Part of me wants to send her a selfie and say I wish she were here. But that sounds like the most douchebag line I could possibly send her.

FIND ME ON THE ICE

So, instead, I wait until we arrive at the bar, End Zone, and I text her and attach a pic of the team huddled around the counter, getting their first drink.

> Me: *Just beat the Eagles' ass. It would have been a better win with you in the crowd to cheer me on. You name the game, and the tickets are yours.*

I hit Send before I can stop myself, and once it is mark Delivered, I get nervous, like a little schoolgirl waiting to see if her crush marked *yes* or *no* on a note. Three dots appear, and I wait for a response. The dots always appear for longer than a technical difficulty, but they always disappear eventually. This time is no different.

When they disappear, I shove my phone in my pocket, feeling vulnerable and defeated. I want to know why she won't answer, why she's so afraid. I want to know what caused the scars on her body, the reason she is so blocked off. I want to know everything. But I can't do that if I can't even get a text back.

"Double whiskey sour, please," I ask the waitress when she meets my eyes.

"Coming right up." She pops the *P*.

Within a minute, she returns with my drink and slides it across the counter with a napkin underneath it. I can see something written on the napkin. I ignore it.

"Eight dollars," she hums with hooded eyes.

I hand her my card. "Open tab, please."

117

"You got it, babe," she says, and I'm already over the advances of women tonight.

I smile sweetly so she doesn't poison my next drink. I laugh to myself as she hands my card back. Picking my drink up, I leave the napkin with what I imagine is her phone number on the countertop and join my team at our tables.

It's become a Nighthawks tradition to celebrate at End Zone after a win. Our tables are always vacant, reserved for us after a victory, no matter how packed the place is.

Everyone is out tonight, including the girls, Laura and Charlotte. Laura is sitting next to Kos in the seats across from me.

Brett shouts as he sits beside me, "What a fucking game tonight was. I thought you were going to destroy that kid, Cam."

"He left walking. He's fine." I laugh.

"Yeah, with two black eyes." Kos chuckles.

Number eight slammed me into the boards and told me to keep my "bitch ass" out of his way. So, the next time the puck was in his stick, I checked him so hard into the boards that it took him a minute to get up after falling to the ice.

He was seething, and I loved every second of it. Our fight was inevitable, but the tension only grew as the time on the clock ran. Third period, he charged Brett and checked him into the boards.

FIND ME ON THE ICE

There's an unwritten rule when it comes to Brett Burns—no one touches him. It's known to almost all players in the NHL. And if by some chance they don't know and they plant Brett on the boards, they quickly find out. He is a golden boy with a slight partying streak but aside from a few nights out with the boys, the only thing he does is dedicate his life to hockey. A lot like myself, but I'm not quite the nice guy he is.

If a player touches Brett on the ice, our defenders will light them up. It never fails that a player wants to test that theory, and it ends the same way every time.

Usually, the defenders of our line are the ones to punish the player that checks Brett. But this one was all mine.

"He had it coming." I smile and take a chug of my drink.

My phone vibrates, and my heart skips a fucking beat at the possibility of it being Nikki. But I'm met with disappointment when I see Olivia's name on my screen. She and I are occasional friends with benefits. But the thought of her in my bed right now sounds like torture. Don't get me wrong; she's hot and great in bed, but I don't want anything to do with her anymore.

> *Olivia: Congrats on the win tonight. Need someone to celebrate with?*

> *Me: No, I'm good. Already got someone. Thanks though.*

Olivia sends back a thumbs-up. The terms of our relationship have always been clear, and I've always appreciated that. We get what we want out of each other—sex—and that's it.

When I set my phone down, the bartender who hit on me earlier walks over to our group.

"How is everyone doing? Need any shots tonight? More drinks?" she asks the table, holding her flirty stare on me before moving on to Brett.

Kos calls out to the table behind us, "MacArthur!"

Matt turns with a shit-eating grin on his face.

"Shots?"

"Fuck yeah!" Matt shouts.

"A round for our group, please." He quickly gets a head count of the players and the accompanying girls. "Thirty-one of them. Your choice of shot."

She smiles eagerly. "Coming right up."

Brett and Kos get into it on what play was the best of the night, and I sit back in my seat in silence, just observing the room and chaos that End Zone is on a Saturday night.

The dance floor is flooded with drunk people trying to have sex through their clothes. Which immediately reminds me once again of Little Dove.

The way she felt in my hands. *Fuck*. It was pure ecstasy.

I wish that night hadn't gotten interrupted. I would have brought her back to my place and licked every inch of her body and fucked her until she couldn't take it anymore.

I want to know what her panting sounds like and the whimpers that would escape her when I gently squeezed her throat.

I'm suddenly aware of the tightness of my pants, and I adjust myself accordingly. If I get this hard from just thinking about her, I can't imagine what it would actually be like to be with her.

I need more from her than just one date. I need more than her ass pressed up against my hard cock through layers of clothes.

Jesus Christ, Cam, get it together, I think to myself, once again adjusting in my seat.

This girl is going to be my ruin.

The waitress appears with the tray of shots and hands them out to all the players and the girlfriends.

Kos raises his glass. The second it starts its descent to the table, everyone else does the same. We each set it on the table for a millisecond before throwing it back.

Before the waitress leaves, I order another double whiskey sour and quickly down the rest of the one I still have.

When the second one appears, I drink a third of the glass in a few large gulps, catching a side-eye from Kos.

I read his expression without any words needing to be said. *You good?*

One sharp nod from me, and his focus goes back to Laura, who is already dancing in her seat to the music. Not in the way a sober Laura would. In the way drunk Laura wants to dance the night away with Kos.

Not two minutes after I notice that, she is dragging him to the dance floor. They are followed out by the other couples and a few of the single guys who take only a second to find a girl.

I'm not feeling up to dancing tonight. In fact, I'm not feeling much up to partying tonight in general.

Nudging Brett, I lean into his shoulder to speak over the loud music. "Hey, man, I'm going to grab an Uber. I'm fucking beat."

"You sure, bro?" Brett asks, looking a bit concerned because we always leave together.

"Yeah, I'm sure. Get home safe," I tell him before I pull my phone out and order an Uber. It's two minutes away.

Sliding out of the booth, I start heading over to the guys to say my good-byes when I'm stopped by a smokeshow of a redhead.

"Care to dance?" she asks me, her words slurring together.

She's hot, but she's got nothing on Nikki. No one in the world is as beautiful as that damn woman.

"I'm good, thanks." I point to Brett. "I'm sure he would love to dance though."

Brett smirks at the girl, and she's already swaying her hips and walking over to him.

My phone alerts me that my ride is here. I quickly say good-bye to my teammates and hype them up about our win tonight. The cold air is refreshing when I open the door and walk outside.

When I slide into the backseat of the car, my Uber driver, Bryan, greets me, "Hey. How's your night going?"

I pull my phone out of my back pocket and set it in my lap. "All right. Yours?"

He merges into traffic. "Pretty good. Been super busy, so I can't complain about that."

"Very true," I say in an upbeat tone.

Picking my phone up, I do the one thing you shouldn't do drunk—text the person you're into.

> *Me: Little Dove, I can't get you out of my fucking head. I should have kissed you that night so I would know what your lips tasted like …*

Three dots appear and disappear a moment later.

Fuck. What do I have to do to win this girl over?

"We're almost there," Bryan announces.

"Thanks, man."

My fingers hover over the keys to message her again. But the continuous line of blue texts in our messages are getting pathetic.

"Thanks for the ride, man." I hand him a twenty and hop out of the car when it comes to a complete stop.

"Anytime. Have a great night!" he exclaims.

I gently shut the door and make my way up to our condo. My exhale turns into a sigh as I shut the door behind me and toss my keys on the counter.

Nikki. Nikki. Nikki.

Images of her from our date flash in my mind. She looked so fucking gorgeous. I have no idea how I made it through dinner without making a move on her. I wanted to for sure, but I need to be patient. She deserves to be wined and dined and fucked like the woman she is.

So, I will have to keep my filthy thoughts to myself—at least for now. Just thinking about her again has me itching to get out of these boxers and joggers.

My feet carry me to my bedroom before I can stop the thought that's growing in the back of my mind.

If I can't actually be with her and touch her, I can at least do this. I kick my joggers and boxers off, followed by my socks. Grabbing the back of the neck of my shirt, I pull it over my head, feeling my muscles stretch from the soreness of the game tonight. I quickly retrieve a hand towel from my bathroom. Crawling into bed, I reach into the nightstand and grab the bottle of lube.

If Nikki walked into my bedroom right now, what would I do?

I squeeze a quarter-sized drop onto my left hand and let it sit for a second to warm up. Then, wrapping my hand around the already-stiff shaft, I slowly slide it up and down.

I would physically tear her shirt in half, right down the middle, and throw it on the ground. If she were here, she would be mine. If she wanted a shirt afterward, it would be from my closet.

My tongue would savor the taste of her mouth as I unhooked her bra. I would pick her up with ease and set her high on my waist, high enough for me to suck one of her peaked nipples into my mouth, rolling it just sharply enough between my teeth before soothing any ache with the warmth of my tongue.

I pump myself harder and faster and grab my balls with my other hand, massaging gently.

I would throw her down onto my bed and strip her pants off of her, tempted to tear those, too, so she had no choice but to show me her perfect ass all the time while she was here.

I would leave her panties on her just for a little longer. She would already be panting, anticipating my next move.

"Get on all fours," I would demand as I pressed the fronts of my thighs against the edge of the bed.

She would hesitate with a challenging gleam in her eyes before obeying. I would memorize this image. Burn the picture of her arched back, naked breasts, and pink hair flowing around her shoulders into my brain forever.

I squeeze my balls tighter and continue my ruthless stroking of my thick cock.

"Now what?" she would ask and be interrupted as my hand smacked against that perfectly round ass.

She would yelp, and my dick would fucking throb. Her breathing would become needy and ragged.

"Do you like that?" I would ask her, pressing my wet lips against her ear.

She would nod before whimpering, "Yes."

"What a good fucking girl you are, Little Dove," I would praise and smack my hand against the same spot as before, knowing the sting was more intense this time.

Smack. Smack. Smack.

She'd finally speak up, her voice sexy and breathless. "Fuck, Cam, it's too much right there."

With my big hand wrapped around her reddened cheek, I'd lift her ass higher into the air as my left hand grabbed the base of her neck, pulling up slightly.

"One more, baby. I know you can take it," I'd encourage her.

Her blue eyes would lock on to mine as she stared up at me, pupils completely blown.

Her nod would struggle against the hand I had wrapped around her throat.

"That's my girl," I'd groan.

I wouldn't give her a second to be scared before I landed my hand on her ass again, slightly weaker than before. And not a moment later, I would have my tongue running back and forth over the raw and delicate skin.

I pump myself harder, already feeling pressure building deep in my groin. Switching hands, I feel my orgasm nearing more and more by the second. I'm not going to last much longer.

Kissing, sucking, licking, I'd devour the bare skin of her round ass. Without warning, I'd kiss her panties that covered her soaking wet center.

Faster and faster, I massage my balls as images of Nikki flash through my mind.

I'd run my tongue up the red thong, inhaling her scent. And I'd be fucking done for.

The pressure explodes, and I groan as those blue eyes fucking ruin me. I come into the towel and wipe myself off when I'm done.

My muscles relax into the bed as I come down from my high. I don't know what I'm doing with myself, what she's doing to me. Before I met her, my life was very simple—hockey and one-night stands. But I turned down three potential hookups tonight because I can't get this girl out of my fucking head. Simple is easy and predictable, and nothing about Nikki is simple.

My phone vibrates on my nightstand, and I pick it up, expecting it to be Kos or Brett. But it's not. It's my Little Dove.

My heart fucking flutters, and I want to slap myself. But I can't help the giddiness when I read her message.

Little Dove: Hi, Cameron.

NIKKI

The last week has been equal parts amazing and terrifying. Cam and I might have said good-bye to each other after our date, but that lasted as long as it took for me to walk to the door of my shop.

He texted me with a picture of me walking away from him.

> *Cam: Who knew watching you walk away would be so hard?*

At first, I thought it was solely sweet and innocent—until he sent a follow-up.

> *Cam: Extra hard.*

By the time I had the courage to turn around and smile, he was gone. As was the sudden urge to respond. It was for the best—to refrain from responding to his messages and advances. Which would prove to be much harder than expected.

Every morning, I receive a selfie of him in bed with sexy, messy hair.

I was even gifted with a video one morning of him saying, "Good morning, beautiful," in a raspy, sleepy voice.

That alone was a struggle to ignore.

Not to mention, the *good night* messages and selfies of him in an empty bed. And photos before and after games and practices.

I had been doing so well until last night.

But when he sent that text last night, it made me cry. Because I was so horrendously terrified to let anyone in, to talk to anyone for more than five seconds.

I typed out and deleted a text over and over for an hour before just messaging him.

Me: Hi, Cameron.

I chose that over ones that felt more honest and true, like: *You should stay as far away from me as you can. It would be better if you forgot about me. I like you, Cameron, but I can't keep talking to you. My ex would kill me if he found out I was alive and had been hiding from him all this time, and I don't want you to die too.*

So, instead of using logic and reasoning to keep distance between him and me, I started a damn conversation.

And we haven't stopped texting since.

Cam is fascinating to me, mentally and physically. I swear he was molded and shaped after the Greek gods, which is a total bonus. But I'm mainly drawn to him because he also carries demons many don't. Ones that can only be seen by someone who has dark ones of their own.

I don't know how I recognized them in him. Was it the barriers I could see behind the facade of confidence and smirks, or was it the way I intuitively felt comfortable with him? Whatever it might be, I sense them in him, the shadows of a dark past. It calls to me in a way I desperately wish I could ignore. I think Cam survives by being the life of the party and by making every second count because, at one point, maybe time was something he thought he didn't have. I can relate to that for sure.

Maybe I'm projecting my own feelings onto him—who knows? Either way, something in him and something in me are calling to each other, and I think it's only a matter of time before we answer.

As if he can sense my thoughts about him, he texts me as I walk into the library.

Cam: Good morning, beautiful. How'd you sleep?

Unable to wipe the shit-eating grin off of my face, I wade through the sea of kids walking out.

My fingers hover over the keys as I debate on telling him the truth or the answer that I just started typing— the bullshit one.

This morning, I finished reading a book where the main character's whole arc was about finding herself, being confident and unabashedly herself in every situation. So, I'll take a page out of her book this time.

> *Me: First of all, it's eleven o'clock, and I have been awake since seven o'clock. Our versions of morning are two very different things, LOL. As for the sleeping, I didn't get much last night.*

> *Cam: Did you have a hot date?*

Not a moment later, another text comes.

> *Cam: Please tell me you didn't have a date last night.*

I respond with a smirk on my lips.

> *Me: Just a date with my demons.*

Three typing bubbles appear, then disappear and appear once more.

> *Cam: Ahh, I usually see mine on a scheduled slot at ten o'clock on Saturdays and nine o'clock on Sundays.*

Me: Are you always so sarcastic?

Cam: Usually, yes. I'm sorry you couldn't sleep, Little Dove. If I were there, you would sleep like a baby every night.

Me: Because I would be so exhausted from being around you all the time?

Cam: Because you would be exhausted from coming for me over and over again.

Me: That's cute, Blue Eyes.

Cam: ???

Me: That you think you could make me come, LOL—and more than once at that. I think you should try stand-up.

Cam: Has any man ever made you come, Little Dove?

I have had orgasms that made me see stars, but always at my own hand or toy, never by the touch of a man. Trey and I were intimate in the beginning, but when he started hurting me, thankfully, his desire to touch me sexually seemed to die, and he never pushed it. I think he found exterior sources for that service, and I was thankful enough not to ask. I think he made me come once or twice, but I don't know if a man can make you come the same way a vibrator can. I genuinely believe that because no man—of the two I have slept with—has ever come close with me.

Me: Yes.

Cam: That took you far too long to answer. You thinking about it means no. You wouldn't have to guess if you were coming with me. Oh, to hear my name on those lips …

We stayed up late last night, texting each other questions constantly. Anything you can think of, we asked, and I memorized every single one of his answers. I didn't mean to, but my brain held on to these little facts like they were life or death.

I love talking to Cam. But sometimes, I forget, if only for a second, that this isn't real—that it *can't* be real. It's hard to remember that with Cam. It's so natural and easy to talk and flirt with him. He makes me comfortable when I'm talking to him, and I hate when reality makes that comfort turn to fear. When I get caught up in it, like I am right now, terror sinks into my bones, and I'm reminded of who I really am and what I'm hiding from.

Me: I've got to go. I'll text you later.

I turn my phone off and shove it into my pocket with a huff.

"Everything okay?" the librarian, Susan, asks me, and it dawns on me that I stopped walking in the middle of the corridor and never moved.

See, this is the problem. A distraction. He is distracting me. I was so focused on his every sexy word that I forgot about my surroundings—a mistake I can't afford.

I silently sigh. "I'm okay."

Susan totally doesn't believe me. She raises an eyebrow and says, "Darling, you are here multiple days a week, and I like to think that I have gotten to know you, Nikki. And I have never seen you smile at your phone, not once. Nor have I seen that smile turn upside down so fast. Boy troubles?"

I chuckle and wince at the tightness in my neck this morning. I must have slept wrong. "I always have boy troubles, Susan."

She pulls our secret stash of Nutter Butters from a drawer in her desk and holds the package out for me.

The first week I was in Duluth, I practically lived in this library with Susan when I wasn't with Chloe. I was overly thin at the time, having lost weight from the stress of being under Trey's hand and then from being on the run with almost no money. She insisted on me constantly taking snacks from her. Then, one day, she opened a package of Nutter Butters, and I had never had them before. My mom was allergic to peanuts and never had them in the house. I thought they were the most delicious thing I'd ever tasted. She must have noticed my adoration of them because there has not been a day where I have approached her desk and not left without a few in hand.

"Want to talk about it?" she asks as I take a couple from the package.

I shrug. "Not today, Susan."

She tucks the package back into her drawer without taking one. "Can I give you a piece of advice?"

Nodding, I bite into one of my Nutter Butters.

She looks me square in the eye, and I can't help but admire every little wrinkle in her face, of the markings of a life well lived. "Everything in life is fleeting. We might walk outside tonight and not get a chance to see tomorrow. Don't waste a second of your precious life frowning over some boy. Drink lots of wine, eat delicious food, and love absolutely recklessly."

A lump forms in my throat at her words. I want it to be that simple. I want to forget about Trey, and in moments, I do, but as her wrinkles and smile lines show a life of love and laughter, the scars from glass and metal show the pain of mine. I want more than anything to love without abandon, but I'm afraid that will cause far more hurt than not loving at all.

"That's good advice, Susan. But I think it makes more sense for someone else." I smile kindly.

"No. That advice is yours, whenever you're ready to take it." She grins. "Can I tell you a story?"

"Of course."

"As you already know, I live right over there." She points at her home across the small lake through the window. "When I was about your age, I almost died in that lake."

Instant anxiety thrums in my chest when I think about it. Aside from Chloe, Susan is the only person that I have here, and I can't imagine not being able to talk to her.

"I was walking home from the grocery store near here and didn't want to walk around the lake to get home. It was mid-winter, and the lake had been frozen over for a couple of months. I assumed I would be fine, as I had seen kids skating on it and people walking across it before."

I sit down in the chair beside her desk, listening intently to her story.

She continues, "I made it about halfway when I heard a sound that I can still hear clear as day right now. The ice cracked beneath my feet. But I didn't fall through—not yet at least. I froze in place, terrified to take a step and terrified to stay still. But I knew I only had one choice—I had to try to get across. So, I took off. I made it one step before the ice fell out from beneath me, and I plunged into that ice-cold water. It was so cold, much colder than I'd expected. And I went fully under and was completely disoriented for a moment before I luckily resurfaced. I started hyperventilating and screamed for help. And then it was as if I could hear my dad's voice in my head. I had grown up in that house, and for years, he would give me a speech of how to climb out of the lake if I fell through. It was like he had known that at some point, I would be faced with that exact problem, and he'd spent those years preparing me. I took a few deep breaths and did my best to put my mind at ease as I worked through the steps he had taught me."

Her eyes glaze over as she recites her memory, and I listen in awe at every word. I can't imagine how horrifying that was, how helpless she must've felt.

"I held myself up on the ice by my arms, and I took a few more deep breaths for the exertion to come. My dad said that you have to become a seal, kick as strong and fast as you possibly can. I dug my elbows into the ice and lifted my body as horizontal as I could get it. And then I kicked for my life. It took a moment, but I was able to propel my torso and up to my hips out of the water. I caught my breath for a second before carefully squirming the rest of the way out. I resisted the urge to try to stand and instead rolled across the ice, following the steps I'd previously taken, until I was a good ten feet from the hole. Then, I gently stood to my feet and took off back to land and ran home."

I didn't even notice that she had placed a hand on my arm while she was speaking until her finger brushes against one of my scars. She looks down at the marks on my arm.

"I was terrified, and I wasn't sure that I was going to make it out of that water alive. I felt helpless and trapped and so terribly scared. But I fought like hell and escaped. You'll escape whatever you're going through too, sweetie. I'm sure of it."

My eyes burn as tears well up, and the lump in my throat bursts.

She pats my arm. "It'll be okay. If you ever need a helping hand from a little old lady, you know the two places to find me."

I smile at her kindness. I can't help but picture her fighting Trey. The image quickly turns sad.

As if she can read my mind, she says, "I might not look like much of a fighter, but I own a few things that will take care of the fight for me." She playfully unholsters two imaginary hand guns from her hips.

Leave it to Susan to be my unseen hero.

"I'll keep that in mind," I assure her.

She rubs my arm and nods her head. "Go do something reckless that doesn't happen between the pages of a book and tell me about it tomorrow."

Without a word, I stand up and take off outside. Grabbing my phone, I dial Mr. Reckless himself.

I shut the door of my car on the first ring and feel my heart plummet to my stomach, hoping he answers while also hoping he doesn't answer.

Second ring.

Holy shit. I should hang up right now and block his number. This is definitely something I should not be doing.

Third ring.

I feel like, at this point, if he hears it ring and I hang up, he'll know I chickened out.

Fourth ring.

Okay, I give up. I'm hanging up.

"Hello?" he answers.

"Shit," I mumble.

He laughs instantly. "Were you hoping I wouldn't pick up?"

I hold my face in my hand as I admit, "Yeah, sort of."

I can hear the smile in his voice as he asks, "And why is that? You're the one who called me, Little Dove."

"Yeah, I know. It was impulsive." I sigh, feeling like I'm being way too honest right now. "I should go."

"Nikki, wait." He stops me. Silence echoes between us before he says, "What are you doing right now?"

"Sitting in my car outside of the library. Why?" I ask.

"I just want to know so I can picture you. Better yet, answer this."

My phone vibrates, and the FaceTime option flashes across my screen.

"Cam, I'm not answering that," I tell him matter-of-factly as my thumb hovers over the green button.

"Please," he begs.

Susan's voice echoes in my head. *"Go do something reckless that doesn't happen between the pages of a book and tell me about it tomorrow."*

The uplifting sound when the FaceTime call connects fills my car. Sitting up taller, I hold the phone in front of my face.

How is he so beautiful?

"Happy now?" I tease.

He smirks. "Very."

"Hmm," I hum as I hold his gorgeous stare.

Those blue eyes are like a trap that doesn't want to let me go. His brown hair is getting longer, and I have a feeling that when he wears his helmet, it sticks out from it in every direction. I just want to run my hand through it. I bet it's so incredibly soft.

Oh my God, get your shit together.

"So, you were sitting in your car outside of the library and thought, *I should call the hottest hockey player I know and hope he doesn't answer?* Seems a little odd, Little Dove. Miss me or what?" He smiles and flashes those perfect pearly whites.

Black silk surrounds his head, and I ask him, mostly in shock, "Are you still in bed right now?"

"Yeah. We had a game last night. Today's a rest day, so here I am"—he moves the camera, scanning over his bed quickly, and I see his shirtless chest and the top of his abs—"resting."

"Did you win?" I ask him even though I already know the answer from watching some of the game last night, unable to stay away.

He mocks me, "*Did we win?* Of course we won."

I squint and smirk. "Are all hockey players cocky assholes, or is it just you?"

"All of us, babe. We're a special breed." He bends his head, and his neck cracks like a glow stick.

"I wish my neck would crack like that," I exclaim. I've had a kink in my neck all morning. I tried popping it, but it didn't work.

He bends the other way, and it cracks even more. "Come visit. I'll get all of your kinks out."

A picture of Cam's hands rubbing my neck flashes into my mind, and my cheeks flush. I hate every second of it, wishing I could force it to go away.

"That's okay. I can get them out myself," I say, knowing the double meaning of our conversation.

He stretches, and the most delicious groan leaves his lips. "Ugh, Nikki, you kill me."

"How so?" I softly ask.

"You don't back down from my teasing. You match my level, and it's fucking sexy. Talk about something else," he says before throwing a pillow over his face.

I try to ignore the flutter in my chest from his words. "Like what?"

His voice is muffled from the pillow. "Anything that doesn't involve you touching yourself."

My cheeks burn, and I'm glad he's not looking at me right now. "Why? You don't like to think about it?"

My jaw drops as he pans the camera down his body to the sheet that's tented up where the dips of his hips disappear beneath the black silk.

"Trust me, I want to hear all of the wet details sometime, baby, but right now, I don't want you to think that's all I want. So, tell me something sad or something gross—anything."

I try to come up with something fast, but with my mind still stuck on what he just showed me, I can only come up with, "My ex-boyfriend … he was abusive, um …" My throat tightens as the words I want to say fight to break free. "I could share endless stories about what he did."

He moves the pillow and meets my gaze in the camera. "Tell me one."

"We used to have this glass coffee table in our living room. One night, he was upset with me." I stare at the ceiling, avoiding eye contact with Cam at all costs. "He slammed me into it. Glass went everywhere." I gulp as my eyes water. "It hurt so bad. Every time I moved, the pieces dug deeper. No matter how used to the pain I got, I was reminded of its intensity with every breath. I lay there forever. It felt like hours passed before he helped me up."

Taking a few shaky breaths, I force my gaze to meet his. Saying that out loud was scary, but also so refreshing.

Cam is seething with anger as he takes in what I confessed. At the center of his rage is sadness for what I went through, but not pity.

"What's his name?" he aggressively whispers.

I smile. "That is a story from the past, Cam. I want to leave it there."

The look in his eyes could kill a man. He nods and looks at me so intensely that I can feel it across my skin and in my chest. So clearly, as if he were here next to me.

"I have wondered about what caused those scars since the moment we met. Thank you for telling me. I won't let another scar mark your skin, Little Dove," he declares, as if he can make it so.

I let him think that I believe that. The truth is, no one in this world, no matter how great their intent might be, can truly protect you. The only defense against harm you have is yourself.

"Thank you," I whisper back, wanting more than anything to wish that to be true. "Your turn."

He smiles sweetly, vulnerably. "For what?"

I lean back in my seat and get comfortable. "I told you a bad story from my past. What's one of yours?"

12

CAM

I wasn't ready for the honesty of Little Dove's story. I was expecting her to say something stupid, like *naked grandmas*. Not the fact that her ex was abusive.

She doesn't want to tell me his name right now, but eventually, I hope she'll share it. Because I would love to pay him a visit. And I know I would have some assistance from the team too. He wouldn't walk away from it. He would need to be carried, if he left alive at all.

How could someone hurt her?

Looking at the screen, I study her face, every beautiful inch. And then I realize I can do one better. I take a screenshot of her looking right at the camera.

Perfect.

I knew what story I wanted to tell the second she asked, but I need a moment to build up the courage.

"I don't let anyone touch my back," I tell her, forcing the words out of my mouth.

"Why?" she genuinely asks.

"It's full of scars, much like your own. But mine were caused by a whip." My voice is shakier than I'd like. But I've only shared this story with one person—Kos. "My dad used to whip me after practice, after games, whenever he felt like it really. He was my coach and would punish me for fuckups or mistakes or if he thought I had an attitude. He thought I had one most of the time. He was a cop, so I used to think he would always get away with it forever."

"Was?" she asks, and I know what she really wants to know.

"He's not dead, unfortunately. He's in prison, getting what I imagine is treatment much worse than death. He tried to kill himself the first night there, but the guards got to him in time."

She doesn't say *sorry*, and I just now realize that I didn't either. But I think we both know that *I'm sorry* is a phrase used when someone doesn't know what else to say.

"Good. It would have been too easy of an out for him. A cop in prison? I'm sure he wishes he were facing death instead. But he deserves whatever pain he's getting for what he did to you," she says with anger.

As the wave of exposure crashes into my chest, I don't shy away from it. I embrace it and feel it all.

"I'm glad you called, Little Dove. I wish you were here right now," I confess.

146

She hesitates, and her lips open and close before she finally says, "Me too."

A maniacal laugh leaves my throat as Knox is pulled away from me and is escorted into the penalty box.

"Sit your ass in the box, bitch."

He cross-checked Kos into the boards and earned himself two minutes in the sin bin. Which puts us on a power play, five on four, not including the goalies. The second he connected with Kos and he went down, I was already on Knox with my gloved fist, pounding into his face. Owen Knox, number twenty-two on the Washington Wild, has been a pain in my ass this entire game, and I can feel the fight between us brewing. That was just a warm-up. The second he lit Kos up, a target was planted on his back.

Kos skates to the face-off, and the puck is dropped. It flies out to Brett, who takes off toward our zone. I swing wide, and Kos cuts down the center. Brett kicks it over to Kos, and I take off toward the net. Kos shoots, and it goes slightly to the right. The goalie covers it, and the whistle is blown. We set up for the next face-off, and when the puck is in Jensen Donnelley's stick, the defender shoots it down the ice, giving us a moment to race to our bench. We are overdue for a line change.

I rip my helmet off and spray my head with my water bottle. I am so fucking hot right now. Throwing my helmet back on, I take a few large gulps of water and catch my breath. When my next shift arrives, I skate onto the ice.

The announcer shouts through the speakers that our power play has ended and the Wild is at full strength.

Knox skates out of the box, and I notice he doesn't head for the bench. He's staying in, which isn't in his best interest.

Number eighty-one gains possession of the puck and flies toward their zone. I take off and see Knox slap his stick on the ice. Eighty-one passes to Knox, who prepares to shoot and is surprised when my stick meets his at the puck, mid-swing. I barrel into him, checking him as hard as I can.

His teammates try to get to me, but mine are already there to hold them off. Their own scraps start, and I focus on the one in front of me.

Knox flies backward, but doesn't fall. Instead, he digs into the ice and skates toward me with fury in his eyes. The moment I have waited for has finally arrived. I am going to kick his ass, and then we are winning this fucking game.

Our gloves fly to the ice, and the linesmen kick them out of the way so we don't trip over them as we fight.

"I hope you can hit better than you shoot," I say to him when he's a few feet away.

He doesn't say anything back, and as he pulls his arm back to swing, I beat him to the punch, literally. I block his hit with my arm and slam my fist into his face. Immediately, I deliver a second one before he has a chance to recover.

He grabs my collar, and I grab his. We are locked together, and our fists are flying. He lands a good one to my jaw and then my nose. For a split second, I consider the chance that Knox might actually win.

But there is no way that is happening. I drop his collar and slam my left fist into his jaw, followed by my right hook.

He falls to the ground, and I drop to the ice next to him and laugh.

"That's the best you've got, Knox? I've got another one in me if you want to go again."

The ref pulls me off of him, and the crowd goes wild. The sticks smack against our bench as our team cheers on my victory.

"Woo!" I scream into the abyss of sound echoing in the rink.

We're both escorted over to the penalty box to sit for two minutes for roughing.

As I'm sitting in the box, counting down the seconds until I can leave, I can't help but think of Nikki.

I scan the crowd even though I know she's not in it. We've texted off and on the last week since our FaceTime. Each day, I find out new things, little and big.

149

She loves chocolate and hates kiwi. She hasn't been able to visit her parents in a few years and misses them dearly. She has nightmares, like me. She has gone to the library daily since our call, and I would love to know what she's reading. Is it nonfiction, like *Hockey for Dummies*? Or is it straight porn on pages? I want to know what she reads to escape, and I intend on finding out soon.

I wish she were here, cheering us on. She should be in the bleachers, wearing my jersey and screaming my name.

The thought of her stays in the deep recesses of my mind during the remainder of the game. When the final buzzer sounds, we take the win, four to one.

When we get to the locker room, Kos slaps my back. "What the hell got into you? You were on fire the last part of the third. That fucking shot you had was fucking filthy. The goddamn tendy didn't know what to do!"

I laugh, replaying the final breakaway I had tonight. "Fucking right."

"Well, whatever flipped that switch in you needs to keep flipping it. We're taking the Cup this year, boys!" he cheers and screams, and we all follow suit.

After a couple of drinks at End Zone, Brett and I Uber home. He decided to bring some chick home with him, who practically already has her hand down his pants in the car.

"Can you fucking wait until we get to our place?" I scoff.

Brett just laughs. "Fuck off, Costy."

Thankfully, we quickly arrive at our condo.

I tip our driver and jump out of the car. "Don't rush up."

The girl is more sober than Brett, who is already swaying side to side as they walk behind me to the door.

She probably thinks she's going to get a night of great sex. But Brett is already fucking sloshed and will probably pass out in the next thirty minutes.

When I finally shut the door of my bedroom, I grab my phone and fall onto my back on the bed.

I somehow find myself in the Photos app, staring at the screenshot I took of my Little Dove earlier. She is breathtaking in every way.

Biting my lip, I set the photo as my new home screen. I definitely can't change my lock screen, or I'll get shit from the guys, which won't ever end.

I want to call her and ask her about her day. But I don't know if she's up right now or if she would even pick up. I sent her a text after the game, saying we won and that I wished she had been there. I sent a kissing face emoji, and I'm now wondering if it was too much. Leave it to Little Dove to have me overthinking an emoji.

The buzz of the drink I chugged before we left is really starting to kick in, giving me more courage than I usually have. Which leads me to pressing her contact on my FaceTime call log.

It rings once, and I wonder if I should have texted her first.

Second ring.

Third ring.

I'm starting to regret calling when she answers.

It's pitch-black, and her voice is a raspy whisper when she says, "Hello?"

Shit. I woke her up.

"Hey. Are you sleeping? Go back to sleep. We'll talk later," I softly tell her.

A soft light floods the room as she turns on her lamp on her nightstand. She squints as she looks into the camera, completely bare-faced with her hair in disarray. With certainty, she is the most beautiful girl I have ever met.

"Is everything okay, Cam?" she asks with concern etched in her voice.

Nodding, I assure her, "Everything's fine, baby. Go back to sleep. Call me tomorrow."

She yawns and asks, "Do you need to go?"

That's when I notice the rapid rise and fall of her chest and the sliver of fear in her sleepy stare.

"Not at all."

She rolls onto her side, and I struggle not to look at her breasts that are now pressed against the thin layer of her tank top. Sometimes, when I'm around her, I feel fifteen again. Like I have no self-control and am seeing a woman's body for the first time.

"I was having a nightmare actually. You called at the perfect time. How was the game?" she asks as her eyes still struggle to stay open.

"It was good—really good actually," I tell her. "What was your nightmare about?"

"The usual," she sighs.

"Still don't want to tell me his name?" I ask, trying to hide the desperation in my voice.

"I don't ever plan on it." She closes her eyes. "In my dream, I had just gotten home after getting my hair done. He didn't approve of it and made sure I would never color it like that again. He chased me with a knife and cut all of it off with the blade and then stabbed me in the stomach. It felt so real. Then, I woke up when you called."

"I'm glad I did. I'm a hero." I smile at her before genuinely asking her, "Are you okay?"

She shrugs. "It was just a bad dream."

"That doesn't mean that you're okay."

"I'm a little shaken up, but I'll be fine. I hate that about you, you know?" She rolls her eyes.

Laughing, I ask her, "What do you hate?"

She groans. "That you can read me. That you can see me so damn clearly. It's aggravating."

I can't help but see her. She's a beacon of light. I knew it the day I saw her. I was instantly drawn to her and not just because of the attraction I felt toward her. She gets my pain and my past without needing me to explain what it feels like. She already knows. I don't have to put on some front with her or wear a mask. We seem to strip each other of those layers and be true to ourselves, the good and bad.

"You're aggravating," I say, teasing her. "I disagree though. I think it is the furthest from aggravation. No one ever sees me, not in the way you so easily do. They see Cam Costello, a starting forward for the New York Nighthawks, someone invincible. Which is true. I am bulletproof, by the way."

She giggles, and my heart jumps.

"Talking with you has been all I look forward to outside of hockey lately."

"Such a sap, Blue Eyes," she coos.

Rolling my eyes, I can't hold back the smile she seems to conjure out of me. "Tell anyone, and I'll deny it."

She mockingly gasps. "Your secret is safe with me. *For now*."

"For now? For always," I demand.

"Fine. For the foreseeable future. Are you just getting home?" she asks me.

"Yeah. We always grab a few drinks at a bar nearby after a win." I hear a moan through my door, and I guess Brett has more left in him than I thought. "By the way, in case you couldn't already tell, Brett has a guest over tonight."

She giggles, and it has got to be the cutest sound I have ever heard. I immediately want to hear it again.

"But not you?" she asks as her laughter dies down.

"No, not me, Little Dove," I say, feeling a spark in my chest at the thought of her being jealous if I did.

But in all honesty, no one has even come close to comparing to her since the night we met.

"I haven't brought anyone home since you kissed me," I say as I stand up and set my phone down on the bed.

I pull my hoodie over my head and toss it onto the floor.

"What are you doing?" she asks with shock in her voice.

I can see from the little screen of me in the corner that she can see my bare chest.

"Getting ready for bed." I laugh. "But if you want a show, all you have to do is ask."

"Hmm," she hums with a smirk on her lips.

I kick my joggers off and climb into bed, lying on my side, like she is.

"Tell me about your day," I softly demand, not wanting her to stop talking.

Her eyes flutter shut as she says, "I worked at the shop this morning until about eleven. Chloe hired a couple of teen girls to work the afternoon shifts so that I don't always have to be there if I don't want to be. So, I went to the library and talked to Susan, the librarian, for a little bit before coming back here and passing out." She seems to relax, sinking further in her bed as she talks. "Then, Chloe showed up and woke me up. We ate pizza from the restaurant that is by us and watched *The Princess Diaries* and *The Princess Diaries 2*. And now, I'm FaceTiming you and about to fall asleep again."

I want to ask more questions to keep her talking. I don't want this to end yet. But by the time she finishes the short speech about her day, her voice is barely a whisper.

"I can let you go back to sleep, baby," I offer.

Her brow furrows, and her lips frown slightly. "Stay." She lays her phone down, and all I can see is the ceiling. "Good night, Cameron."

"Good night, Nikki." I can't hold back the smile on my lips as I hear her breathing even out as she falls back asleep.

My body is exhausted from tonight, and I am the perfect amount of intoxicated because I feel like I'm floating. I close my eyes and am very thankful that I haven't heard another sound from Brett's room because hearing her calm and peaceful breathing is the most soothing sound in the world.

156

I feel sleep closing in, and I quickly plug my phone in so it doesn't die while I'm passed out. I don't want to be the reason the call ends. I lay my phone beside me and get comfy as I drift into slumber with Nikki at my side.

13

What have I gotten myself into with Cam?

I can't stop going over everything that has happened since that night we met at Fireflies. Of the risks I took that night and have been taking since. But I can't stay away from him, and it's frustrating. I wish I could easily push him out of my life. But I have spent what feels like forever keeping people at a distance and pushing everyone away.

Talking with Cam makes me feel like I'm waking up after a long sleep. The way he can so easily understand me is shocking. He makes me vulnerable, and that is a horrifying thought.

The trauma he has faced is horrendous, and I can't imagine going through that—getting whipped by my own father. I love my parents so dearly. They are the best parents in the world. Which is why they had to believe the lie that I died. If they knew I was out here in the world, alive and well, they wouldn't stop searching until they found me. I couldn't put them at risk of being caught in Trey's line of fire.

Which is exactly what I'm doing to Cam by letting him get close to me. I can't stop the battle inside of me between wanting to be near him and wanting to protect him. It's exhausting.

The bell of the shop door dings, and Holly walks in. Chloe decided to surprise me, and she hired two eighteen-year-old girls to help work at my shop so that I'd have time to step away. It's four o'clock, and we close at seven tonight. The shop is pretty quiet on Wednesday nights, so Holly should be fine by herself. We usually only have high schoolers who hang out in the evenings anyway.

I was super anxious when Chloe told me that she hired staff. But she said that teenagers only cared about themselves, and, well, that's true enough. She only hired female employees so that I would feel more comfortable. I love spending time in my shop and was hesitant to share that time with outsiders. But without them, I wouldn't be able to head over to Chloe's at mid afternoon.

"Hi, Nikki!" Holly chimes as she joins me behind the counter. "I just have to use the restroom quickly, and I'll be all set."

"Sounds good. Thanks, Holly." I smile at her as she turns and walks to the back room to use our staff restroom.

Holly is also opening tomorrow morning for me so that I can have fun tonight with Chloe and sleep in. I am loving having these new additions to the team more and more.

When Holly returns, I give her an overview of what needs to be done tonight and what needs to be prepared for tomorrow. Then, I change and meet Chloe out front when she texts me.

"Hiiiiii!" she squeals as I get in the passenger seat.

"Hey. What're the plans for tonight?" I ask her with excitement as I buckle in.

"Okay, I thought we could either do a marathon of the Twilight movies or the Fifty Shades series," she says and takes off for her house.

"Two very different vibes," I mutter as I consider her proposed options.

"I have a drinking game planned for either, so I'm good with whichever option you pick," she says proudly.

"Oh, perfect. I was worried I would have to come up with that myself." I laugh.

I'm in need of a vent session, and the alcohol will definitely help loosen my tongue.

I would rather watch Fifty Shades, but just the thought of it makes me think about Cam and what he likes in bed. Which I guess, now, I'm thinking about anyway.

"Fifty Shades," I announce my choice.

She clicks her tongue. "That's my girl."

161

Closing my eyes, I inhale deep and sigh louder than intended.

"What are you thinking about?" Chloe softly asks.

Leaning my head against the window, I give myself a second to just feel—feel the overwhelming emotions that have ahold of me.

Excitement for the way Cam makes me feel. Yet simultaneously, I feel fear and dread when I think of him. Not his fault, of course. But I cannot think of Cam without thinking of Trey. Of what would come if he found out I was alive. I'm not only putting myself in danger every time I talk to Cam; unknowingly, Cam is in danger too. It's like walking a tightrope, and you know that someone will eventually grab your ankle and pull you off of it and into the darkness below.

I hate that they coexist in the same space in my brain. One cannot consume a thought without the other. It would be a lot easier if Trey was dead. I should have killed him instead of killing myself. But unfortunately, that is not how it played out.

"It's not fair, Chlo," I whimper as she pulls onto her street.

Her hand lies on my leg, and she says, "I know. I wish I could change it for you—I really do. I love you, and I'm always here for you, Nikki."

"*Nikki*." I utter the name with disdain.

I'm grateful for the life Nikki has, for the friendship she has with Chloe. But sometimes, I can't help but feel so lost inside of this world that she created because of my desperation. I love my shop. I love her. I love sleeping and waking up without Trey by my side. But I hate the constant feeling of having a bag over my head or a pillow on my face, the constant suffocation of this safe and lonely life.

I have everything I could want, except for my parents. I miss my father's cooking and my mother's hugs. I miss the comfort of their scent and the warmth of their home. Loneliness is a feeling I am well accustomed to, a friend in its own right. If I'm lonely, that means that everyone I care about is safe.

"I love you too, Chlo, always," I tell her sincerely.

She smiles and pulls into her four-car garage. "Do you think you'll live like this forever?"

I sigh. "I would like to say yes. But I think, one day, he will find out. Somehow, someway, I think it's inevitable."

We get out of the car and walk into her home. We work our way to her kitchen, and Chloe sets her purse down.

"What do you think he would do if he found you, found us?" She attempts to mask the fear in her voice, but it's there nonetheless.

With the utmost serious stare, I say, "I don't have to think, Chloe. I know for a fact what he will do. If I'm lucky, he will kill me for running from him."

She quietly asks, "That's your idea of luck?"

163

I chortle. "My death alone is lucky. Him not killing the people I love is lucky. I can accept my own death. I cannot bear any of yours."

She sharply inhales. "There is no way he can find you. Nothing exists in your name. You look like a completely different person. He's looking for Morgan Dove. He would have to look for someone who doesn't exist to find you. But if you want, I can hire security for each of us to be with us twenty-four/seven."

"That would draw attention to me, and that is the last thing I want. I have a gun of my own, which is the only protection I need," I assure her.

Besides, a cop can probably sniff a security detail from a mile away. That would do nothing to stop him. But I don't need to worry her more than I already have.

"I just wish I knew how my parents were doing," I sigh.

She holds her finger up and unlocks her phone. She straightens up with a big smile on her face. "Here. Look for yourself on my accounts."

She leans across the kitchen island and hands me her unlocked phone, and I open up her social media, immediately searching for my mom. I click on her page and scroll down to the most recent post. When Trey's face appears, my heart drops. I click on his profile that's tagged in my mom's post, and I try to prepare myself for what could be there. Maybe he's found someone new, which would be horrifying in its own way, knowing what someone else might be going through. Maybe he hasn't moved on at all, and maybe he still cares about his poor dead wife. The latter is what I find.

The most recent post is dated a day ago.

> *Not a day goes by that I don't miss you dearly. I love you forever, Honeybee.*

I feel sick to my stomach.

I scroll down and find another post very similar to the last. But this one has a photo with it—a photo of us. Sadness washes over me, and I'm confused by the intensity of it. I look so happy in that photo, so overjoyed with love and life. But I remember that night with great detail. He choked me until I passed out. He grabbed me from behind and put me into a headlock.

When someone looks at that photo, they see a loving couple. But what they don't see is his fingers pinching my back, the bruises on my arms underneath the sleeves of my dress, or the recently healed broken ribs. They don't see the darkness that haunts the photo.

I scroll to the next photo and feel a sucker punch to the stomach. It's a photo of my sweet mother and father at a restaurant with Trey. Heavy bags sit beneath my mother's eyes, and my heart breaks for the pain she's feeling at my hand. She doesn't even know that she's sitting right next to her daughter's killer. I mean in the sense that my parents think I'm dead. I wouldn't be here if it wasn't for him. He did kill me, a part of me at least.

As I read the caption, unadulterated rage floods my veins, spreading through me like wildfire.

> *Sunday lunch with the Doves is the best part of my weekly routine. We miss her so much.*

That should be *me* at lunch with *my* parents. Not the imposter of a loved one that Trey is. The phone shakes in my hand as the thought of him with my family becomes too much.

I scroll again and see another photo of them all together. And another. And another.

Do they not see him for the monster he really is? Can they not tell, even now?

Those photos, those moments and memories, should be *mine*.

"Take a breath, Nikki. It'll be okay." Chloe tries to soothe me.

I snap, "Okay?! Okay?! How in the hell will everything be okay? Trey is living my life with my own family! While I'm in hiding! Oh, yay, some days, I get to pretend to be normal and kiss a stranger at a club. Oh, yay, I can start falling for a stranger who will never know who I really am. What if we have sex? Will he be saying my name?! No! He'll be saying the one I made up! This"—I wave my hand over my face—"is a lie. The person people meet and like and call their friend doesn't exist! I don't exist! He took everything from me!"

I collapse to the ground as tears pour down my face, and wet sobs and screams tear through me.

"I might not actually be dead, but he killed the person I was, Chloe. He killed her, and I'm left living in this fake life." My sobs continue to fill the silence of the room. "I know how lucky I am that I got out and that I found you. You saved me. But this fear that every shadow is him, the fear that he's walking into my shop when that bell dings, is exhausting. I'm fucking exhausted."

Forcing deep breaths into my lungs, I stare at the ceiling with my head against the kitchen cabinet. Chloe opens one of them without saying a word and grabs a clean plate.

"Here." She juts the plate toward me.

"I am really not hungry right now, Chlo." I can't help but chuckle at the ridiculous offer.

She scoffs, "Stand up and take the damn plate, Nikki."

Closing my eyes, I sigh and stand up next to her and take the plate from her hand. "Okay, now what?"

She turns and grabs another plate from the cabinet. Turning back to me, she has a devious grin on her face, and I can't figure out what she is up to.

She lifts the plate above her head with both hands, screams, and throws the plate against the ground a little ways away from us. "Fuck you, Trey!"

The porcelain plate shatters, and the pieces fly everywhere.

"What in the hell are you doing?!" I shout at her.

"I will give my maid, Gwen, an extra thousand dollars on her next check; don't worry. Now, shut up and throw the damn plate!" she orders.

So, I do.

I lift the white ceramic above my head, close my eyes, and take a deep breath. A deep, guttural roar booms from me as I let the plate fly from my hands. The second it reaches the ground, it explodes.

Chloe places another plate in my hand and nods. "Again."

I lift it up and start my downswing as I shout, "I hate you!"

Crash! The plate practically disintegrates.

She hands me another.

"You fucking broke me, you piece of shit! You deserve to burn in hell!" I scream and shout as the plate breaks apart and settles into the pile of shards on the floor.

Chloe continues to hand me plates, and every time I destroy a perfectly good piece of china, I shout at the ground and say everything I wish I could tell him. My rage fades by the time we get to the last plate, and sadness replaces it immediately.

Sadness, sorrow, unhappiness are emotions I typically fight to feel. Being mad is easier than being sad.

Anger is an emotion that you can feel and process without feeling the vulnerability and rawness of despair. It is easy to stay mad at the world and live in rage at the bad parts of your life, but to open yourself up and feel the pain and loss and treachery this world tortures you with takes strength and bravery.

Chloe pulls me into a hug, and I sink into it, tired from the constant battle no one knows I fight.

"I can't make him go away. I wish I could, Nikki. I wish I had a hit man on speed dial to take this burden off your shoulders." She rubs up and down my back, and I burrow deeper into her hug as my tears stain her shirt. "But I can give you whatever you need and want. If you want to live in Hawaii for a year, let's go. If owning a Lambo and a thousand dogs will make you happy, I'll make it happen. I can't give you that life back, but I can make this one everything you dream it to be."

"Thank you," I whisper and pull her in tighter. "Thank you."

I owe her absolutely everything. She is my best friend, my guardian angel, my savior. She is the sole reason I have made it this far, and I can never thank her enough.

"Come on. I'll make some popcorn. We've got a date with Christian Grey." She pulls back and rubs my shoulders.

"There is no way I can enjoy watching a movie with this mess in here. You make popcorn and get the movie ready, and I'll clean up."

"You're going to take a thousand dollars away from Gwen?" she challenges me.

"No, you are still giving her what you promised." I laugh. "But I physically cannot sit still with this being here. If it makes you feel better, I can leave one piece."

"Two," she bargains for no reason.

Laughing at the stupidity of this, I agree, "Fine, two pieces."

Walking over to the sink, I grab the broom and dustpan from the storage beneath it.

"I want extra butter and salt!" I demand as I sweep the plate fragments into the dustpan.

Buttery goodness fills my nose, and I work faster, needing to devour that popcorn as soon as I can.

Chloe brings the trash can over, and I dump the first scoop.

"What do you want to drink?" she asks.

It has been a while since I let myself get drunk, so let's continue the fun of the night. "Whatever will get me drunk. Host's choice."

She clicks her tongue and winks at me. "You got it!"

She hurries away with new gusto, and I go back to my work. I like cleaning; it's calming. Maybe it goes back to the fact that I like to control everything in my environment to prevent unknown circumstances. If the plates are cleaned up, no one can trip on them or step on one.

If I need to run out of this house for my life, I don't have to worry about stepping on sharp plate shards.

When I finish dumping the last load into the garbage can, I remember the deal Chloe and I made. But I can't bring myself to honor it. I can't leave a mess without bone-chilling fear attacking me—a leftover emotion from Trey.

When I find Chloe in the living room, I'm met with her seventy-five-inch television, bowls overflowing with popcorn, two wineglasses, a bottle of orange juice, and a bottle of champagne.

She is on her phone and starts reading me the rules of the drinking game when I sit down next to her. "*Take a sip when Anastasia puts a pencil or pen or other long object close to her lips. Take a sip when Ana bites her bottom lip. Take a sip when you see or hear the word* Grey."

I grab a handful of popcorn and start laughing. "We are going to be drunk in the first five minutes of this movie."

"There are more." She giggles and shares the rest with me, a few of which are phrases that Christian uses frequently. "Oh my God, this list is long. Basically, take a sip every second of the movie."

"Perfect. I will be blackout drunk before we're halfway through the movie." I grin.

Chloe starts the movie, and we are already sipping on our late-night mimosas before the opening scene is over.

"You know we can go visit Cam if you want," she offers as Ana fumbles with the pencil in the interview scene.

I know if I said I wanted to, we would be leaving tomorrow morning. I want to see Cam—I do. But I don't know if I'm ready to take that leap yet. Guilt still twists in my chest every time we talk because I am keeping a secret from him—the truth of who I am.

"I'm not ready," I tell her, trying to convince myself of it as well.

I will never truly be ready to trust someone again. But I want to try. I have to try. I know there are men out there who are kind and understanding. From what I've seen from Cam, he is one of those guys. But I will never forget that I thought the same thing about Trey. But it wasn't until his claws were already hooked so deep into me that he showed me his true self. By then, I was trapped. I won't be trapped again.

It's confusing, you know, to develop feelings for someone again after what Trey put me through. I can't help but compare everything Cam does to what Trey did. To look for the signs of hidden intent.

Part of me wants to be carefree, to take Cam for his word and trust him. Sometimes, I catch myself doing that. But the second I notice those walls slipping, they are reinforced at once. It is a constant battle of *will I or won't I*—will I take a chance and let myself fall for Cam, or will I force myself to stay safe and alone?

"Okay, but tell me that doesn't look a little fun," Chloe says as Christian smacks the crop against Ana's bare skin.

A lifetime ago, I would have tried almost anything during sex. But I don't think I would be able to stop the panic that would attack me, watching someone lift that into the air with the intent of striking me.

"You have fun with that one, Chlo." I tap my glass against hers as Ana bites her bottom lip.

The light buzz of alcohol begins to relax my muscles, and before I know it, the movie is almost over, and I'm eight mimosas deep and about to piss my pants. As I stand up to use the bathroom, it really hits me. I sway and stagger my way into the bathroom, and I pee for what feels like an hour before my bladder is finally empty.

I quickly wash my hands and dry them on a towel before finding my way back to the living room, where I find Chloe already passed out on the couch. I grab one of her throw blankets and lay it over her.

Getting comfy on the love seat across from her, I take my phone out and Google *Cam Costello Nighthawks*.

Images of my handsome Blue Eyes fill my screen along with links to articles, like "Hottest Hockey Players of the Year" by Buzzfeed and "Nighthawks Take Victory over the Wild, Four to One."

Reaching over, I chug the rest of my mimosa and set the glass back down. Instead of reading these articles and looking at these photos, I do something sober me is going to regret.

I go to my Contacts and call Cam.

CAM

"Brett, did you take my last fucking Twix?" I shout toward his room from the kitchen.

"I'm sorry!" Brett apologizes as he walks into the room.

"Bro, I was looking forward to that all fucking day today," I exclaim.

"Hold on. I can fix this," he says before pulling his phone out of his pocket.

That Twix bar was literally the focal point of my thoughts today. Practice was exhausting this morning. Scrimmaging, on top of lifting weights, kicked my ass more than usual.

"Uber Eats will have your bag of Twix delivered in forty-two minutes," he announces with pride.

I laugh at his enthusiasm and effort. "Thanks, man. What's new with you?"

He shrugs. "Nothing at all. Same old, same old. You?"

I can't help the smirk that forms on my lips. "Well—"

"Holy shit. Does Costy have a crushy?" he teases.

"Brett, don't forget that I can beat your ass." I pause and smile at him before continuing, "I've been talking to someone."

"Is this Costy-level talking?" He places his hands on the back of his head and thrusts his hips, humping the air.

"Not exactly," I say, knowing a shit-eating grin is stretched on my face.

Brett slaps the counter. "Well, goddamn, I didn't think I would see the day when Cam Costello developed … oh my God … are those … feelings?" He breaks into laughter.

"Brett, my foot is about to go into your ass in five seconds if you don't stop playing around," I tell him.

He holds his hands up in defeat. "Okay, okay. She must be something special to have you all wound up. I'm just giving you shit. I'm happy for you, man. What's her name?"

Leaning backward against the counter, I grip the edge. "Nikki."

"And why haven't I met her yet?"

"Because she lives in Duluth," I say.

"Minnesota? Fuck, that's a hell of a road trip for a date night," he says with a furrowed brow.

Stretching my neck from side to side, I respond, "True. But I'm actually going to fly out on our next two days off to see her. She called me drunk off her ass last night and asked me to come visit. She's actually the girl who kissed me at Fireflies."

"With the white mask? Phewww." He whistles. "She was a fucking dime. Good for you, Costy," he says.

"Thanks. I've got a picture if you want to see what she really looks like without a mask," I offer.

He books it around the kitchen island and leans against the counter beside me. "Um, yeah, no shit."

I lift my phone to unlock it and swipe up, and Brett spots her photo as my background immediately.

He places his hand on my shoulder and sighs. "Her photo is already your home screen? Tsk, tsk. Goddamn, man, you've lost it for her, huh?"

I roll my eyes. "I haven't lost it. I do really like her though—a lot. I know we don't get real mushy with each other. But, yeah, I don't even find myself looking at other girls anymore, no desire whatsoever. If it isn't her, I don't want it."

He pats my back. "Well, you know she is going to have to meet the family soon enough."

"Why do you think I'm dating a girl who lives states away? You fuckers would run her off." I laugh.

I don't know if I realized how much I have come to care for Nikki. When I'm not texting or talking to her, I miss her. And I just told Brett I'm dating her. Can I even say that? We technically did go on a date when I was in Duluth. That counts, right?

I wonder what she tells Chloe about us. Does she say we're dating? Or am I way in over my head for this girl?

"I'm sure if she can put up with you, she will fit right in. Invite her out for a game or something. I'd really like to meet her, as would the whole team once they find out about her. Not from me—unless you want me to tell them," he assures me.

I'm not sure if I'm ready for their nonstop questions and ridicule.

"All right, man, I'm going to bed. I'm fucking beat," Brett tells me before walking off to his room.

"Good night, bro." I push off the counter and walk toward my own bedroom.

My phone pings when I get inside of my room and shut the door. I pull it out of my pocket to see it's from Nikki.

My cheeks hurt from smiling so big when I see her name on my screen.

Nikki: Are you still up? I can't sleep.

I type out a quick response, but before hitting Send, I change my mind and opt for something a bit more intimate.

178

Falling backward onto my bed, I call her. She answers after the first ring.

"I'm going to take that as a yes?" she asks.

Placing my hand behind my head, I hold my phone up to my ear in my other hand. "That would be a yes. God, I knew I liked you for your smarts."

She scoffs, "You are always such a brat."

I gasp, "Me? A brat? *Never*." I pause, and she remains silent. "What's up? What's on your mind?"

She sighs, long and heavy. "I can't sleep. I am just really anxious tonight, I think."

Now, that, I can understand, especially alone at night. "How can I help?"

She quietly says, "You can distract me."

I bite my bottom lip as a thousand ways to distract my Little Dove flash into my mind. "We could play a game," I offer.

"Like what?"

I smirk. "Truth or Dare."

"What are we, twelve?" She laughs.

"That is so rude. I take Truth or Dare very seriously. So, what will it be, Little Dove? Truth or dare?" I ask her, smiling.

She hesitates. "Truth."

"Hmm." I want to ask her a *good* question to set the tone of the questions. "What is something you've always been too afraid to tell anyone? Dig deep. I want the secret-est secret of all time."

179

Silence pulses between us as I wait for her answer.

"Do you promise to keep this secret with you and take it to the grave?" she asks sincerely.

"Whatever you say to me, at any time, is mine to hear, and I will never share anything without your permission, Little Dove. For always," I say to her, meaning every single word.

"Chloe knows about my ex and almost all the things he did. But she doesn't know everything." She takes a deep breath.

"I won't ever let him hurt you again, Nikki. I will protect you with my life," I promise her.

"I was pregnant," she whispers softly.

My stomach drops at the pain in her voice, and I patiently wait as she finds the strength to continue.

"I didn't know. At least not until after that night I told you about, the one with the coffee table." Her voice is shaky, and I wish she were here or I were there so I could hold her and comfort her through this horrid memory. "I think my body had just had too much. I started cramping really bad in the middle of the night, and when I went to the bathroom, I was bleeding. It felt like it would never end. I knew it wasn't my period. I had never felt anything like this before. And it wasn't. The next day when Trey was at work, I went to the clinic and they confirmed what I already suspected. I had miscarried."

My fingers tremble with rage at what he did to her.

180

She continues, more anger than sorrow in her words this time, "I had to have been barely a few weeks along, five to seven at the most. If I had known—if I'd just *known*—I could have gotten both of us out. He took my baby from me, my poor baby that never even had a chance."

Tears pool in my eyes from the pain she endured, but in addition, I'm sad for what she lost, for what my girl had to go through. I wish I could help her. I just have to prove to her every single fucking day that I am not him and I won't ever become him. I don't have a mask waiting to shift to show a dark and evil side.

I swear, if I ever get his name from her, I will find him, and I will break every *single* bone in his body. I want him to feel more pain than he could ever imagine. I want him to *pay* for what he did to her.

I can't stop the wave of vulnerability from washing over me. "Thank you for telling me. I know how hard that must have been." I wet my lips. I know the words might not mean much, but I offer them anyway. "I'm sorry. I'm so sorry, Nikki. I wish you were here right now. I just want to hold you. I promise you that I will never—*never*—lay a finger on you that you do not ask for. I swear it. Do you understand? I will never hurt you in any way. And I am always here when you want to talk—always, Little Dove."

She sobs, and her breaths are choppy. "I like you, Cam—I really do—and it scares the living shit out of me."

I smile with a heavy heart. "Me too, baby. Me too."

I take a deep breath, absorbing every second of the moment before saying, "Your turn to ask."

She takes a slow breath to calm her erratic breathing. "Truth or dare?"

"Truth."

"Same question to you then," she says.

I don't have to think about what I want to share. She has been so open and honest with me, and I want to do the same.

"You already know the first part of this. My dad was abusive to both my mom and me. But if I took the whips he liked to give, then she wouldn't be hurt. So, almost daily, I would kneel in front of the wall in our basement, and he would tell me what my lashings would be for. He would count them out and force my mom to watch."

I shakily inhale and continue, "I had no escape from him other than school. Game nights were the worst. I would be punished for the errors I made and the ones he made up in his own head. Each error would total a different number of lashings. There's almost no inch uncovered on my back. And I don't let anyone touch them—I never have."

"One night, after practice, the team and I grabbed a bite to eat, and I got home later than I should have. He was beating her. I tried to stop him, but he overpowered me. He broke my leg, and I couldn't get to her in time. I couldn't save her. He killed her… right in front of me. He is not only in prison for what he did to me. But he's also in prison for murdering my mom."

"Oh, Cam. It was not your fault at all. It wasn't your job to save her. It was his job to not hurt you both. He is the failure—*him*. I can't imagine that. I'm so sorry you had to go through that. No one should have to ever find their mother like that." She hesitates. "I love that you want to protect me and keep me safe, Cam—I do. But please don't burden yourself with the guilt of not being able to. The only person you can protect is yourself. And you did that. You protected yourself, and you made it out alive. And I'm so glad that you did, and I'm so glad that I met you."

For a moment, we sit in silence after our trauma dump, no awkwardness at all, just respect for the pain we have survived.

"All right, let's lighten the mood. Truth or dare?" I ask her with a more upbeat tone.

"Dare. And no more heavy stuff tonight." she orders, and I obey.

"I dare you to tell me your favorite thing about me."

She giggles and says, "Okay. Hmm. My favorite thing about you is … how tall you are. You can grab anything off of the top shelves that I can't reach."

I burst out laughing at the completely unexpected response. "You flatter me."

She giggles. "Well, I have a hard time reaching things sometimes at grocery stores or shopping in general. You would be a great help."

"I would love to go grocery shopping with you." I laugh.

My phone dings and I check it quickly. It's a text from Brett that my Twix have arrived early.

"Perfect." She says with glee. "I also love your smile, and your eyes, and that you seem to be able to read my mind. Your hands are insanely attractive for no reason, and I swear, it's annoying how pretty you are."

My heart races, and I bite my lip to try to stop the full smile from breaking free, but it's no use.

"Now, *that* is what you call flattery. I don't usually like compliments, but, fuck, I love them, coming from you."

"Truth or dare, Cameron?" she hums.

"Truth," I tell her.

She hesitates then says, "What is the craziest thing you've ever done?"

"In what context?" I ask, my mind immediately going sexual, but I don't want to assume that's what she means.

She answers, "In whatever context you want it to be."

"Hmm … the craziest thing I've ever done." I tap my finger on my cheek. "I had sex in the locker room once after a game."

"Shut up." She laughs. "With all of your teammates there?"

"God, no," I scoff. "It was after they left. I snuck her in."

She mockingly says, "Wow."

"Are you jealous, Little Dove?" I ask her, praying that she says yes.

"Definitely not." She snaps the t at the end of the word.

Biting my bottom lip, I laugh. "It seems like that. Sure."

She huffs. "Truth or dare?"

"Tsk, tsk, tsk," I scold her. "It's your turn. Truth or dare?"

"Dare," she says confidently.

Blood shoots to my dick at the dare that enters my mind. "I dare you to take your clothes off."

She grins. "Done."

"Nikki, that wasn't even a second," I say, knowing that wasn't enough time for someone to take their shirt off.

"I was already naked. Aside from my thong that I just kicked off," she says with such casualness, as if she isn't bringing me to my fucking knees right now.

"Truth or dare?" she questions.

"Dare," I say with gusto.

She clicks her tongue. "I dare you to take your top off."

It's truly pathetic how easily she turns me on.

"Hold on," I tell her before setting my phone down on the bed and stripping my T-shirt off.

I snap a quick photo and send it to her before letting her see me again.

"Done," I tell her, lifting the phone back up to my ear.

She breaks out into a fit of giggles. "You did not just send me a douchebag selfie. I hope you know you're not getting one back."

"Imagination is a wondrous thing, Little Dove. I don't need a photo to imagine how perfect those tits of yours are."

Fuck, her being states away is hard. I need to touch her and kiss her and feel her body move in sync with mine. I want to connect with her on every level possible.

"Truth or dare?" I give her the choice and save her from responding to my comment.

"Dare," she says, her voice breathy.

"I dare you to tell me your deepest and filthiest desire," I challenge her.

"I don't know that I really have one. You know, I've never really thought about it," she admits.

We will be returning to this topic another time. I want to bring every one of her fantasies to life. Nothing is off-limits to me when it comes to her. If she wants it, it's hers.

"Okay, then I dare you to name five of your biggest turn-ons."

She blows a raspberry before responding, "I used to like my neck to be kissed and licked. My ass to be grabbed and massaged. I used to love being picked up. And I liked skin tracing. Like, if you took your finger and traced it anywhere on me."

Maybe it's for the best that she lives far away. Because I'm pretty sure if she lets me touch her and taste her and eventually fuck her, I'm going to last all of five seconds.

"Why did you say them all in past tense? Do you not like those things now?" I ask her.

"Hmm. I think I still do. It's just been so long since I've been with someone, and it's not like my ex and I had a wonderfully intimate relationship. Besides him, I only slept with one person before, and I think I might have been the first girl he ever touched." She breaks into a fit of laughter. "Oh my God, it was so bad. Like, so bad, Cam."

"I want all of the details, please, at some point." I laugh, unable to stop myself from the contagiousness of the sweet sound of her own laugh. "Your turn."

"Truth or dare?"

"Truth," I answer.

"When was the last time you slept with someone?" she asks with feigned confidence.

I don't hesitate to reassure her. "The night before I met you. I don't want anyone else but you, and I haven't since you kissed me."

Silence echoes between us before she finally says, "I hate how much I like you, Blue Eyes. You were supposed to be my escape that night, a glimpse into a life of carelessness and fun. But here we are now, on the phone at—*oh my God*—two a.m., playing Truth or Dare."

"In my defense, you called me." I chuckle. "But if you hadn't, I would have called you anyway. And I don't want to stop calling you. I don't want you to stop calling me."

"What does that mean?" she softly asks.

"Whatever you need it to mean as long as it never stops."

15

CAM

"Welcome to Duluth. Have a good day," the flight attendant says as I step off of the plane.

"Thank you. You too," I tell her as my palms start to sweat.

Flying states away to see a girl? This is something I can say I have never done, but she deserves it. I would fly to fucking Antarctica if it meant I could get five minutes with her.

When she drunk-dialed me and asked me to come visit, I booked a flight that night without hesitation. It's pretty much all I've been able to think about since then.

Quickly, I make my way through the airport with my carry-on duffel and backpack and order an Uber.

Throwing my hood up onto my Nighthawks cap, I maneuver through the crowds and find the exit rather swiftly, my heart continuing to thrum in my chest with each passing second.

I'm a fucking goner for this girl. I've never had anxiety or butterflies before seeing someone like this before. I wonder if I should have messaged her and let her know I was coming. What if she has plans and is out of town or something? I already checked her shop's hours online multiple times to make sure it would be open. Because if it's open, then she's there. *Right?*

My phone buzzes, telling me that my Uber is arriving. I throw my phone in my pocket, and I quickly find my ride outside.

Throwing my bags across the backseat of the car, I slide into the seat and buckle up.

"Hey, man. How's it going?" my Uber driver, Jared, asks me.

"Good. How about you?" I ask.

"Great. Thanks for asking. Looks like we're about four minutes out from your destination. There's water and snacks; feel free to grab something," he announces as he pulls into traffic.

"Thank you," I say, but I don't take anything.

My leg is bouncing like crazy as I pull my phone out of my joggers and check once again to see that the shop is still open. It's already six thirty, so the shop is open for another half an hour tonight.

God, why am I so nervous to see her?

I've never opened up with someone like I have with her. She's gotten to know my demons pretty well. Perhaps that's why I'm sweating bullets.

It's easy to get girls when you're a pro hockey player—that's not arrogance; it's just a fact. But I've always kept it superficial. It's always at my place so I can control their length of stay and because I'm in my comfort zone. We fuck, and they leave. That's it—simple.

But Nikki and I have only kissed once, and she already knows more about my past than anyone else does—aside from maybe Kos. Everything is different with her, and I want it to be. I don't want to rush anything with her. I want every touch and every kiss to go in slow motion. I want to memorize every second that I'm with her.

The moment her shop is in view, my heart skips a beat. I hope she's going to be excited to see me.

Shit, maybe I should have called her first before dropping in. But it's too late now.

"Have a good night, sir," Jared says as I grab my bags and open the door.

"Thanks. You too." I tip twenty dollars and climb out of the car.

Too late to turn back now. My stomach is in my throat as I approach the door to her shop.

Fuck, what the hell is wrong with me?

With my hat and hood up, I might be able to stay under the radar for just long enough to see her first.

But as I pull the door open and the bell rings, Chloe is already turning to face me from behind the counter.

191

It takes her only a second to recognize me. I don't see Nikki. Hopefully, she's in the back or something. It would give me the perfect surprise.

"Cam!" Chloe shouts across the shop, pulling the attention of the group of girls studying in the corner.

They are not impressed by the interruption and go back to their work.

"Hey. Is Nikki around?" I ask, unable to hold back my smile.

Her lips part, and her eyes widen with excitement as she says, "Yeah—I mean, no. She's at the library. Does she know you're here? There's no way she wouldn't have told me."

A quiet library, where she will for sure not expect me? Perfect.

Shaking my head, I smile. "No, I'm surprising her. Can you tell me where I can find the library?"

She clasps her hands together on the counter. "Oh, she is going to die, seeing you here." She laughs. "Yes, come here. I'll show you."

She walks out from behind the counter and heads toward the front door, and I follow.

"Do you see that building right there with the blue roof?" She points across the street toward the two-story building at the end of the street perpendicular to us.

"Yeah. That's it?" I ask.

"Yeah. Here, bring her a croissant. I know she didn't eat dinner before she walked over there," she tells me as she hustles over to the display case. She bags up a chocolate-strawberry croissant and hands it to me.

"Thank you," I say, turning toward the door. But immediately, I spin and face her again. "Do you think she'll be happy to see me?"

She practically shoves me toward the door. "Oh my God, yes. She hasn't stopped talking about you. But if you say that, I will deny it until I die. You can leave your bags here if you want—easier to walk that way. Now, hurry up and stop wasting time with me."

Laughing, I drop my bags behind the counter, then head back towards the exit. "All right, thank you."

"No problem. Bye, Cam!" she says as I walk through the door and into the softly falling snow outside.

Hasn't stopped talking about me, huh?

The snow is really starting to come down. I hurry across the street and jog once I hit the sidewalk, closing the distance to the library in no time at all.

The door opens with ease, and then it's grabbed by the wind and flung open. Pulling it shut behind me, I throw my hood off of my head.

Now, where would my Little Dove be in here?

A little old lady sits at the desk up front, so I think that might be a good start.

"Well, hello there. How can I help you?" she asks as she adjusts her glasses.

Cradling the croissant in my arm like a prized possession, I say, "I'm looking for a girl who is about this

193

tall"—I raise my hand to my chest—"and has long light-pink hair. Do you think you could help me with that?"

A light bulb goes off behind her eyes as well as a streak of protectiveness. "Uh, yes. And you are?"

"I'm Cam. I stopped by her shop, but she had already left. Chloe sent me over here with this." I hold up the bag.

She narrows her eyes, but nonetheless tells me what I want to know with a smile as she points behind her. "She is in the Romance section to your right, dear. You'd better be on good behavior, do you understand?"

"Yes, ma'am," I tell her as I begin to wander toward the section she pointed out.

For as small as this building seems from the outside, it feels huge. Bookcases and bookcases fill the room. I pass at least ten before I see light-pink hair through the gap between rows of books.

As quietly as I can, I creep into the row behind the shelf she is leaning against. I don't want to spook her too bad, but I want to see what she's reading and get an idea of what she likes.

I carefully crouch and look over her shoulder through the bookcase between us. She isn't reading at all. She is on her phone, stalking my Instagram. More precisely, she is zooming in on an action shot from our last game that I posted.

This feels like the perfect moment to announce myself. "If you want ice-side seats, all you have to do is ask, baby."

"Ahh!" she shrieks, and the look of fear in her eyes as she turns around and meets my gaze stabs me in my heart.

Without a second of delay, I race around the bookcase and kneel in front of her, spinning my cap around so there is nothing obstructing my view of her every micro movement. "I'm sorry. I didn't mean to scare you like that. Are you okay? I'm sorry."

Her chest is rising and falling with such ferocity. I set the bag down and take her hands in mine, rubbing the backs of her hands with my thumbs.

"I'm sorry. Surprising you like this went much smoother in my head."

She bursts into laughter and squeezes my hands. "Oh my God, please don't do that again. I might have an actual heart attack next time. What are you doing here?"

What am I doing here? She doesn't remember drunk-inviting me? Maybe I'll keep that little secret to myself.

"I wanted to see you," I tell her with the utmost sincerity.

"You flew here just to see me?" she whispers.

Nodding, I pull her to her feet and gaze down at the short, pink-haired goddess who has me wrapped so tight around her finger and she doesn't even know it.

Releasing her hands, I bend down and grab her phone, which is still open to my photo, and the bag with the snack in it and hand them to her.

Her cheeks flash red as she remembers I saw her social-stalking me. "Thank you." She opens the bag and looks up at me quizzically. "Ah, that makes a lot of sense now. Chloe told you where to find me."

"She did. She also sent that along. So, what do you have planned for tonight?" I ask her.

I take in every beautiful little feature of her face, the ones that FaceTime can't show me. The small freckles across her cheeks and nose. The small scars on her jaw. The lines by her eyes from years of smiling. Although, I think those smile lines should be more defined. Everywhere I look is as perfect as the last.

"The only thing I was going to do tonight is rewatch *The Princess Diaries*, so lucky for you, I'm free," she says with the sweetest smile on her face.

I thought there would be more awkwardness between us, more nervousness. We FaceTime or text every day. In a way, we already know each other so well. It makes sense that it is so natural between us.

"Good. Because I was really hoping that we could hang out." I slide my hand into hers as she steps toward the exit.

"Hmm. I don't know if that's such a good idea," she mumbles, and my heart plummets. She looks up at me and panics. "Oh my God, I was kidding. Of course I want to hang out with you."

The ache begins to fade as she strokes her thumb over my hand.

"I thought about you a lot today."

All the time, according to Chloe.

"Oh, really?" I tease her as we approach the front desk.

"Heading out?" the librarian asks her.

"Yeah. Do you need help with anything before I go?" she asks and turns, giving the lady her full attention.

How is she always so thoughtful? That small gesture might be overlooked by most, but she always makes sure that whoever she is interacting with feels truly listened to—a habit she probably picked up because she once felt like she was never heard. She gives me the same attention every day while we talk. I will make damn sure she always feels the same way with me.

"Oh, no. I can handle it from here. You two have a good night." She shoos us away with her hands, and I follow Nikki's lead to the door.

"Did you pack any bags?" she asks. "I have clothes you can borrow, but they might be a little tight." She giggles.

My smile stretches on my face from that beautiful sound she makes. "I think I'll have to pass on that this time around. My bags are at your shop. I just have to

197

drop them off at the hotel, and I'm all yours. Do you have a jacket? It's pretty cold out there."

She shrugs. "I'll be just fine. I walked over here, you know."

I don't give her a second to protest before I'm pulling my hoodie up and over my head. "Here, wear this."

She stares at me. "Cam—"

"Please. It will make me feel better," I assure her.

She hands me her phone and croissant and takes the black Nighthawks hoodie from my hand.

She slides her arms through it, and as the extra-large hoodie envelops her small frame, I know that I am eternally fucked. No one will ever look as good in my hoodie as my Little Dove does. She might not be mine yet, but I'm sure as hell hers.

"What?" she whispers.

Smirking, I feel my cheeks warm as I hand her things over to her. "It looks better on you than me. Keep it."

I take her hand in mine again when we step outside, and I'm happy to see the snowfall has lightened up.

She swings our hands between us as we make the brief walk back to her shop. "If you want, I was thinking you could—"

Her hand pulls mine as she slips, and I lift her up with ease.

"Are you okay?"

She giggles again. "I didn't even fall; you caught me."

"Always, Little Dove. Better safe than sorry," I tell her as I scoop her legs and cradle her in my arms. "Now, what were you saying?"

Her soft gaze is locked on to my face, and she remains silent for a moment before breaking it. "I was going to say that if you don't want to stay at a hotel, you could stay with me."

It takes all of my focus to stay on my feet and not let my knees buckle out. "Are you sure you're comfortable with that?"

Nodding, she says, "Yes."

I know how hard it is for her to take a leap of faith with me. "I would love to."

She looks ahead as we approach the shop, unable to hide the smile on her lips.

"If you change your mind at any point, I'll go to the hotel, okay? And nothing will change between us. I won't take it personal, Little Dove, I promise," I assure her so she knows she has control the whole time.

She turns back to me with glistening eyes and whispers, "Thank you."

Nodding, I support her weight and bend down so she can reach the handle. "Can you get that for me?"

She leans down and throws the door open, and I catch it with my foot.

"Thanks."

"Whoa, what do we have here? Cam! What a surprise!" Chloe shouts at us across the now-empty shop.

I lower Nikki to the ground as she laughs. "Shut up! Thanks for the heads-up!"

We approach the counter as I say, "I'm so thankful you didn't say anything because I caught her creeping on photos of me."

Chloe cackles. "Oh my God, I'm so sorry."

Nikki fake glares at her. "Mmhmm."

An awkward silence falls over us before Chloe says, "Well, I'll lock up. You crazy kids have a good night. Cam, your bags are back here."

I step behind the counter and notice that my duffel is unzipped and a complete mess. "Um, what happened?"

"Oh, well, I had to make sure you didn't have, like, a serial killer kit in there or anything weird, you know. All checked out," she says as she walks up to Nikki and pulls her into a hug, whispering something in her ear.

Laughing to myself, I zip my bag up.

"Call if you need anything." She points at Nikki as she walks backward toward the door. "Cam, be good. But remember, I can make you disappear *like that*." She snaps her fingers.

Lifting my hands in surrender, I say, "I believe you. I promise to be on my best behavior."

She squints her eyes before turning around and walking through the door, locking it behind her.

The thought of my girl and me being alone together for the rest of the night is suddenly very real, and I couldn't be happier.

"Have you eaten?" she asks me as she grabs my backpack.

I take it out of her hands and grab my duffel bag. "I've got it. I ate lunch and a snack on the plane. I'll definitely need to grab something in a bit. Do you have something in mind? Are you craving anything?"

She continues down the hallway and unlocks a door that leads to a staircase. "Pizza. But I'm always craving pizza."

We ascend the stairs that lead to a door with more than enough locks on it.

"Pizza it is."

She begins to unlock the door, starting at the top, and I don't question why she has as many locks as she does. She's a single woman who lives alone—that's answer enough.

"I have some fresh dough and toppings in the fridge, if that works. Or we can order from next door," she says as she undoes the last lock and opens the door to the small studio apartment.

Up to this point, I have only seen glimpses of her space from whatever has been behind her during FaceTime. It's small, but it has charm. I'll probably just sleep on the floor tonight. I'm not going to invite myself into her bed unless she wants me there.

"I would love to make pizzas here. Homemade dough? I might never leave," I say with exaggeration.

"You'll be sick of my baking soon enough," she mumbles.

Gently grabbing her wrist, I spin her around to face me. "Never."

She gulps, and her skin flushes red. "Set your stuff wherever you'd like. Um, I-I'll get the pizza going."

She pulls from my featherlight touch and walks to the kitchen.

With my bags in hand, I bring them over to the sofa as I hear her rustling in the fridge. I unzip my duffel and begin refolding the mess that Chloe made. I stack the clothes neatly on her chair and unpack the rest of my bag as fast as I can so I can join her.

"How's it going in there?" I ask.

"Oven is preheating, and the pizza station is ready, just waiting for you, slowpoke," she teases.

"I'm done now." I laugh, dropping everything in my hands.

Walking a few feet toward her kitchen, I step beside her and wait for her instruction.

"I only have cheese and pepperoni," she says as she spoons sauce onto her dough.

"Pepperoni is my favorite," I say as I take a spoon from the counter and scoop sauce onto my dough, smoothing it out.

Silence and tension build between us as we make our pizza. The oven beeps, and she jumps slightly. At least I'm not the only one on edge right now.

"All done?" she asks without meeting my eyes.

"Yeah," I whisper as her gaze slowly rises to mine.

She wets her parted lips before tearing her focus away and going back to the task at hand. She places both pizzas on a baking sheet and slides them into the oven. She grabs her phone and sets a timer.

"Ten minutes-ish. I usually only cook one, so it's a guess," she says as she sets her phone down on the counter.

I take a few steps back and grab the counter with my hands as I lean against it. I can't help but stare at her. Her eyes are so piercing blue, almost haunting. I didn't think pink hair could look so good before I met her.

I let my eyes roam over her body, down my hoodie to her bare feet and back up her perfect face. "You are so beautiful," I whisper to her.

She looks down, and I wish I were close enough to catch her chin to make her meet my eyes so that I could say it again.

"I like you, Cameron," she says softly while looking anywhere but at me. "But it scares me."

"What scares you?" I ask her.

"How much I like you. I've built such a careful wall around my life, around myself. Letting you into that …" She trails off and meets my eyes. "It's terrifying. My ex hurt me … a lot. I know you say you won't hurt me and you won't let anything hurt me. But what do you think

203

he said to me? He said all the right things all the time until he showed me what he really meant."

Gripping the counter tighter, I resist walking over to her and touching her. I know how difficult it is to open up about this. I don't want her to feel suffocated.

"I know you take everything I say with a grain of salt, and that's okay. The only way you'll ever trust me is through my actions, and I'll make sure that they always match my words, I promise. Are you sure you don't want me to stay at the hotel? I don't want to push you."

She smiles, and her face lights up, like the shadows that her ex cast over her fade to the back of her mind. "I want you here, Cam."

Taking slow steps toward her, I hold her intense stare and place my hands on either side of her against the countertop. Gently, I lean my forehead against hers and close my eyes.

"I want to be here too. I like you, Little Dove." I lift my head up and place a soft kiss on her hairline. "A lot."

We spend the next few minutes wandering through her studio apartment on somewhat of a tour. When our pizzas are done, we eat and start *The Princess Diaries* on the couches. At first, I want to sit on the sofa seat next to her. But I opt on the other couch across from her's to prove that I'm not just here for a hookup and to touch her. That I'm here because I really like her. And now I couldn't be happier with my decision. I would like to say that I learn all about her favorite movie, but I can't take my eyes off of her the entire time. When the end credits begin to roll, I make a mental note to watch this sometime in the future to actually remember what it's about.

"So, what did you think?" She turns to look at me on the couch across from her.

I knew I couldn't sit next to her and focus on the movie. Little did I know, that would happen over here too.

"It was good. I really liked the part in the beginning when she met the queen," I say, unsure of my answer.

She licks her lips and smiles. "What was the main character's name?"

Fuck.

"Mila?" I say questioningly.

"Horrible. Just horrible." She laughs. "What was the country's name that she was the princess of?"

It started with a *G* and had something to do with pears. "G-G …"

"Did you watch the same movie I did?" She laughs and stands up, pulling the hoodie off of her and setting it next to her.

Adjusting my hips on the couch, I answer genuinely, "I was watching you far more than I was watching the movie."

"Mmhmm," she hums. "I'm going to change quickly. I'll be right back."

205

I watch her walk over to a dresser and grab something red out of it before walking into the bathroom and shutting the door.

My need to touch her is going to be at an all-time high if she walks out here in something short and tight. Thank God I'm sleeping on the couch. I would have the hardest fucking time keeping my hands off of her.

When the door opens, I catch my jaw from fucking dropping. She is wearing a silk tank top and shorts set *without* a bra. Her nipples are poking through the red top, taunting me.

She smirks and is well aware of what she is doing.

"Comfortable?" I ask her mockingly, my eyebrows pinching together.

She smiles villainously. "Very. You?"

"At the moment, not very," I mumble, lifting my hips as my pants tighten from my growing erection.

Standing up, I grab a blanket and and say, "I'll take the couch."

When I turn around, she's mere feet from me.

"Cam."

"Yes, baby?" I whisper as she takes the blanket from me.

"I can change if this is too distracting," she offers.

"No, please, God, don't change," I beg of her. "I just need a second to … adjust."

I will never get used to the sight of her.

She bites her bottom lip, grinning.

"I want to go slow, Little Dove," I tell her as every fiber of my being itches to feel how soft her skin is right now.

She looks at me like she's waiting for the punch line. "Okay, that works for me. Can I ask why?"

I take a step toward her and another until we are so close that our bodies are pressing against each other in the utmost torture.

Hooking my bent finger under her jaw, I lift her gaze straight up to mine. "When I fuck you for the first time, I want you to trust me completely. I want every cell in your body to respond to mine. I don't want you to hold back because you doubt what I feel for you, what I would do for you. I want you to want me without fear."

She wets her parted lips as her eyes darken and soften at the same time. "Okay. But what are we supposed to do right now?"

"What do you mean?" I ask her as I run my fingertips up her bare arms.

She closes her eyes and bites her lip. "What are we going to do right now? Because I am so turned on that I'm about to go to the bathroom and take care of it myself."

I smirk at her as an idea comes to mind. "How would you do that?"

She hesitates. "With my vibrator."

"Hmm," I moan as her breath quickens. "Can I see it?"

She narrows her eyes before walking to her nightstand and pulling it out. "Why do you want to see it?"

I reach out to take it, and she pulls back but gives in after a second. Tucking it in my arm, I grab her hands and gently sit her down on the couch she sat on during the movie. I set the vibrator next to her and walk over to my couch.

My hard-on is already threatening to bust the seams of my boxers. *Fuck*.

"We don't touch each other," I say as she watches my thumbs slip into my joggers, and I push them down my thighs. "But we listen to each other. You tell me what you want me to do to myself. I'll tell you the same."

"You want me to masturbate in front of you?" she asks shockingly as I pull my shirt off and over my head.

Grinning, I hook my fingers into my tight boxers. "I want you to use that vibrator and make yourself come as I tell you how desperately I wish it were me. How I wish I could taste how sweet that perfect pussy is between those thighs."

She slowly reaches for the vibrator while holding my stare. "I've never done this in front of someone before."

"You'll be perfect, baby," I praise her as I begin to push my boxers down. My almost-full erection springs free, and I sit down on the couch with my knees falling open.

Little Dove's eyes are locked on to my hardened cock.

"Are you happy with what you see?"

She nods.

"Good. Then, run that along the inside of your thigh," I demand.

She listens as I wrap my hand around my shaft, pumping lazily. It is not going to take me much to come with this happening in front of me.

"Good. Now, the other leg," I order as she drags the tip of the vibrator from the inside of her thigh toward the apex.

Her breathing is loud and heavy, and I can't wait to hear what she sounds like when she falls apart with her toy pressed between her legs.

"Cam, you-you're huge," she moans, and I all but fall apart at the seams.

"Don't worry, baby. It'll fit," I assure her. "Now, press it against your clit."

She hesitates and gasps the second it hits that bundle of nerves.

"I'm not going to last very long," she whispers.

"That's okay, baby. *Fuck*, I wish I could burn this image into my mind." I tighten my grip on my cock and pump harder.

Her breaths are already so uneven and labored. I think she's going to come faster than I thought.

"I want to taste you so badly."

"So, do it," Nikki says, and it takes every ounce of willpower I have not to tear those little silk shorts off of her body and tongue-fuck her until she comes in my mouth.

"Nikki," I warn.

"What? You don't want to do it?" she asks as a spark lights in her eyes.

She's getting off on teasing me. Little Dove, Little Dove.

"Don't test me, baby," I groan as I cup my balls with my free hand.

She throws the vibrator to the side and stands up. I contemplate what I would let her do. If she were to storm over here and grab my cock, would I be able to push her away? Say no to my Little Dove? I honestly don't know.

But she doesn't take a step. Instead, she yanks her shorts down, revealing a see-through red lace thong, and kicks the shorts off.

"*Fucking hell.*" I pump faster. "Grab the toy," I demand, knowing I'm moments from coming. Even if it kills me, she is coming first. "Touch your pretty little clit."

I watch her sit down and push the toy against herself, jumping from the sensation.

"Fuck, Cam," she moans, and I know she's on the edge.

Standing up, I walk over to her and drop my arm beside her head and cage her legs between mine as I continue to stroke myself with my left hand.

210

"Keep going, baby," I order as I lean my forehead against hers. "There you go," I praise as she begins to writhe in place.

"Cam. Fuck. Fuck. I'm going to come. Fuck," she moans as her legs start to quiver between mine.

Pulling back slightly, I hover my lips over hers. "Come for me, Little Dove."

I pump harder and feel my spine tingle as my orgasm nears.

She falls apart beneath me. "Cam. Fuuuck. Fuck, Cam."

And it is my fucking undoing. I throw myself down on the couch beside her as I feel my balls tighten, and I plummet over the fucking edge of sanity.

"Fuck, baby," I groan as I come on my stomach.

I roll my head to face her, and she is panting and staring so intently at me.

"That was … fun." She grins.

"Good. We can do that anytime." I smile as my heart rate begins to slow.

"Can I get you something for …" She trails off, pointing to my stomach.

"I've got it. You relax," I say as I carefully stand and walk over to my shirt on the ground. "I'm going to clean up quickly, if that's okay."

"Of course," she says as she stands up and walks over to the bed with a shy smile on her lips.

16

NIKKI

My heart rate feels deadly as Cam walks backward into my bathroom, completely naked. I cannot believe what just happened. My skin is humming from the tingles erupting all over my body.

That vibrator and I have had lots of practice together, but, holy shit, I have never come like that from it before. I know that Cam is the reason why, and I knew the second the vibrations touched me that it was going to be intense. But when he leaned over me and his breath hit my lips, I saw fucking stars in my eyes.

Oh my God. The way he looked, sitting across from me—the way he was looking *at* me—I wish I had taken a photo so that I could stare at that image forever.

The water starts in the bathroom, pulling my mind to the present.

Cam is so attractive, and I sometimes forget that when we text or talk on the phone. But in person, it is so much different. I know how to talk to Cam and how to open up and listen, but I don't really know how to interact with him up close, especially after everything we've shared.

I don't think I'll ever get used to how he towers over me. I think, at first, that intimidated me, but now, it feels protective and comforting. Then, there are his stunning blue eyes that contrast his dark brown hair and tan skin. I could look at him forever and never get tired of it.

Deciding I don't want to seem like all I've been doing is sitting here, thinking about him, I stand up and slide my shorts on. Grabbing my vibrator, I walk over to my side of the bed and stow it back in its drawer right as the bathroom door opens.

"Will you sleep in bed with me?" The question leaves my parted lips before I can stop it.

Cam stutter-steps as he walks over to the couch, and a smirk lifts a corner of his lips up.

"What side is yours?" Cam asks. He grabs a pair of underwear from one of his bags.

I can't resist watching him with his backside turned to me—an impeccable backside at that. He catches me staring as he turns around, and smiles.

"I-I don't care. I practically sleep in the middle, to be honest," I mumble as he walks over to me, wearing only black boxers. "But you can have this side."

I step away from him and walk over to the light switches and turn them off. The only light that remains is a lamp in my living room.

As I spin around, I'm startled when Cam is right in front of me instead of by the bed, where I left him.

Silence surrounds us, and it makes everything else more noticeable—the charge in the air, the way our chests rise and fall, and the way he carefully closes the distance between us.

Without a word, he lifts his hands to my face and cups my jaw on each side, and his thumbs begin to stroke my cheeks with a featherlight touch.

I pull back from him out of instinct, immediately feeling guilty for reacting to him that way. I can't always help it, being triggered by things that remind me of Trey. Sometimes, I'm not even aware of it consciously; it's my body that is reacting. Whether in fear of what could happen or fear of what previously did.

Cam has never made me feel scared of him, and I have to remind myself of that before I lean further into his touch. What we did on my couches was intimate, but this feels so much more vulnerable.

Taking a deep breath, I'm suddenly overcome with emotion from what I feel for him. I didn't want to fall for Cam. Well, I guess that's not entirely the truth. I wanted to fall for Cam, but Trey made me not want to. But I can't control it anymore, and I'm not sure I ever could.

Cam's eyes bore into mine with such ferocious sincerity and adoration. His lips part, and he leans down toward me so slowly that I know it's because he's giving me a second to pull away if I want to. But that is the last thing I will do right now.

I lift my head against his hands, and it's all the permission he needs for his lips to melt into mine.

He kisses me gently and sweetly, but I can feel the passion in the touch of his fingertips, in the way his body lines up with mine, and in the way his lips aren't saying a thing.

He knows he doesn't need to always fill the silence. Instead of saying something he thinks I want to hear, he touches me gently, showing me how soft and tender he will be with me. It shows me so much more than a compliment could. Our bodies speak to each other in a way our words never will.

His forehead rolls onto mine for a brief moment before he pulls away, biting his smiling bottom lip.

"How long do I have you for?" I ask him as I walk over to the bed and pull the comforter and top sheet back.

"My flight leaves tomorrow at two p.m.," he says as he waits for me to crawl into bed before he does the same.

We both roll onto our sides and face each other. It's exactly what we do when we FaceTime, except that I can reach out and actually touch him now.

"Okay," I breathe. "Will you be back?" My hand quivers beneath the blanket with nervousness.

He smiles at me. "As soon as I can."

"Good. I'd like that," I say softly.

His blue eyes are locked on to mine, and I can't look away. They look so different right now than they did when we first met. Granted, we were in a dark club with flashing lights. But if anyone had looked close enough, they would have seen what I saw too. A wall, a mask, a barrier, whatever you want to call it, sat between his eyes and mine. But as we lie side by side, nothing sits between us. It's an odd feeling—to be so exposed to someone else—but it feels right with Cam.

Reaching his hand out to me, he runs his fingers through my hair and tucks the runaway strands behind my ear. "Can I hold you while we sleep?"

I nod as my cheeks redden and my stomach flutters. "Yeah."

I roll over onto my back and then the other side and inch backward to him.

His fingers wrap around my waist, and in one movement, he pulls me flush against him and adjusts his arms, one tucked under my head and the other wrapped over my waist.

I'm not only enveloped by him, but by the scent of green apples, amber, and musk. Closing my eyes, I inhale through my nose, feeling waves of comfort wash over me with each breath.

"Good night, Nikki," he whispers into my ear.

Nikki. There's that damn name again.

I don't deserve the care and tenderness he has given me when I've been lying to him this whole time. But I'm not ready to open that box of secrets yet.

Bliss. The only word I would use to describe waking up in Cam's arms.

"Nikki?" Cam whispers as my eyelashes flutter open, and I realize that my head is lying on a very firm yet surprisingly comfortable chest with my arm draped across his torso.

I haven't felt this well rested in years, nor have I slept that tranquilly. "Mmhmm?"

The deepest chuckle vibrates against my cheek.

"How long have you been awake?" I ask as I lift my seemingly heavy head and turn to look at him. I swear his eyes might be bluer in the morning, or I'm just imagining it.

He yawns and says, "About a half hour."

Crossing my hands on his chest, I lay my head down on top of them. "Why didn't you wake me?"

His tongue swipes his bottom lip before the cheesiest smile spreads across that perfect face of his. "You were sleeping so peacefully. There's no way I could have woken you and ruined that, especially when I was lucky enough to hold you during it."

Butterflies the size of dragons soar in my stomach. "So, you were watching me sleep?"

"Absolutely," he says without pause.

I don't have to guess what Cam is thinking or feeling; he tells me, and more importantly, he *shows* me.

The backs of his fingertips caress my cheek. "I will always stare at you. I can't help it. My eyes were made just to see you. In a room full of people, I would spot you in a heartbeat."

I know people can die from heartbreak, but can the opposite of that kill you too? Because my heart feels like it's going to explode.

My cheeks are burning. "What if I didn't have pink hair? It wouldn't be nearly as easy."

He glares at me in the most adoring way. "Your hair color has nothing to do with the way I am drawn to you. I do like the pink though; it suits you."

His heartbeat kicks up—I can feel it under my hands. Pride and joy blossom in my chest because I know that I am the reason.

But guilt finds me immediately. I want to tell him that I feel the same way. That I never thought I would be able to start to trust someone again after Trey. I want to grab his sexy face and kiss him senseless. But I can't let him give himself to me when he thinks I'm *Nikki*.

Sliding my hands up his chest, I press two kisses on his bare skin and breathe him in before meeting his eyes. "You are perfection, Cameron."

I sit up and crawl out of bed and make my way to the bathroom. I know myself well enough to know that I can't lose Cam—it would hurt too much. He wiggled his way past all the walls I had built and latched himself on to my heart. I just have to figure out the plan, how to ensure my safety and to make sure Cam knows the truth about who I really am.

After I gather myself and change, I find Cam in my kitchen, drinking water, still shirtless, but it seems he decided to put pants on at least. Not that I minded the shirtlessness. Hockey players must be the fittest athletes on the planet. Cam is pure muscle.

After we grab breakfast down at the shop, we spend some time with Chloe, and Cam learns how to make from-scratch chocolate chip cookies and blueberry muffins. Chloe and Cam get along so well, and that brings me more happiness than I could have imagined. Before I know it, the morning and afternoon have passed, and Cam has to be on his way back to New York. We share another sweet and loving kiss and an endless longing look before he leaves.

And I have had an ache in my chest since.

"You're literally sulking." Chloe laughs.

I chuck my spoon at her, trying to hide my smile. Lucky for her, it was before it went into my ice cream. "I am not. Shut up."

She sets her pint down and crosses her legs up on my couch. "You *are*. Awww, Nik's in loooove."

"*Nik's* not anything," I groan.

She takes a deep breath. "Have you thought about telling him?"

Rolling my eyes to her, I say, "Of course I have thought about it, Chlo. But it's not just about me. It's not that simple, and you know that."

"Why can't it be?" Chloe asks with ease.

More than anything, I want it to be. If it only involved me, I would want to have the conversation about who I really was. But it'd immediately put my family in danger.

What Cam and I have already done is dangerous enough.

I should cut it off where we are.

A cold shiver runs down my spine at the thought. I don't want to stop talking to Cam.

My eyes burn from frustration as Chloe takes my hand in hers. "I know. I know. I'm sorry. I shouldn't have pushed it."

I shake my head, and a tear falls down my cheek. "No, it's fine. I'm so torn, Chlo. I don't know what to do."

Rubbing the back of my hand, she says softly, "Yeah, you do. The bottom line is, you like him, and you want to see him. So, let's go."

"What do you mean?" I scoff.

She lets go of my hand and types rapidly into her phone. "They are playing tomorrow night. We're going."

I laugh and begin to stand when I'm yanked by my shirt back down to the couch.

"It's about damn time that you get a little piece of your *own* happiness, Morgan! We're going to this game because you deserve to smile. And I've never seen you smile like you do with Cam." She shoves her phone into my hands. "You pick the seats. I'll book the plane and make sure we have signs up for the shop's closure."

Blinking the tears out of my eyes, I lift her phone up and look for the seats farthest from the ice. Not that I don't want to see Cam play, but I don't want anyone else to see me. So, I select the absolute farthest row and add two tickets into the cart and hand it back to her.

"Good. I'll get everything ready. Don't stress for a second about the shop. Our customers are the best and most understanding. We'll give the regulars a free drink when we see them again," she assures me as she stands up and walks away into the kitchen.

I often think about where I would be right now if I'd never met Chloe. But I always have a hard time picturing it. Maybe because I don't want to imagine what it would be like. She's right, as she annoyingly usually is. I deserve to be happy too. I just don't know how far I'll let myself fall into comfort and love before it's too late and everyone else falls with me.

Walking over to my bed, I notice something black tucked under the corner of the comforter. Pulling it back, I find Cam's hoodie, and I freeze. Gently, I bring it up to my face and breathe it in, feeling my shoulders relax as I exhale.

Cam is ruining all of my plans of staying hidden and tucked away. But the only place I find myself wanting to be lately is with him. He understands me—better than he even knows. He knows true terror and pain; he knows what it's like to be hurt by someone you love.

I inhale again and know that two paths lie ahead of me, and I need to choose one—either I will be forced to say good-bye to the first true comfort that I have found in years or I need to reveal the truth of who I am.

"I swear to God, Nikki, you are never in charge of buying the tickets again," Chloe complains as we continue to climb the never-ending stairs to our seats.

I laugh. "You told me to pick."

She turns around and scolds me with her stare. "Well, I didn't think you would *literally* pick the last row in the rink."

Shrugging, I turn and follow her down the row into our seats as the light show continues in the dimmed rink.

This is the first hockey game I've ever been to. I've watched bits and pieces of games that my dad used to have on the TV, but I couldn't tell you a single thing about it. My dad would probably fangirl if he ever met Cam. My dad is a big hockey fan. Well, he's a big fan of pretty much every sport, but he has a soft spot for hockey.

The crowd goes crazy as I turn around and sit down, and I quickly find the reason why. Silver-and-black-and-white jerseys decorate the ice as the Nighthawks fly onto it. The cheering is almost deafening, and I wasn't expecting to feel so exhilarated.

I recognize the Nighthawks logo on the jerseys, and I immediately start looking for Cam.

They seem so far away that it's almost impossible to even tell what the jerseys say, so I'm forced to rely on the Jumbotron.

And then I see him, and the noise seems to stop. The camera follows him as he glides on the ice, handling the puck with such grace. It's mesmerizing, watching him in his true element.

The camera locks on to a different player, and I sigh. I wish I could bribe whoever's controlling that to stay on

Cam the whole night. Every time I get a glimpse of him, I feel my stomach flutter.

My mind and my heart are in a constant war right now. I know what I feel for Cam is real and evolving. And I'm afraid that my heart might win in the end, and that scares me more than anything. I push the never-ending thoughts away and focus on the present.

I glance over and see Chloe completely unaware of the fact that we're at a game right now. She is so zoned into her phone with a smile on her face.

"Who are you texting that makes you look like that?" I nudge her with my shoulder.

She locks her phone and stares at me. "Nobody."

"And you expect me to believe that? Spill," I demand.

She bites her lip and looks around before leaning into me and whispering, "I kind of met someone."

Pulling back, I playfully slap her arm. "And you're just *now* telling me? When did you meet? Where? Who is it?"

She looks around again, and I'm beginning to wonder if she's having an affair with a big celebrity or something.

"Nik, this is super secret. No one can know," she warns me, as if she isn't protecting the biggest secret I'll ever have.

I don't even say a word. I just stare at her in bewilderment.

She rolls her eyes. "Oh, you know what I mean. It's just a big deal, and he would get into so, *so* much trouble if this got out." She leans back into my ear. "It's my dad's business partner."

I gasp, and my eyes fly open. "Oh my God, Chloe! Which one?" I start laughing. "Your dad is going to kill you."

"Mark Ledger. It's a good thing that my other *daddy* will protect me." She winks.

"Nope." I laugh. "Don't do that again. Horrible. Keep it in your bedroom. And instead of picking a lower-level business partner, you picked the one who works with your dad every single day? You're *bad*."

She smirks. "I know."

Our attention drifts back to the ice as the announcers say something completely inaudible.

Number nineteen flashes across the screen as the teams skate off of the ice. Grabbing my phone, I snap a picture of the ice down below and send it to Cam.

Me: Good luck, Cameron. XO

Just a few minutes later, the announcer shouts into the mic, "Are you ready for some Nighthawks hockey?!"

The rink explodes with cheers from the thousands of attendees. The announcer quickly tells us the visiting team's starting lineup with almost no excitement.

A beat of silence passes before he roars into the mic with immense enthusiasm, "Let's meet your starting Nighthawks! Number sixteen, Alec Kostelecky!"

The crowd cheers and hollers.

"Number nineteen, Cam Costelloooo!"

"Woo!" I scream along with everyone else.

Cam flies out onto the ice and joins Alec at his side. I don't know how Cam makes skating so attractive, but it's one of the hottest things I've ever seen. But that could totally be because I know exactly what he looks like out of that uniform.

The rest of the team is announced, and the US anthem is sung before the teams are ready for the puck drop.

I can't take my eyes off of him. The way he is so completely in the zone and exactly himself. It's a turn-on to see him do what he loves.

The whistle blows, the puck drops, and my heart races as I realize that I'm totally screwed. I'm falling for a Nighthawk, and I don't think he'll ever let me go—and I don't want him to. I'll find a way to make it all work out. I have to.

The first period flies by, and I have a feeling I am going to become a huge hockey fan—or rather a huge hockey-player fan. The score is zero to zero as the teams go toward their locker rooms.

"Having fun?" Chloe asks me as I take a sip of the water we grabbed at concessions before the game.

"Yes, a lot of fun." I pause. "Thank you for making me come tonight."

She smiles at me, and I see pride in her stare. "Don't mention it. If being at a Nighthawks game makes you smile like that, I'll buy season passes, and we'll fly out for every game."

"Maybe someday." I grin at the hopeful hypothetical.

Scanning the crowd around us, I make a quick check for any unwelcome surprises. The only person raising a semi-red flag on my radar is this guy in a suit on the steps, studying the crowd.

I pull my gaze away from him, but my focus remains. I track him in my peripheral vision, and my hairs stand up on my arms.

"Everything okay?" Chloe asks as she sets her hand on my bouncing knee.

"Man on the stairs to our right. He's been standing there and looking around," I whisper to her without moving my head.

"I'm sure he's just looking for someone he knows. Maybe he just got here." She tries to calm my nerves.

But her attempt fails miserably as he takes a step up to our row and turns our way. I stick my hand in my bag to wrap my fingers around my bottle of pepper spray, and then I remember I couldn't bring it in because of the damn bag checks.

Shit. I clench a pen and click it to expose the pointiest part.

He's only a couple of seats away when I dare to look up. My stomach twists. He's looking at me like he knows who I am, like he's here for me.

I grip the pen tighter in my hand and get ready to fight.

"Are you Nikki?" the man shouts over the deafening noise of the crowd.

Thump. Thump. Thump.

My heart pounds against my rib cage as I nod my head.

"Would you and your friend come with me, please?" the man asks with an enthusiastic smile.

"Why would we do that? We don't know you," I snap and quickly calm my growing fear.

If this were an attempt from Trey, he wouldn't have done this. He would have waited until after the game to make his move. He would have grabbed me in the chaos of the emptying rink.

"Mr. Costello sent me to bring you both to new seats," he tells us, less friendly than before.

What is Cam doing?

Guilt burns my chest as I realize I was rude to this man for no reason. But I'm taking enough risks as it is. I don't need to be taking any additional ones by following a strange man simply because he requested it.

"Cam sent you?" I ask him again simply because I don't know what else to say. "Where are you taking us?"

"Down to the glass."

Chloe grabs both of our purses, and I release the pen instantly.

She stands up. "Thank God. Let's go!"

Before I can protest, she grabs my arm and pulls me up out of my seat and begins to follow this guy.

"Chloe, what the hell is wrong with you?" I shout-whisper to her.

"Cam went out of his way to do this for you. Take it for what it is and stop overthinking it, Nik. Enjoy it, please," she says sweetly.

My heart contracts as I let my fear fall away. Fear that this was all a setup from Trey. That he knew about Cam and this was an elaborate plan.

I can't believe Cam really did this for me, that he went out of his way to move me to a better seat. I honestly didn't think that I would find someone after Trey. I swore love and men off for good. I swore to keep to myself and stay hidden. But it's impossible to be invisible around Cam. He sees me like no one ever has.

"Right this way," the man orders as we continue to descend the stairs.

After what feels like a short hike, we reach the glass and are brought to two empty seats next to the Nighthawks bench.

Did he pick these seats on purpose, or did they just happen to be free?

The players skate out onto the ice, all beginning to circle and shoot pucks into the net. My eyes find my number nineteen instantly. He's already looking my way.

Cam winks at me as he glides across the ice and blows me a kiss, and I swear, if I wasn't in an ice box right now, I would actually *melt*.

CAM

S *he's wearing my hoodie.*

    My stomach feels like it's floating as I grab a biscuit with my stick and throw it into the net. Had I known she was here during the first period in the worst seats in the house, I would have moved her to the ice much sooner.

It took free season passes, signed jerseys, and a meet and greet with me and Kos to get the people in my girl's and Chloe's seats to give them up. But it was so worth it. Kos doesn't know I volunteered him yet, but he'll get over it. He loves meeting fans of the team.

I wanted Nikki as close as possible. One, so that I can look at her as much as I want. Two, because I know how these games can sometimes get. Alcohol and idiots are always a bad mix, and hockey seems to attract a lot of them. Now, I can make sure no one tries anything stupid.

The whistle blows, and I skate toward the bench. The second line is starting this period. I feel her stare on me before I even look up. With my stomach in my throat, I meet her gaze, and I can't help the smile from stretching across my lips as I see her sitting there, wearing *my* hoodie.

I can't get over it—how perfect she looks, wearing it. I never want it back *ever*. I want it to be the only thing she wears. That way, everyone will know who she belongs to, who protects her.

She blushes and bites her bottom lip, and the image of her wearing those sexy red PJs with her mouth hanging open and the toy between her legs flashes in my mind.

Fuck.

"Where's your head at, Costy?" Brett taps his stick to my chest.

Refocusing on the task at hand, I do my best to push Nikki out of my mind. "Sorry, man. I'm here. Let's go."

Starting line is readying for the puck drop as I join Kos at his side on the bench. We've got less than a minute before our shift.

Substitutions in hockey are quick. We're maybe on the ice for forty to fifty seconds, tops, at a time. Our energy is used in short bursts to be the most effective as many times as possible during a game.

The puck drops, and we gain possession. Number thirty-three on the Philadelphia Patriots steals it and takes off toward their goal.

After one more attempted shot on our end, our line is hopping over the barrier and taking the ice. Kos scoops the puck up and dribbles it around one of the Patriots' forwards. The Patriots take it back after Brett's shot is stopped by the goalie.

After a couple more unsuccessful shots, Kos and I are back on the bench, waiting for our next turn. A Patriots' player checks one of ours into the boards right in front of Nikki and Chloe. Nikki glares at the Patriots' player with more anger than I anticipated. I chuckle at her frustration. I'm glad she's getting into the game.

It was a clean hit, so there's not much to be upset about. But then he looks at her and winks.

This motherfucker winked at *my* Little Dove.

She pulls her gaze away, as if it was hurting her to continue to look at him, and her eyes fly to mine, a soft smile forming on her lips.

She holds my gaze for a moment before waving, her smile stretching wider across her cheeks.

I wave back at her gleefully, then force myself to refocus on the game.

The rest of the second period flies by, and when the clock times out, no points mark the board on either side. Not for a lack of trying, mind you. Our defense and offense are so equally matched that we can't seem to get the edge on each other.

The third period starts with my line on the ice. The energy in the building right now is tangible, and the tension between the Patriots and us is explosive.

The puck drops, Kos scoops it, and we fly into our zone. Kos kicks it to Brett, who dangles it and fakes out one of their defenders. Brett fake shoots the puck. Their goalie falls for the move, and I skate toward the opening. Brett slaps it to me, and in one swift movement, I throw it into the net.

The buzzer sounds, and the boys pile into me with resounding cheers.

We skate off toward the bench for the routine high fives after a goal. I lead the line as we bump the gloves of our teammates on the bench.

Instead of stopping at the end of the bench, I skate past it and stop at the glass in front of Nikki. She lifts her fist to the glass, and my heart bursts. I bump the glass where her fist is. I want this every single game for the rest of my career. I want her in that seat. I want her to be a part of the routine.

The player who winked at her earlier skates up to me as we line back up and says, "I bet she has the sweetest ass on her."

Gripping my stick tighter, I resist knocking him on his ass on a dead puck.

"Keep fucking chirping, and I'll knock your teeth in," I growl at him.

"She would be on her knees, begging me for it, if I wanted. She looks easy enough." He grins, and all I can see is red.

The puck drops, and he gains possession. We all fly down the ice. They miss a shot, and it rebounds off of the goalpost toward the boards. His teammate grabs it and shoots. MacArthur blocks it, and it rebounds off of him and glides toward the benches.

Number eighty-four—the guy begging to get his teeth knocked in—takes off after it, and I'm right on his tail. Digging my blades harder into the ice, I gain as much momentum and speed as I can. He's not a foot from the boards in front of Nikki before I put every ounce of rage into smearing him into the glass. The sound from him hitting the wall is deafening in the rink. But the audience's shouts and cheers immediately take over.

With his face still against the wall, I grit my teeth. "Say one more thing about her, and you won't be walking out of this arena."

He falls to the ground as I pull away.

"Now, who's on their knees?"

I spit on the ice next to him and look up to Nikki. Her face is a mix of confusion, fear, and adoration. I can't tell what she's thinking, and it's driving me crazy.

My team flocks to my side, ready if a fight breaks out. I know I have a target on my back for that hit now. But

I also know that Reed and Jensen will be with me. And they aren't letting any of the Patriots get away with anything. Luckily, the Patriots didn't try to get me back for that throughout the rest of the third period.

The game ends—Nighthawks one, Patriots zero. The next time we play them, a bloodbath is going to happen since it didn't tonight. Their team is going to get me back for the hit I put on eighty-four—or at least try until it's an all-out brawl. I know that's what we would do for our boys. But I guess that usually depends on how the other team would handle it at the next game.

As we skate off the ice, I look over to Nikki, who is already staring at me with the biggest smile on her face. I wink at her and grin.

We play again tomorrow, and I *need* her here. I play better with her. I *am* better with her. I hustle to my phone and shoot her a text.

> Me: *Please don't leave yet. I'm going to hop in the shower quickly. I'll be right out.*

She responds instantly.

> Nikki: *I'll wait for you in the lobby.*

"So, you want to talk about the girl you wouldn't stop looking at throughout the game?" Kos asks as I strip out of my gear.

Smirking, I walk over to the showers. "Hopefully, you'll meet her tonight. We can talk about her then."

"Do I know her? She looks familiar," Kos asks.

"She owns that coffee shop in Minnesota," I say as I start the shower and step into the warm water.

"So, that's where you disappeared to on your last off days." Kos shouts to Brett who's on the toilet, "Dammit, Brett, I owe you a hundred bucks."

"Woohoo!" Brett cheers.

"You guys had a bet going?" I laugh. "Fucking stupid."

The guys continue to give me shit as I wash my hair and change into gray joggers and a Nighthawks T-shirt and hoodie before rushing out to find Nikki.

Me: On my way to you.

When I walk through the exit door of our locker room, I see Chloe and Nikki standing with their backs to me. I want to scare them, but then I remember how Nikki reacted when I snuck up on her at the library. I never want to make her feel that genuinely fearful of me again.

"Hello, beautiful," I say to her as I approach them.

"Oh, hey, Cam," Chloe says, taking the compliment for herself.

Nikki laughs as she turns around and takes me in. "Hey."

239

She pulls her bottom lip between her teeth, and I can't help the feeling of needing to touch her, but I restrain myself. For now.

"Did you enjoy the game?" I ask her, dying to know what she actually thought of it.

"I loved it, honestly! I've only seen hockey on TV. This was a much different experience. It was a lot of fun. You're really good too," she says as she stares up at me with those stunning blue eyes. "Oh, and thank you for the seats."

I sometimes forget how much shorter she is than me. I'm six foot four; she's got to be maybe five-three.

"I told you if you wanted seats on the ice, all you had to do was ask. I'm glad you enjoyed it. Do you guys want to come again tomorrow night? We play the Washington Wild. It'll be a good game." *Please say yes.*

"We would absolutely love to. Thank you so much, Cam, for being so generous," Chloe says mockingly as she looks at Nikki.

She's nervous. It's cute as hell.

"We would love to come," Nikki answers, blushing.

"Our team has a tradition after home-game wins. We go to End Zone, a bar in town, for a couple of drinks to celebrate. Will you come with me?" I ask Nikki. "Chloe, you are more than welcome. I'm sure the guys would be thrilled if I brought someone else along for them to flirt with all night." I laugh.

Nikki nods. "I'm down to go for a drink or two. Chlo?"

She winks at Nikki and says, "I am exhausted and going to head back to our hotel. You go have fun. I have to FaceTime someone and go over business stuff anyway."

"At ten o'clock at night? Must be really urgent." Nikki smirks.

I wonder what conversation is happening between the words here, one that I'm not privy to.

"Super urgent. Can't wait. I really need to go show him the value of his investments with the company and what he's going to be getting out of it," she says, and I look away, giving them privacy.

"Are you sure?" Nikki asks Chloe, and I can sense her nerves for leaving her friend.

"One hundred percent. Get out of here, you two lovebirds," she coos.

"Okay, text or call if you need me," Nikki tells her as she takes a step toward the door.

I move to join her, but Chloe grabs my wrist and yanks me down to her level.

What kind of superhuman strength does this girl have? That hurt my arm more than I'll ever admit.

"Listen here, Cam. If you hurt her, make her cry, make her want to cry, or so much as upset her for a millisecond, I will make your death look like an accident and pay off whoever is necessary to make sure it stays that way." She shoves me toward Nikki, who is now staring at us with a humorous smirk on her lips. "Have a great night, you two! Nikki, call me if you need a ride."

Remind me never to piss that girl off.

"Love you," Nikki tells her.

"You too, babes. Have *fun*," she says with a heaviness I didn't expect.

Hooking my fingers with hers, I grab my keys from my pocket. "I'm glad you're here."

We step outside into the cool yet refreshing air.

She kicks a rock with her shoe. "Me too." She looks down and fluffs the hoodie. "You forgot this at my place."

Staring ahead at the dark parking lot, I say, "I didn't forget anything." That hoodie is hers for good. "I don't want it back either. It looks too damn perfect on you."

"Okay, deal." Her thumb strokes mine, and actual tingles shoot up my arm. "Is the whole team going to be there?"

I unlock the car as I walk her around to the passenger door and open it for her. "Yeah."

She nods and gets in the car without another word. I hustle over to my side and start the car.

"Do people take a lot of pictures and stuff with you guys after the game?" she asks in a slightly shaky voice.

I pull out of my parking spot. "Sometimes. It depends on the night. Don't worry though; I won't leave your side," I assure her. "We don't have to go if you don't want to. Seriously, I will drive somewhere else."

She furrows her brow. "No, I want to go. And I don't want to be the reason a Nighthawks tradition is broken."

"Are you sure? I don't care what anyone else thinks, Nikki, only you."

She rests her hand on my arm and takes a deep breath. "I'm positive. Plus, I want to meet your friends."

"You got it. And don't get too excited." I chuckle. "They have a tendency to be assholes. But they'll be nice to you and accept you right away. I know that for a fact."

"They haven't even met me yet," she says worriedly.

"They don't have to. I know they will love you for exactly who you are. And on the insane point-zero-zero-zero-zero-one percent chance they don't, I'll make them."

"The same way you, uh, showed that guy on the ice earlier?" she asks.

"That was different. He was quite literally asking me to do it," I say as I pull into the parking lot of End Zone.

"He asked you to hit him into the boards so hard that he couldn't get up for a minute?" she retorts, and I can't tell if it bothered her or not.

Throwing the car into park in a spot, I turn and face her. "He said how sweet of an ass you must have and how he would have you on your knees for him. I gave him a warning to watch his mouth, and he decided not to listen. No one gets to talk about you like that. Ever. I won't tolerate it."

She looks at me, taking shallow breaths with a big doe-eyed stare and parted lips. Silence builds between us as she continues to look at me while a war seems to be going on behind her eyes.

But then she is flying over the middle console, grabbing my face, and kissing me aggressively. Like she can't get enough of me—and I *fucking* love it.

I cup her cheeks in my hands and kiss her just as hard back. This girl fucking owns me.

The sound of our lips smacking together fills my ears. The sound of heaven.

I run my tongue across the seam of her lips and feel them lift into a smile against mine right before she pulls away slowly.

I contemplate saying *fuck it* and taking her away from here, anywhere but into a room full of people. I want to keep her just to myself. If we stay alone any longer right now, I'm going to rip her fucking clothes off and devour her, but I don't want to rush her.

"Ready?" I ask her, and she gives me a sharp nod.

She grabs her purse and gets out of the car, giving me a second to adjust my suddenly snug boxers.

As I step out of the car, the cool air seems to help calm everything down, including the bulge in my pants.

Nikki stares at the building with wide eyes.

"What are you thinking?" I ask her as I reach her, and we start walking toward the entrance.

"It just looks very busy in there, is all. I'm not used to such ... crowds," she says quietly.

"It'll be okay. I've got you," I assure her as I open the door for her, letting her step inside before me.

Kos finds my stare from across the room, and I glance down to Nikki to give him a heads-up that she's here. Then, hopefully, he'll give the rest a warning to behave. But the more hockey players you add together, the wilder we seem to be.

Nikki looks up at me as we make our way through the full bar toward our tables. I nod and smile at her. Taking her hand in mine, I interlock our fingers.

For the time it took me to look down to her and back up, the entire team has turned to look our way with faces of excitement and shock. They couldn't be any more fucking obvious if they tried.

Laura is sitting next to Kos and looks like she's vibrating in her damn seat. She's so excited. Dear God, maybe this was a mistake. I laugh to myself. They're a lot to take in when you first meet them.

"Oh, oh, oh. And who is *this*, Costy?" Brett asks, and I know damn well he's doing this for show since he knows all about her.

I glare at him before scanning across the rest of them—a warning to be on good behavior. "This is Nikki. Nikki, this is the team."

245

"Hi," she says softly, giving them a quick wave. "You guys played great."

Brett sits up. "You should have seen how excited Cammy boy here got when he found out you were here. Like a kid on goddamn Christmas, I swear."

I'm going to kill him.

Brett props his head in his hands with a sly smile on his face. "And is she your sister orrrr … just a friend orrrr …"

"She's my girlfriend. Any other *questions*, Brett?" I snap at him to shut him up.

Nikki squeezes my hand, gently giggling.

Brett holds his hands up in surrender. "None from me. Guys?" He looks around to the other players.

Almost everyone's hand shoots into the air with a stupid smile on each of their faces.

"We're going to the bar to get a drink," I announce as I spin Nikki around with me. "Try to be less weird when we get back. Thanks."

We make our way through the crowd, and I watch every wasted guy with extra caution. She is already nervous enough. No one is touching her and making her feel worse.

She approaches the bar, and I stand directly behind her, wrapping my arms over her shoulders.

One of the bartenders walks up to us. "What can I get you guys?" she shouts over the music.

"Vodka cranberry, please," Nikki orders and shows her ID.

The bartender nods and looks at me.

"Just water."

"Ten dollars," she shouts to us.

Nikki goes for her card, and I grab her whole wallet out of her hand and shove it in my pocket.

"Nope. Absolutely not."

"Here." I slide her a twenty from my own wallet. "Keep the change."

"Thanks," she says and gets to work on our drinks.

I don't move an inch. Nikki is pressed so perfectly against me right now. I could stay in this spot forever.

I hand her wallet back to her. "I know you can take care of yourself. But I want to."

She tucks it in her purse and wiggles in my arms as she twists and turns around to face me, her back now pressing into the countertop. "Girlfriend?"

My face heats up. When she didn't immediately bring it up, I thought she was going to let it slide without comment. I guess I should have asked her about that first. But it doesn't change the fact that that's what I think of her as, regardless if she thinks of herself that way.

"Yeah, my girlfriend. I don't want to even think about another guy getting your attention. I can promise you no other girl has gotten or will get mine." I pause. "Do you not want me to call you that?" I ask her with bated breath.

She tilts her head side to side with pursed lips. "Hmm." Her finger taps her chin, and her smiling blue eyes look up at me. "I think I like it."

"Think?" I lean down, closing the distance between our faces.

"We'll see." She smiles and squints her eyes.

She bites her lip as the bartender slides our drinks across the countertop. She turns around to grab it, and I lean down and kiss her ear from behind.

"Do you know what you do to me every time you bite your lip, Little Dove?" I whisper into her ear.

The effect she has on me has little to do with the biting of her lip. It's every single thing she does. The way her hand fits into mine, the way her smile gives me fucking butterflies, and the way she understands my demons yet accepts them anyway.

She nods and shoves the little straw into the cup before turning around and taking a drink. With a devious little smirk, she says, "Yeah, I know. And?"

I want to show her how good I can make her feel, how good a firm smack on her ass or the sting of a bite can feel on her skin.

I lean down until my lips are hovering over hers. "You are driving me mad—you know that?"

She nods, and her lips press into mine, slow and soft. My heart thumps in my chest so hard—harder than a simple kiss has ever made it. But nothing with Nikki is simple, and I don't want it to be. What we have isn't simple or ordinary. It's special; it's everything.

I take her hand in mine again as we walk back to the team. They are acting exactly the same as when we left, everyone staring at us like we are their entertainment for the night.

There's only one chair empty across from Kos—my usual seat. Looking around, I try to spot an empty chair that we can steal, but I don't see anything.

Brett notices, hops off of his, and offers it to Nikki. "You can have mine."

She shakes her head and sits down in my chair and holds her arms out. "You can just sit here."

She laughs, and I smirk. No way am I crushing her in this chair.

Shaking my head, I say, "Nah, not happening. I have a better idea." Before she can protest, I hook my arm under her legs and around her waist and lift her up as I sit down on the chair and place her in my lap. "There we go."

"You're ridiculous." She smiles.

I kiss the side of her head as the guys seem to chill out and go back to whatever their conversations were before we got here.

"Where are you staying tonight?" I say and then get a brilliant idea to throw in before she answers. "Would you want to stay at my place?"

She doesn't move or say anything for a moment, and my palms start to sweat because maybe she doesn't want to. But then she nods, and I immediately relax.

"How have you been, Nikki?" Laura asks with the biggest smile.

"I've been really good. How about you guys?" she asks.

My hands are awkwardly hanging to my sides, so I decide to put them in a more useful place—on the tops of her thighs. She wiggles her hips, just enough for me to feel it, but not enough for everyone else to notice.

Stroking my thumb on her thigh, I brush it off, thinking she is just adjusting to get comfy. Until she does it again. And again as she sits forward to take a sip of her drink on the table.

My dick presses up against her, getting harder every time she moves.

She leans back and sets her drink down, and I lean into her ear.

"Little Dove, don't play with me right now."

She shrugs her shoulders, as if to ask, *Why?*

Then, she wiggles her hips again in my lap.

"Because I really want to *play* with you, and if you keep that up, I'll do it *right. Here.* And I don't think you want all of these people to watch."

18

NIKKI

This. I deserve this and everything that comes with it. I deserve to be cherished the way Cam cherishes me. To be flaunted and *loved.*

I don't know exactly how I'm going to get Trey out of my life yet, but I will find a way to keep my parents safe and myself safe, one way or another. I'm tired of living in fear of him. Maybe I could get in touch with my parents and tell them what happened and why they need to leave their home. If they come here, Chloe and her family could help protect them. My mind can't stop trying to come up with a plan, but I do my best to push it away for the time being.

When I agreed to come here with Cam tonight, I still had a lot of reservations. Seeing him on the ice was incredible. Watching him pummel that player right in front of me was intimidating and a little scary, but I know that Cam wouldn't hurt me. But the power he holds and the fact that, if he wanted to, he easily could hurt me, is a thought I had a hard time ignoring when that guy was lying on the ice after Cam's hit. And that was a full-grown six-foot man, and he did that kind of damage from one hit. I wasn't scared of Cam, just Cam's strength.

But every time he's with me, he is so soft and gentle and loving. He never makes me doubt his intentions. Even in the times where his intentions are PG-13, like right now. Granted, I am playing a large part in the reason he's reacting this way.

When he sat me down on his lap, I saw flashes of the night he and I masturbated to each other. Feeling him beneath me for the first time is electrifying. And every time I shift or move, I can feel him get harder. It's addictive.

I consider his comment about him *playing* with me here in front of everyone. I don't necessarily want that, but the thought of it is erotic.

As I lean back, my back sits flush against him. Turning my head, I whisper into his ear, "So, when do you want to get out of here, hotshot?"

"*Now,*" he insists. "But, uh, I'm going to need you to walk in front of me."

My face burns as I realize what he just said. "Okay. Hold on. Let me finish this quickly. I don't want to waste it."

He growls in my ear, "Hurry, Little Dove. The longer you're on my lap, the harder I'm getting. It's all for you, baby."

I take three large drinks, draining the cup almost completely.

"We're going to head out, guys. Brett, do you need a ride?" Cam asks him.

"That'd be great, man. Thanks," he says and downs his entire glass of beer.

I finish my drink and set the glass down, feeling the buzz as tingles dance over my skin.

"Are you ready?" Cam asks me and lifts his hips, pressing into me.

I gulp as the tingles are replaced with overwhelming nerves for what is to come tonight. I know what I want, and I know what I'll let him do, which are two very different things.

Until I sort Trey out, I'm not ready to tell him the truth about everything. Which also means that I'm not letting him fuck me and moan my fake name. It would feel so wrong. He doesn't deserve to be lied to either. He said he wouldn't fuck me until I could trust him without fear. Well, I won't let him do the same until he knows the truth.

Standing up, I hook my purse over my shoulder. "It was nice meeting you all. Laura, it was great seeing you again!"

Laura smiles at me. "You too! I miss stopping in there with Jack! You'll have to build a second location here."

I laugh. "Yeah, I'll get right on that."

Nikki's Coffee makes a good amount of money, but not enough to put up a second location that's states away from the first.

"Good-bye, Cam's girlfriend!" one of the guys in the back shouts. "Send your hot friends my way, please."

I giggle and smile at him. He couldn't handle Chloe. She would chew him up and spit him out.

Brett stands and turns to me, reaching for my hand. "Come on, babe. Let's get going."

"Funny," Cam says as he slaps Brett's hand away.

His lips press into the top of my head, and his fingers wrap around my waist before he gently guides me away.

"See you tomorrow, boys," Cam announces.

"Use protection!" one of the guys shouts to him.

One of the players shouts embarrassingly loud, "Don't be silly; wrap your willy!"

"Oh my God," Cam groans as we pick up pace with Brett on our tails.

The cold air causes goose bumps to shoot up all over my arms. I should've grabbed a coat, but when we left for the game, Cam's hoodie was warm enough.

We hustle to the car, and Cam gets my door for me. The car is already surprisingly warm. He must've started it from inside. Brett dives into the backseat and sits in the middle with his arms across the backs of our seats.

Cam gets in and shivers. "I'm sorry, Nikki. They can be a lot to handle sometimes."

"Oh, don't be. They're funny." I smile at his worried face.

Brett laughs. "What did you expect, Costy? That's the first time you've ever brought a girl to meet the team. Of course they weren't going to go easy."

First time?

"You're saying he's never brought a girlfriend to meet you guys?" I ask, shocked.

Brett shakes his head. "I'm saying he's never kept someone around long enough to become his girlfriend to then bring to meet us."

"Brett, shut up," Cam begs him.

"What?" Brett shrugs. "Not my fault. I'm just speaking the truth. Clearly, you're special to him, or you wouldn't be here. I can tell you that. And he damn sure wouldn't spend the few days off we get during the season to fly to you."

My heart races, and my stomach flutters at his words. I knew Cam was a bit of a player. But I didn't know I was the first girl he'd invited to meet everyone, let alone the first girlfriend they knew about.

Cam shoots Brett a glare through the rearview mirror, which seems to shut him up.

"Is that true?" I ask Cam as he pulls into a parking spot at what I'm guessing is their condo.

255

He throws the car into park and looks at me with such intensity. "Yes. Only you."

He might have only said three words, but it felt like so much more. *It's only* you *who has met them. It's only* you *who I have claimed as my girlfriend. It's only* you *that I want.*

"All right, I'm going to head inside before you guys start going at it right here," Brett says, exiting the car.

I grab my purse and open my door, breaking the tension before Cam and I do just that.

As we walk toward the skyscraper of a building, I shoot Chloe a text.

> *Me: I'm staying at Cam's tonight. See you in the morning?*

She answers right away.

> *Chloe: YESSSSS!!! Oh, my pleas to the heavens have come true! Go have fun! Be safe! I want every detail tomorrow!!!*

> *Me: OMG. You go have fun with your dad's friend, LOL.*

> *Chloe: Already on it! Don't worry! Good night, babes! XOXO*

Locking my phone, I drop it into my purse and focus on what's right in front of me. Cam, Brett, and I make our way to the elevator and then their condo. When he opens the door, my jaw drops. It's beautiful and surprisingly clean. I've seen almost every inch of this house on FaceTime, but it doesn't come close to comparing to how it looks in person.

The floor is black marble with matching countertops. It's modern and sleek, and it looks like the perfect bachelor pad. White cabinets line the kitchen with state-of-the-art appliances. I wonder how much cooking is actually done there.

"Your guys' place is so nice," I tell them as I kick my tennis shoes off.

"Thanks. I had it all to myself before Cam invited himself to live with me." Brett chuckles.

"Shut the fuck up." Cam laughs. "I did not. You practically begged me to."

"Yeah, yeah," Brett mocks as he walks off to some other part of the place.

"Do you want something to drink?" Cam asks.

"Water would be great."

He nods and walks toward the stunning kitchen. When he reaches up to the top of a cabinet to grab a glass, his shirt and sweatshirt lift up, revealing a deep V carved in his hips and perfectly toned abs.

How can someone like him even exist?

He fills the glass from the fridge and hands it to me, grabbing my free hand and walking backward toward a closed door.

"I love you being here, in my place." He bites his lip. "Do you have to leave?"

How did I even end up here in the first place? I think he hypnotized me and convinced me to put all of my guards down for him. There is no other logical answer for the way I feel for him. It's overwhelming.

"I have to," I say as he opens the door to his bedroom. "You know that."

He smirks. "Doesn't mean I can't try to convince you to stay." He closes it behind us.

"Hmm." I roll my eyes. "And how do you plan on doing that?" I drop my purse to the ground by the door.

He releases my hand and pulls his sweatshirt over his head, taking the shirt with it. "I can't tell you my secrets. You'll have to wait and find out for yourself."

"Hmm," I hum, at a loss for words. "Okay. Good luck."

He throws his clothes on the ground and grabs the TV remote, turning the TV on. "I don't need luck."

"You're pretty cocky for someone who hasn't even truly touched me yet," I say, snarky.

He's in front of me in the blink of an eye, towering over me. He steps toward me and pushes me back until I'm leaning against his closed door with his arms caging my head in.

"You think I haven't wanted to?" He leans down and breathes me in. "It's all I think about. I dream of it every night—what you will feel like when I fill you with my cock, what your moans will sound like when you're begging for more. Touching you is all I have wanted to do, Little Dove."

My breaths are panting in and out as his face is inches near mine. "Me too."

He smirks and brushes his lips against my cheek. "Me too what? What do you think about?"

Fucking hell.

"Say it," he orders.

Huffing, I whisper, "I think about what your tongue will feel like between my legs. I think about what your kinks are and if I would like them too. I think about what it's going to be like the first time we fuck because—let's face it—you're huge and it's probably going to hurt."

He moans, and the vibrations tickle my cheek. "*Fuck.*"

The fingers of his right hand trail down my stomach and hook under the bottom of the sweatshirt, lifting slowly. His callous fingertips graze my soft skin as he lifts it higher and higher until my bra is exposed. He pulls it up and over my head until my arms are stretched up above me. He doesn't take it off the rest of the way. Instead, he clasps my wrists in his hand and holds me there.

A deep and sexy chuckle leaves his lips. His hooded eyes explore me. "You are so beautiful."

His free hand reaches out and trails across my skin, and I can tell without looking that it's over one of my scars. He does it again to a different one. And another.

How can the touch of his fingertip feel so good?

He hooks his finger under my bralette. His darkened stare meets my eyes as he lifts it up, and my breasts bounce free.

"*Fuck*, baby," he moans and cups my left breast in his hand, kneading it.

His thumb brushes over my nipple, and I gasp at the unexpected jolt of pleasure. My eyes flutter open and shut as he continues to flick my nipple over and over.

His forehead presses into mine, and the heavy breaths from our desperate need mix together.

"Tell me," Cam groans into my mouth. "Tell me you're mine."

When I hesitate, he pinches my nipple between his fingers.

"Cam."

"Tell me that no one else will ever touch you like this." He rips the hoodie and bralette off of me and grabs my other breast, doubling the intensity. "Tell me you're mine, like I'm yours."

"Fuck, Cam. That feels so good," I whimper, and he freezes.

As I slowly open my eyes, he is staring at me, waiting for me.

Nodding, I try to find words, find coherent thoughts, but my brain is mush. "Please."

"Tsk, tsk." Cam flicks my nipples at once, and I gasp. He leans down until our lips are just barely touching. "Tell me, baby."

"I'm yours, Cam. Only yours. Now, please, don't fucking stop," I beg.

His lips crash into mine, and in one swift motion, he lifts me up and sets me on his hips, carrying me over to the bed.

His tongue tastes my lips, and I part mine, letting him in. He lays me down on the bed as his tongue explores mine, and we kiss with ferocity.

His fingertips grab my jaw, and he pulls away and runs his tongue up my stretched neck. "Lift your hips."

I listen and lift them up as he grips my leggings and panties. He pulls them both down to my ankles, tossing them onto the floor.

"Fucking hell, baby. Look at you. You're fucking *perfection*," he growls.

Biting my lip, he runs his hand from the inside of my ankle and up my leg, leaving a trail of goose bumps in his wake, reaching higher and higher until he finds the apex of my thigh, bordering the spot I desperately need him to touch.

"You're fucking soaked for me, aren't you, Little Dove?" Cam's husky voice asks.

I nod as my head leans back, anticipating his next move, which comes instantly. I moan as he runs his fingers between my legs.

"Cam …" I beg him for more as I look at him.

He lifts his wet fingers to his lips and sucks his fingers clean with the sexiest gleam in his stare. "Mmm. I just knew you would taste *so* sweet."

Fuck. Fucking hell. Screw everything. I want him to fuck me now. I need him to fuck me now.

"Put your head on the pillows," he says as he kneels on the bed.

I sit up and inch backward until my head is on his black silk pillows.

"Open those pretty legs for me, baby. I want to see all of you," he says as he pushes his joggers and boxers down his hips, his massive erection springing free.

My mouth starts watering.

Forcing my legs open, he squints at me and whispers, "More."

He takes his pants and boxers off and throws them off of the bed before he moves closer. I push my knees further apart, completely exposing myself to him.

"No one else is ever looking at your perfect pussy. No one else will ever taste it and feel it stretch around their cock. Your pussy is mine. You're mine, Little Dove. Do you understand?" He grabs his length and pumps it slowly.

I've never wanted to be claimed so badly before, to be obsessed over, to be owned. But I want to be his more than I've ever wanted anything else. Him being possessive yet respectful like this is the sexiest fucking thing I've ever seen.

"I understand," I whisper, on the verge of pouncing on him if he doesn't hurry up.

He releases himself and grabs my knees, placing them over his shoulders as he lies down on the bed in front of me. "I want to hear every moan and scream. Don't hold back. I don't care if Brett and the entire building hear you. At least they'll know exactly who you belong to."

My nerves explode as he runs his tongue up my center, savoring me. He moans, and my legs flinch from the vibrations. He latches on to me and tastes every inch of me, lapping me up. His fingers graze my entrance, and I throw my head back. His finger plunges inside of me and thrusts, quickly joined by a second finger. They pump in and out of me as his mouth suctions on to my clit, his tongue flicking rapidly against it.

"Ahh, fuck," I moan and grip the sheets as he picks up pace from my praise.

A third finger slides into me, and I gasp at the new sensations and pressure. He pumps faster, and his tongue flicks over me harder and harder. I'm not going to last much longer like this. A shiver runs down the length of my body, and I know my climax is coming, faster than I'd like.

Looking at Cam, I'm hit with a new wave of pleasure at the sight in front of me. His dark blue eyes are locked on to mine. His dark hair falls over his forehead, and his arms are flexed. The vision is enough to send me over the edge. I hold his stare, and he releases my clit, only to suck on it again harder, tugging slightly.

"Fuck, Cam," I scream as I plummet over the edge.

His assault doesn't slow as every nerve in my body explodes, waves of never-ending pleasure pulsing through me over and over.

"Give me one more, Little Dove," Cam demands as he devours me again, the sensations more intense than before.

His fingers continue to thrust in and out of me as he sits up and hovers over me. His thumb presses my clit, matching the rhythm of his fingers.

His long cock rubs against my stomach as he leans his head down to mine, our foreheads rolling together. Reaching down, I grip him in my hand, which can't even wrap around his hardened shaft, and pump him, feeling a drop of pre-cum fall onto me.

"Fuck, baby. Just like that," he moans, and his eyes roll back.

I can't help but stare at him, at how he reacts to every move I make. As I pump him, base to tip, I run my thumb over the tip, and his thumb works me harder and faster.

"Keep going. Don't come yet. I'm almost there," he growls as his breathing picks up.

I cup his balls with my other hand, massaging him as I continue to work his full length.

"Your pussy is so tight. I can't wait to feel you stretch around my cock," he groans, and I feel the second orgasm approaching.

He circles his fingers inside of me without missing a beat, his thumb changing direction. And that's all it takes.

"Make me come for you," he orders, and I grab his shaft with both hands, pumping him in long, hard strokes.

"Fuck, baby. Fuck. Yes," he moans deeply.

His thumb twitches, and I'm hit with an explosion of pleasure. My head digs into the pillow as I come around his fingers.

"Fuuuck," Cam calls out as he comes over my breasts and stomach.

We quiver as our orgasms tear through us and our breaths pant against each other's lips.

"Cam," I whimper. "That was …" I trail off. "The best."

His breathing slows, and without a word, he kisses me gently and passionately. He kisses me until I only know myself as Cam's girl. Not someone in hiding. Not someone with a fake name. But as someone who is undoubtedly *his*.

He pulls away and pushes off of the bed, turning to walk to the bathroom. And I see them—every mark on his back. Every inch is covered in scars, long marks stretching across his skin. His dad did that, hurt him. I can't imagine having a father like that. The person he was supposed to be able to trust broke him. I can't imagine the physical pain he felt, let alone the loss of any trust of a loved one. To him, anyone can hurt anyone. No one is assumed to be safe. He lives with that fear—that anyone can turn on him at any point.

A lot of which I can understand and relate to. He understands my darkness so well because he has a very similar darkness of his own.

He walks out of the bathroom with a towel in hand and cleans me up, wiping the wetness from between my legs before cleaning up the cum he decorated my skin with.

He throws the towel in the bathroom and grabs the shirt he had on earlier. "Here."

Taking the shirt from him, I slide it over my head and envelop myself in the scent of Cam. "Thank you."

He gathers his clothes on the floor and tosses them into the hamper, followed by my panties and clothes. I guess I'm sleeping commando tonight.

He grabs boxers and wiggles them over his hips before grabbing the TV remote and asking me, "What do you want to watch? Movie? Show?"

"Movie," I say as he hits the lights and joins me in bed.

He pulls the covers back, and I crawl underneath them with him. I lay my head down on his chest, and he grabs a few strands of my hair, twirling them between his fingers as he searches for a movie to watch.

"You're the first person, aside from Kos and Brett, who have seen my back fully. In showers after games, my back is always kept to the wall and is draped with a towel the second I'm done. No other girl ever has. I would blindfold them or keep my shirt on. But I wanted you to see me, every part of me," he says casually, as if it wasn't the most vulnerable statement in the world.

"Thank you," I say, kissing his chest.

"For what?" he asks as he clicks on a Marvel movie.

Laying my arm over his waist, I pull myself in tighter against him. "For trusting me enough to show me."

"Always, Little Dove. I meant everything I said tonight. It wasn't just sex talk," he says as the movie starts, and he sets the remote on the nightstand.

Gulping, I say what I shouldn't, something forcing me to acknowledge that I'm falling harder and harder. "Me too."

"I'm glad you're coming to tomorrow's game." Cam says quietly.

"Of course. There's no where else I would rather be," I confess.

He smiles. "Good."

"Try not to get into any fights over me tomorrow." I laugh.

"As long as everyone's mouth stays shut about you, that won't be a problem," he says. "But it's hockey, so someone is bound to chirp and get their ass kicked. Just the way it works."

"It's kind of exciting," I say, remembering the adrenaline I felt when Cam smashed that guy.

"Oh, so you like the fighting then?" He chuckles.

I nuzzle into him. "It's beautiful in a way. The way the game works. It's an eye-for-an-eye balance. If someone hurts your guy, you hurt them back. The violence is expected and, in a sense, controlled. And if anyone gets out of hand, they are punished for it. Retribution and justice are demanded. I wish that would apply in other aspects of life sometimes. If you hurt someone, you get hurt back."

He rubs my back, and I relax in his arms.

"I am your retribution." He kisses the top of my head. "If someone dares to hurt you, they will answer to me."

My eyes well up with tears, and a lump forms in my throat. "Thank you."

CAM

"How'd you sleep?" I ask Nikki as she stretches in bed.

"So gooood," she groans. "You?"

"Best sleep I've ever had." I smile at her from the end of the bed.

I woke up about an hour ago with her passed out next to me. Mouth open and drool everywhere. Still the cutest image I could ever wake up to. I went for a quick run on the treadmill to warm up my muscles for the day.

"Why are you all sweaty?" she asks and throws the covers off of her, clearly forgetting that she's only wearing my shirt, which is now bunched at her waist.

My eyes instantly fly to her bare pussy on display. Her face reddens as she remembers. With bright red cheeks, she hops out of bed and walks to the bathroom.

"Is it okay if I use your shower?" she asks, still seemingly embarrassed.

"Of course," I respond, and she shuts the door.

The water starts running, and I hear the shower start not a second later. There's no way in hell that I'm missing out on this. Without second-guessing it, I storm to the bathroom and open the door, tearing my clothes off as I shut the door behind me.

"Cam?" she asks as the last of my clothes finds the floor.

I grab the curtain and gently pull it back. "Is it okay if I join?" I ask her as I step into the scalding hot water.

She laughs. "Well, since you're already here, it would be rude of me to say no."

I smirk. "It would be extremely rude."

The water flows down her body, and I let myself take it in. The beads fall off of her breasts, and a stream runs down between her legs. Her hair is soaking wet, all pushed back. She is the sexiest and most beautiful woman I have ever seen.

"Don't look at me like that," she says as she takes my shampoo bottle and squirts some into her hands.

"Like what?" I tease.

"Like you're thinking about last night," she says as she massages the shampoo into her hair.

Placing my hand on my chest, I admit, "I'm not thinking about last night at all."

She rinses her hair out and arches her back to get the top of her head, and I physically stop myself from reaching out to cup her perfect tits.

She ignores me for a moment before saying, "Then, what are you thinking about?"

Taking the conditioner bottle, I squeeze some out in my hand and signal for her to turn around.

She listens, and I rub the conditioner in my hands and then run it through her hair, giving her a little head massage while I do it.

"I was thinking about what you would look like while pressed against this shower wall."

Gripping the sponge, she tries to turn around, but I catch her shoulders, stopping her. Sudsing the sponge up with body wash, I wash her back, rubbing the sponge in circles over her skin.

When I finish her back, I palm her asscheek in my hand and run the sponge over the other one. Releasing her cheek, I clean that one. I glide the sponge up her ass as I hook my fingers around her hip bone and pull her back into me. Her bare ass bounces against my dick. Gripping the sponge, I swipe it across her neck, down her shoulders, over her breasts and now-hardened nipples, and down her stomach.

I run my tongue down her wet neck and nip her shoulder. "Can't forget to clean this." Squeezing her hip, I rub the sponge between her legs. "That's better, huh?"

She pulls out of my grasp and grabs the sponge from me, turning around to face me with parted lips and blown pupils.

"My turn," is the only warning I get before she grips my already-hard erection.

She squeezes the sponge above it, letting the soap and bubbles soak my cock. She pumps me back and forth, ridiculously slow. As she continues that sweet torture, she cleans my shoulders, chest, and abs with the soapy sponge.

She mimics me and tells me to turn around as she says, "If this isn't okay, please stop me."

I consider it, not letting her touch my back. But if I'm ever going to let anyone, it's going to be her. I want to share this with her. I want to share everything with her. No boundaries, no limits.

"It's okay," I assure her.

She places the sponge on the top of my spine and very slowly zigzags across my shoulder blades. My stomach flutters as she continues to clean my back. Letting her do this feels more intimate than anything we could ever do sexually. It feels like she's washing my soul, cleansing the dark marks my dad left on me.

As she reaches the top of my ass, she leans in and presses a kiss against my back, which touches my fucking heart.

Facing her again, I cup her face in my hands and kiss her, parting her lips with my own and plunging my tongue into her mouth. Her tongue rocks against mine as her hands find my dick again.

Her lips leave mine, and I open my eyes to find a sight I wish I could revisit at will—her on her knees with her mouth open.

She flicks her tongue against my tip, and I rest my hands on the shower wall behind her, letting the water fall down my back from the rainfall showerhead.

"Fuck," I groan as her tongue runs up my shaft.

Her eyes are locked on to mine as she takes my tip into her mouth and sucks. She grins right before taking half of it in her mouth, bouncing it off the back of her throat.

Then, as if a switch were flicked, she sucks me like she needs to survive. She takes as much as she can down her throat over and over.

"Fuck, baby. Just like that." I grab her hair, wrapping it between my fingers. "You can take more than that."

Pushing my hips forward, she does just that, taking my cock further down her throat until she gags. Pulling away and out of her mouth, I ease up, but she doesn't. She grabs my dick and lifts it up while pumping, taking my balls in her mouth. She flicks her tongue against them and then sucks them deeper into her mouth.

"Fucking hell, Nikki. Yes, just like that. Come on, baby. You're going to make me come," I praise her.

As her blue eyes meet mine again, I lose it.

"Fuuuck," I growl.

She feels me start to come and takes me back into her throat before running her tongue over my tip as I spill into her mouth. She swallows and releases me with the biggest, proudest smile on her lips.

"That was"—I throw my head back—"fucking amazing."

She licks her bottom lip. "Good."

"Come here," I groan and grab her hips.

I lift her up and press her back against the shower wall, lining her pussy and my mouth up perfectly. "Hook your legs over my shoulders."

She slides them over my shoulders and settles her heels against my back as I adjust my grip on her, shifting my hands to her ass.

"My turn." I smirk and plunge my tongue into her sweet pussy.

I physically crave the taste of her, and I will never get enough of this. I widen my stance slightly, holding her weight on my shoulders and hands.

"Fuck, Cam," she moans and places her hands on my head.

I pinch her clit between my tongue and my teeth before rubbing my tongue rapidly back and forth as she moans louder and louder.

"Cam. Cam. Fuck," she whimpers.

God, my name is perfect on her lips.

My tongue continues to work her sensitive clit, and she moans more and more, faster and louder.

"Cam, I'm going to—oh fuck!" she shouts, slouching over into my hold on her.

I lick and lap at her pussy until I get every single drop from her.

She sits up and gazes down at me with a serene look on her face. "Can we do this position again sometime?"

I lower her back down to the floor. "Abso-*lutely*."

She leans back and washes the conditioner out as I stare at her—at *my girl*. I'm obsessed with her—truly, undeniably obsessed.

The Nighthawks don pink-and-black-and-white jerseys tonight for our once-a-season charity game. A percentage of home-game tickets and merch sales are donated to charity, but tonight, every single dollar earned from tickets to concessions to merchandise will be donated to the National Breast Cancer Foundation. Including these bright pink game-worn jerseys that will be auctioned off online during the game and announced afterward.

"Costy," Brett hollers at me, nodding to the benches.

Looking to see what he's pointing at, I'm met with a stomach of butterflies and my pink-haired girl.

She and Chloe are sitting down in the seats I got for them—the same ones from last night. The same couple had these seats again tonight, and it was easy enough to convince them to give them up again because two seats with the same vantage point were available on the opposite side of the rink. Plus a few hundred dollars, and they seemed to love the idea of those seats even more.

The announcer starts in about sponsors and whatnot before announcing the visiting team, the Washington Wild. He moves to our starting lineup, starting with Kos. The arena cheers for him.

When the announcer shouts my name into the mic, I burst out onto the ice through the smoke and lights.

Punching my stick into the air, I skate up to Kos and join him in line. But not before sneaking a glance at Nikki.

She's clapping with Chloe and shouting. And I notice she's not wearing my hoodie. But she's wearing a Nighthawks jersey. I spot the number nineteen on the sleeve.

My jersey, number nineteen, on my girl. Fucking hell, I think I'm in love.

The rest of the lineup is announced, and the first period is underway. We gain possession first, and Kos scores in the first play, firing up the arena. The Wild attempts to score on us, but MacArthur is a brick wall tonight, not letting a single puck through. The first period ends one to zero.

The momentum continues throughout the second period, earning us two more goals—both scored by me—and the Wild stays at zero.

The third period starts with my line on the bench. But in no time, our shift is up, and we are back on the ice.

Kos kicks the puck over to me, and I barrel down the boards toward their open goal when I'm blindsided and knocked into the wall.

I fall down onto the ice, and the whistle is blown. The crowd gasps when I don't get up right away, but I need a second. My boys skate over to me and assess me.

I lift my glove up, and Kos helps me up. I shake it off and get my head back in the game.

Coach glances my way, looking for an answer to the unasked question, *Are you in or out?*

I nod and line up for the drop. Looking over to the penalty box, I finally see who hit me—Owen Knox, number twenty-two.

Finding the one person I need to check on, I look at Nikki, who looks horrified and worried. I nod to her, and she nods back with a sad smile. I'll be okay. I just need to finish this game with a win and maybe an ice bath tomorrow.

Knox is fucked when he comes back in. He is getting lit the fuck up.

The next two minutes fly by, and Knox drops onto the ice, right into the action. A mistake on his part.

The second he has the puck in his stick, Jensen lays him out on the ice. Knox bounces back up and throws his gloves. The second mistake he makes.

I think I could take Knox in a fight, but you know who he can't take in a fight? Jensen fucking Donnelley.

He's our enforcer. The biggest and strongest motherfucker out of all of us. He isn't picked for fights; he picks the fights.

Jensen smiles and drops his gloves, which the refs kick out of the way.

Knox swings, and Jensen ducks before landing a punch on Knox's jaw. Knox grabs Jensen's jersey, and Jensen does the same to him, locking them at arm's length. But Jensen yanks him forward and punches him straight in the nose. He throws one, two, three more times, connecting each one, before Knox falls down, and the fight is called. If he wanted a fair fight, Knox should have picked it with me.

The game ends in a victory for the Nighthawks, beating the Wild five to zero—a blowout. We all hustle in and out of the locker room, excited to celebrate at End Zone. But I'm more excited to get to Nikki.

I find her in the lobby, waiting for me with Chloe. When she sees me, she takes off for me, weaving between everyone else.

She throws her arms around me and cheers, "You won!"

She pulls away, and I lean down and kiss her. "That we did. I think you're my lucky charm. You have to be at all of my games now."

"Sure, if I lived here, I think we could arrange that. But that would be a lot of days to close the shop, and we can't afford to do that," she sighs.

"I know. I'll take what I can get," I say as Chloe walks over to us. "Come on. Drinks are on me."

"I love the sound of that," Chloe says with a smile. "Bill is picking us up at twelve for our flight; otherwise, we are free."

"Perfect," I say and throw my arm around Nikki's shoulders as we walk outside.

I only have two hours left with her, and then she's gone again. My heart constricts at the thought.

The same thought won't leave my head the entire ride to End Zone.

As we walk inside the packed bar, Nikki asks me, "Is everything okay?"

Grabbing her hand, I rub the back of hers with my thumb. "I'm going to miss you."

She smiles, and her eyes crease at the corners. "I'm going to miss you too, Cameron."

We all make our way inside and wade through the sea of people to the bar to order our drinks. Nikki orders her vodka cran, and Chloe orders a negroni. Since I drove tonight, I just order a water.

The bartender makes our drinks at record speed. We grab them and turn to walk to our table when a familiar face stands in front of me with a mean scowl.

Owen Knox, who's backed by two of his teammates.

I lean down and whisper to Nikki, "Take Chloe to the table. I'll be there in a minute."

She then whispers to Chloe, who walks away without her. My brow furrows, and she simply shakes her head.

"Who is this beautiful lady, Costello? Care to introduce us?" Knox smirks.

I spot Kos and Brett standing up and making their way over to us.

"No, I don't think I will," I snap, and he smiles.

"Dirty play tonight, having Jensen fight for you," Knox spits out.

Laughing, I tuck Nikki further behind me. "You're the idiot who threw down your gloves with our biggest defender. Did you want to get your ass kicked or what?"

Kos and Brett emerge from the crowd and join me, tucking Nikki between them. I doubt the Wild players would go after her, but I'm not taking that chance, and I'm thankful they aren't either.

"Say one more thing, Costello," Knox snarls.

"Did you have something in mind? Or just anything in general?" I mock him.

And he swings. I catch his fist and throw his punch to the side. Something he doesn't know about End Zone is that they have a zero-tolerance fighting policy. Another thing he doesn't know is that we've become pretty good friends with the bouncers and staff here.

The bouncers, TJ and Jackson, are over to us in a heartbeat. They grab the Wild players and throw them out of the bar, quite literally.

Turning around, I check in with Nikki. "You okay?"

She nods and smiles. "I was ready."

Chuckling, I ask, "What do you mean, you were ready? They weren't going to get near you."

She lifts her hand out of her purse and shows me the can of pepper spray she is death-gripping and quickly stows it away again.

I laugh and grab her free hand. "Come on, killer. It's almost time for you to leave."

We find our seat at the table. She sits in the same seat she did the night before—my lap. But this time, she behaves and doesn't wiggle a thousand times.

She and Chloe each finish their drink, opting out of a second one, and by the time Kos and Laura are done talking about Jack's increasingly impressive hockey skills, it's time for them to leave.

Chloe's phone lights up on the table.

"It's Bill. He's outside," she mumbles to Nikki.

"Come on. I'll walk you out." I kiss the back of her head.

Hand in hand, we walk with heavy steps to the door. A man in a black car waves at them, and Chloe waves back. That must be Bill.

They push the door open, and I follow them out, feeling my stomach twist. Chloe gets in the backseat and leaves the door open for Nikki.

She spins and looks up at me. "Can you visit soon?"

Nodding, I tell her, "We have a couple of off days coming up. I will then, but after that, it's pretty strict for the next couple of months."

She sighs, "Okay. I—" She pauses, stopping herself. "I am going to miss you."

I lean down and kiss her forehead, breathing in the sweet smell of Nikki. "I'm going to miss you too, Little Dove."

Pulling my phone out, I open my camera. "Come here."

I hold my phone out to take a selfie. She looks scared in the image, but then suddenly, she seems normal and is smiling for the photo. I press the button and snap it. Quickly, I send it to her so she has it to look back on, too, during our time apart.

Her phone beeps, and she pulls it out, staring at the screen with the biggest smile on her face. "It's perfect."

"All right, I'll see you soon, baby," I say before grabbing her face and pulling her in for a gentle, long kiss.

20

NIKKI

"What colors are you doing?" Chloe asks me as she holds the hottest-pink nail polish to ever exist.

Twirling two bottles in my hand, I can't help but think of him. If I can't be at the next game, I can at least support him from here.

Chloe chortles and smiles at me. "You are too darn cute—you know that?"

"Oh, shut it." I roll my eyes and walk over to my chair.

Chloe joins me in her chair next to me. "I'm happy for you—*so, so* happy."

I smile at her, even as a sharp sting slices my heart when I remember I'm playing with fire. I need to find a way to get my parents to safety without Trey finding out. But here's the thing about my dad: he is a papa bear through and through. When he finds out that I'm alive and I have been in hiding, he will want to eliminate the reason why, and I think he would be able to do just that. But I don't want him to go to prison for it, and killing a cop would carry a hell of a sentence.

Trey Roark, a cop, is great at many things, including reading people, interrogating, and so much more. These skills enable him to read the slightest and most minute changes in someone's demeanor or tone. If my parents knew, he would know something was off, and he wouldn't stop until he found out why.

I just need a little time to find a way to get them out of there safely without completely kidnapping them. But if it comes down to it, I know Chloe would help me— with the financial backing of Zonama.

The nail techs work fast, and within forty minutes, we're leaving the salon with perfect nails. Chloe's is a simple, modern design of hot pink and white, and mine are black with silver accents.

Cam would like these and think they were cute. He might be biased, as they are inspired by the colors of the Nighthawks.

It's been a little over a week since I saw him in person, and I've come to the understanding that I didn't know what love was with Trey. I knew he was possessive and controlling, but for a long time, I thought that was how he expressed his love. But I was very wrong. That wasn't love at all.

Love is a six-foot-four dark-brown-haired and blue-eyed hockey player who refuses to touch you until you trust him completely. One who gets you ice-side seats so he can see you during his games and who shows you his scars and makes yours feel beautiful. Love is knowing that he will never hurt you because it would hurt him too.

"What do you want to do today?" Chloe asks, pulling me from my thoughts.

"Bake," I answer honestly, wanting to do something that I know and love.

"On your day off, you want to go to work?" She laughs. "Of course you do."

We arrive at my shop a few minutes later, and I find Holly helping a few customers at the register. And I spot one of my favorites, who is holding …

Oh my gosh.

"Who is this little cutie?" I shriek as I see Charlie holding an adorable baby.

He turns around with the absolute biggest smile I've ever seen. They are the proudest parents.

"This is Arlo." He swoons.

"Oh my gosh, you guys, he's perfect." I wave my fingers, smiling at the little guy.

"Thank you. He's been amazing," Charlie adds.

"I'm happy for you both. You've been waiting so long," I tell them, feeling like a proud aunt to Arlo.

"Thank you, Nikki," he murmurs.

The happy new dad and his perfect newborn baby boy get the usual coffee order and leave me with a feeling of hope.

"So, what are we baking this morning?" Chloe asks with feigned excitement.

Chuckling, I say, "I was thinking white chocolate raspberry cookies. I've been craving them."

"Oh, so we're baking for *you*, not the store?" she teases.

"For both—a happy medium." I smile and grab all of my ingredients and tools. "Holly, do you want to take your break?"

She usually has to wait for the next shift to come in to step away.

"That'd be great. I have a couple of errands I need to run." She beams. "Thank you."

"Of course. See you in a bit," I say as she walks to the back to grab her things.

"And then there were two," Chloe says hauntingly in my ear.

Stirring my dry ingredients together, I zone out as I move through the motions. It isn't until I'm done scooping the batter out onto the baking sheet that I realize Chloe is staring at me.

"What?" I ask her, confused as to why she looks confused.

With the shop now empty, she hops up onto the counter. "I want you to be happy."

Scoffing, I throw the pan in the preheated oven. "I am happy."

She frowns. "But truly happy, as *you*. I know how hard this has been for you and how hard it's been for you to let yourself be happy with Cam." She hops off of the counter and leans against it. "You know we won't let Trey hurt you. I say, go for it. Call your parents, tell them the truth. Tell Cam and live your life without thinking of Trey."

Glaring at her benign optimism, I say, "Chloe, I can't risk anything happening to my parents, or Cam, or you by being naive in thinking that Trey wouldn't act on the anger he would feel for me lying to him. I know who he is and what he does. He would either kill me so that no one else could have me or he would kill all of you so that I wouldn't have anyone else. You don't know him and what he's done, what he's said." My eyes well with tears of anger, pain, and frustration. "Every scar on my body is from him. Every time I flinch, it's because of what I went through with him. He will never let me be happy and not be with him. Those two things will never ever coexist."

"I'm sorry," Chloe whispers. "I just want to help."

"I know you do. But I'm the only one who can fix all of this. I don't know how yet, but I will. Because I love you and I love … Cam. I won't lose you both because of him. I won't."

She throws her arms around me and pulls me into the tightest hug. "I love you too. And Cam does too. He'd be an idiot not to." She pulls away. "Come on. Let's get your mess cleaned up."

By *let's*, she means me. I quickly rinse out the bowls and utensils I used and stow away the ingredients while Chloe sits on the counter on her phone.

The bell rings as the door is opened, and Holly walks through. "It's getting chilly out there."

"Holy FUCK!" Chloe screams, and I nearly jump out of my skin.

"Please don't do that. My God," I scold her.

She glances up at me, and my heart sinks from the look in her eyes. You know that when someone gives you this look—one of absolute fear and sadness—they are about to tell you something that they know will hurt you.

"What?" I whisper as my heart starts to race in my chest.

She turns to Holly. "Did you have a good break? Nikki and I are going to have a meeting in the back if you don't mind watching the front."

"No problem," she says and runs her stuff to the back quickly.

I stare at Chloe and beg her to say something.

"Thanks, babes," Chloe tells Holly before grabbing my hand, all but running to my office in the back.

"What in the hell is going on?" I demand as Chloe shuts the door behind us.

288

"Sit down," she orders, holding her phone close to her chest.

Knowing she is the most stubborn person and won't tell me anything until I do, I sit down on my couch and try to calm my now-shaking hands.

"Chloe!" I snap. "Tell me."

She takes slow, calm steps over to me and slams her eyes shut as she hands me her phone and whispers, "I'm so sorry."

"Sorry for wha—" My heart plummets to the ground, shattering into a million horrified pieces.

On the screen is the headline "Has This Nighthawks Bachelor Settled Down?"

And beneath the headline is a photo—a photo of Cam and me at the bar at End Zone with his arms around my shoulders, my face clear as day.

Cold chills settle over my skin as a feeling of the inevitable doom smacks me across the face. I scroll down the article and am slapped with another photo—one of Chloe and me in our seats at the second game with the caption, *Mystery girl spotted with friend, Zonama heiress Chloe Dupont.*

Clenching my jaw, I fight the lump in my throat trying to burst free. I'm an idiot—the biggest, stupidest fucking idiot. Trey's going to see this. I don't know when, and I don't know how, as tabloids aren't his thing. But someone is bound to see it and show him how similar this woman looks to his wife. But he'll know. He'll know it's me and not a doppelgänger.

"Breathe," Chloe whispers and takes the phone from my hand.

Laughter rumbles deep from my chest, taking over until I can't control it. "It's funny really. I did it to myself." Tears stream down my cheeks as I continue to laugh hysterically.

"Stop. It is not your fault. It's his fault for putting you in this position." Chloe grabs my shoulders, trying to calm me.

"I knew I shouldn't have gone down to those seats or out to that bar. I knew it, Chloe. But I refused to really think it or believe it because I wanted—"

"To be happy! And to be loved!" she cuts me off. "We will figure this out. We won't let him hurt you."

Meeting her worried gaze, I say as calmly as ever, "You won't have a choice. He will find out where I am, and he will come here. And I don't want you to be around when he does."

She scoffs, "I'm not going anywhere."

Storming off of the couch, I grab my keys from the front and rush to my loft, flying up the stairs with Chloe hot on my heels.

"What are you doing? Talk to me. Please," she begs as I open my door.

"You have your security, right?" I ask her as I lock the door behind us.

She nods.

"Good. Call them and keep them with you twenty-four/seven. Don't think this is just about me. That picture of us might as well have had targets on it. You were an accomplice in keeping me from him. Call them and tell them not to let you out of their sight," I tell her.

"He can't just kill all of us and get away with it," she mocks.

I turn around and face her, holding her stare with intensity. "Do you think he doesn't have the resources or reputation to back himself up? He can make your death look like a freak accident and be the one to arrest your so-called killer. Don't you understand? I'm already dead. He can kill me, and nothing will change. I already don't exist."

I walk over to my nightstand, and she remains quiet. I open the drawer, grabbing my pistol. I pop the clip out and make sure it's fully loaded, aside from the chamber.

"There's no way he knows where we're at right now, so just take a breath. We have some time to get a plan together."

"I already made your plan for you. Call your security and go home. I'm closing the shop, and I'm going to wait. He will come for me. And when he does, we're finishing it once and for all. I'm done living in fear of Trey. I'm done hiding. I'm taking back my fucking name and my fucking life. This is between him and me. When he comes, I'll be ready."

CAM

"Cam, wait up!" Laura calls me right before I'm about to step onto the ice for practice.

"What's up?" I ask her.

She cringes. "I have a favor to ask you, and I know you're not going to love it."

Dammit. "What do you need?"

"For you to stay here after practice for an interview," she mumbles.

I'm off for the next three days, and I want to spend them with Nikki, not sucking up to an interviewer for good press. She thinks I'm off but that I have to stay here for team bonding. But I'm flying out tonight because I like surprising her. But this job comes with things like this, and sometimes, it's hard to complain about it because of the amazing pros I do have.

"What's the interview about? Did Kos already say no?"

Usually, he is the one to do most of the one-on-one interviews. Everyone wants to talk to the captain of the Nighthawks.

She sighs. "This interviewer requested you personally. Have you not seen the article about you yet?"

"What article?" I ask with hesitancy. "I haven't seen anything."

She holds her finger in the air as she unlocks her phone and searches for it. "This one." She hands her phone to me.

I read the headline on the screen. *"Has This Nighthawks Bachelor Settled Down?"*

What the fuck?

"This is news?" I laugh. "That's why the interviewer requested me?"

It was inevitable that pictures of Nikki and me would get posted and shared, but I'm still surprised at the uproar from it.

She takes her phone back. "Everyone wants to know who the mystery girl is that stole your heart. So, will you do it? If not, I need to let them know."

"Yeah, I'll do it. I gotta go though. It's here after practice?" I ask, stepping onto the ice.

"Yes," she says, smiling, and answers a call on her phone. "Hello?"

I skate away and make a lap to warm up. *The girl who stole my heart, huh?*

I wonder if she's seen the article yet and what she thinks of it. The public eye is daunting and invasive at times. I'll call her after practice and the interview.

Coach blows the whistle and divides us into teams to scrimmage. A lot of our practices are straight scrimmage because it's one of the best ways to improve our skills and prepare us for games.

We scrimmage for an hour before Coach calls it and releases us for the night. I have no hope left to escape before the interview because Laura is already waiting with a strange woman and a cameraman on our benches. Laura waves at me, and I lift a glove, waving back.

"Good luck, Costy. Don't forget to show off those pearly whites." Brett smacks my back as he skates past me.

"Sure you don't want to do it?" I jokingly but not jokingly ask him.

He laughs. "Absolutely not. Besides, I'm not the one with a new girlfriend or a new scandal or a new injury. They don't care about me right now. Thank God."

I skate over to the waiting vultures with a big, flashy smile. "Where would you like me?"

"Hi. I'm Natalie. Please, have a seat here, and we'll set up around you. It will just be you on camera today. I'll be asking you questions off-screen." She beams.

Sitting down on the bleachers, I pull off my helmet and set it down beside me, shaking my hair out.

Natalie and the unnamed cameraman set up their equipment and clip a mic on my jersey. Laura is sitting down, typing away on her laptop. She should have at least told me what questions would be asked.

"Are you ready?" Natalie enthusiastically asks.

"As I'll ever be." I smile.

She positions herself to the right, behind the camera. "Don't stress. We can redo as many takes as we need. Just look at me the whole time and pretend the camera isn't there."

Yeah, I know how interviews work. I've done a handful already. But I know she's going to ask about Nikki, and that alone has me nervous in a different way.

I nod, and she fires the first question at me. "This season has been incredible for the Nighthawks. You guys are undefeated so far. What are you all doing to keep your streak?"

"We put in a lot of work this past off-season, on and off the ice. It shows in our game play and in our teamwork. The bond we have together is unbreakable. We go into every game with a clear mindset, ready to work for every goal and not to expect a win. The time we've dedicated to our craft and to the team is paying off."

She nods with a big smile. "Perfect. The chemistry of your team is undeniable. No matter who is in the game, you play at the exact same level." She pauses awkwardly.

"What do you do in your free time? Any secret hobbies or skills you're working on?"

Shrugging, I generically answer her question. "In my free time, I'm often watching other teams' games, trying to learn their strong suits and potential weaknesses."

"What about your personal life? Anyone special?" she asks and winks at me.

I give her what she is pushing for. "Yes, actually. I recently started seeing someone."

She oohs and aahs. "What's her name? How did you guys meet?"

Nikki in that tight gold dress flashes in my mind.

"Her name is Nikki. We met at a club in town during their masquerade opening night a few months back."

Natalie waves her hands toward herself, asking me to give her more.

"She's amazing and so down-to-earth. She knows what really matters in life and what doesn't. I've never met someone so strong and resilient. She makes me look at everything differently in the best possible way."

Forcing my swallow over the new lump in my throat, I continue, "She is everything I never knew I needed or wanted in life. I'm incredibly grateful to Laura, Alec Kostelecky's fiancée, for introducing us that night."

She makes me happier than I ever thought I could be. She makes me look forward to every single day because she's in it. Life before her was routine and boring.

I refused to let anyone in because I didn't want to feel pain anymore from the people I loved. I've been that way since the man I was born to trust and love took the life of the one and only person who truly did love me—my mom.

After my dad hurt us, I assumed everyone had that darkness within them even if they didn't know it yet. Maybe everyone does. But it's a choice you make every day. You choose to do or not do evil things. You choose to protect or to hurt the ones you love. You choose right or wrong.

But I didn't have that choice when I was younger. He chose for me. He chose to whip me whenever he pleased. He chose to hurt my mom whenever he wanted to, and one day, he chose to take her life. But when he killed her, he also chose to go to prison for the rest of his life. He was a cop who had gotten away with so much for so long.

When I was young, I tried many times to tell people who he really was—school counselors and nurses. But no one would listen, and if they did, it was shut down the second it reached the station. After all, he was a beloved cop in the community who could *never do those things*. I just had an active imagination and was mad at him and trying to get him into trouble—or at least, that was what I was always told.

He broke every trust I ever had—with him, with peers, with those I was supposed to be able to go to for help. He made me give up on anything good.

Until that night at Fireflies, I did a good job at keeping everyone at arm's length. But Nikki snuck into my life, and I don't know if it was the scars that graced her skin or the darkness I recognized in her eyes, but I was hooked. I knew it the moment we met, but I was too scared to really see it. To see that we were inevitable.

Whatever shitty paths life had taken us down, we found our way to one another—to the only person who would understand us without saying a word.

After everything she has been through, she still chose to take a chance on me. If I were her, I don't know that I would have been able to do that. But every day, she shares more of herself with me, and I, with her. Who knew pink hair and bright blue eyes would make me believe in love again?

"Wow. That is so sweet," Natalie adds. "Have Laura and Nikki known each other long?"

Nodding, I answer, "Nikki owns a coffee shop that Laura used to go to when she and Jack lived in Duluth."

"Oh, so she's not from here?" Natalie retorts.

"Nope. She still lives there and runs her coffee shop. I visit her when I can, and vice versa," I answer.

"Long distance must be hard. Any tips or tricks for keeping a relationship healthy during those times apart?"

"Communicate. FaceTime has been our go-to almost every night. We connect about our day and talk about our plans for our next time together. It's hard, but it's not impossible. It's an easy sacrifice to make when it's for someone you love."

I did not just say that.

But I'm not wrong or lying. I was just too afraid to admit it to myself.

I love her. I *fucking* love her.

I love the way she melts in my arms when I hold her. I love the way she smiles when she catches me staring. I love the way she has opened herself up to me and slowly trusted me with her heart and her body. I love everything about her.

She was made for me to love.

I've never felt anything like how I feel for her. It consumes me. Every thought and every second of every day, she is there in my mind. When I lie in bed at night, my body aches to feel her next to me. When I wake, I want nothing more than to kiss her and feel her lips on mine.

The thought of loving someone used to scare me, but I think I was just waiting to love her. Because loving her isn't scary. It's the most freeing thing I've ever done. I'm going to continue to love her every single goddamn day.

I need to tell her how I feel. I need to show her. Words are but a promise to her and me, but actions are their fulfillment. I'm going to kiss every inch of her body, trace every scar with my tongue. I'm going to show her what love *feels* like.

"That's all the questions I had. Anything else you would like to add?" Natalie asks.

Shaking my head, I tear the mic off and hand it back to her. "Nope. Thank you so much. This was … enlightening. I need to go. Let Laura know if you need anything else from me, please. Thanks."

I grab my helmet and take off for the locker room. My flight leaves in two hours, and I need to pick up flowers before I get there.

I love Nikki Satinn, and nothing is ever going to change that. She and I were fucking made for each other.

On my way out of the arena, I try calling her, but she doesn't answer, so I leave a voice mail.

"Hey, baby. I'm coming to see you. There's something really important I need to tell you, and I have to do it in person. I miss you. I'll be there in a few hours."

I love you, I want to say, but don't. I want to see her reaction when I tell her for the first time, and then I want to kiss her senseless.

22

NIKKI

F*uck.*
    "Chloe, he's on his way here right now. What am I going to do?" I beg her to give me the perfect answer.

I left my phone unattended for a few hours to reset myself, and I came back to a nightmare. Cam is on his way here right now and might have already landed. He can't be here when Trey comes.

"Take a breath. Let's start with that," she says calmly as she locks the door to the shop and hangs the sign up, saying we're closed for the next week.

We weren't sure how long to close for, but we figured that was a good start. Chloe also let our staff know that we would be closed but that they would be paid for what they were scheduled.

My throat clenches, and my eyes well with tears when I imagine what is to come. "He can't be here, Chloe."

She walks over to me and sits on the counter next to me. "Why is he coming here?"

My brows slam together. "What? What do you mean?"

"Why is he coming to visit Duluth, Minnesota, on his few days off when he could be resting and relaxing, like he was planning to?" she asks.

Taking a slow, long breath, I answer her honestly, "Because he wants to see me."

She clicks her tongue and winks at me. "Exactly right. Because he cares for you and wants to spend whatever free time he has with you. So, you know what you are going to do? Continue to face your fears."

"I'm scared to lose him," I whisper.

Horrified. Terrified. Petrified. Whatever you want to call it, I am that.

What if he thinks less of me and leaves? I know Cam isn't quick to judge, but I can't help but consider that as a possibility.

But it's time. He deserves the truth, and I'm going to give him it. I'm going to tell him who I really am, why I'm here, and why I've been so scared to tell him how I really, truly feel about him. That I love him.

Nikki Satinn has served her purpose. She kept me and my family safe for as long as she could. But Nikki can't save me anymore. It's time I take that mask off once and for all.

When I checked my phone and listened to Cam's voice mail, my heart dropped. If Trey hurts him, I will never forgive myself. I haven't texted or called Cam back yet. I don't know how to tell him not to come without breaking my own heart—or his.

My phone buzzes on the counter next to me. Which is the only warning I get before a knock sounds on the door behind us, and I jump off of the counter as I feel phantom spiders crawling across my skin.

Turning around, I prepare for the worst. It's Trey. He's here for me.

But instead, I get the best.

Cam.

He wiggles his fingers at me with the biggest smile.

I walk over to the door as Chloe tells me, "I will give you guys some space. Call me if you need me, okay?"

Nodding, she leaves me to deal with this mess of my own making. I unlock the door and let him in, relocking it behind him.

"Look, Cam, I need to—ahh!"

I shriek as I become airborne as he swings me around in circles.

"I've missed you," he whispers into my ear before lowering me to the ground and pulling me into a hug with my head against his chest.

Inhaling deep, I breathe him in and sigh, "I've missed you too."

He releases me and steps back. "I hope you listened to my voice mail and this isn't an unwelcome surprise."

Laying my hands on his abs, I kiss his chest and assure him, "You being here is never unwelcome."

"Good." He leans down and kisses my forehead. "I'm sorry to surprise you if that's not okay. But after practice today, I couldn't stop thinking about you while I was doing that interview. After that article was published about us, the first thing I wanted to know was if you were okay."

I stopped listening at the word *interview*.

"What did you just say?" I interrupt him. "What interview? Did you talk about me in it?"

"Of course I did. Everyone wants to know who you are. And when I was telling the interviewer about you, I couldn't stop thinking about something I have been wanting to tell—"

"Cam, please. What did you say about me?" I beg him to answer.

His brows furrow, and his shoulders tense. "What's going on? Why are you upset?"

Frustration rattles me to my core. "Please just tell me. I need to know *exactly* what you told them."

Cam reaches out to grab my hands, and I flinch. I flinch from Cam. But not because of Cam, but because of the emotions and feelings being stirred up right now.

"I'm sorry," I mutter.

"Nikki, what is happening right now? What am I missing? Is it about the sign on the door?" he whispers.

I cackle. "*Nikki.*"

Oh fuck, I'm losing it.

"I will tell you everything, but *please* tell me what you said—every detail. Nothing is too small."

"I told them how happy you make me. How you are someone I never knew I needed but that you've changed my entire life. You make me look at everything differently in the best possible way." He pauses. "I told them your name and that you run a coffee shop here. If I can help spike business, I want to. I want you to be as successful as you can be. I know how important it is to you."

Ripping my phone out of my pocket, I call Chloe and wait for her to answer.

She picks up on the first ring. "What's going on?"

All of the words try to come out of my mouth at once, but nothing makes it past my lips.

"Nikki?" she fearfully whispers.

Opening my mouth, I force the words out. "He knows where I am. He knows where to find me."

Saying those words out loud sounds much scarier than they did in my head. It makes them real.

He knows where to find me.

Cam whispers, "Who? What is going on?"

Chloe gasps. "How? What happened? Nikki?"

Tears well in my eyes until a drop falls over the edge of my lashes and rolls down my cheek.

"Nikki?" Chloe shouts in the phone as it slips out of my hand, caught mid-drop by Cam.

"C-Chloe, what is going on right now?" Cam stutters into the phone.

"What else did you tell them?" I ask, my voice sounding unrecognizable.

"Chloe said she's coming back. She turned around," Cam says, still confused.

I reach my hand out, and he sets my phone in my grasp.

I tell Chloe, "Don't come back. Please. I'll call you in the morning."

"Are you sure? I'm right outside. Whatever you need, I'll do it," she says, and I can hear the sadness in her voice.

"I need to talk to Cam. Come over in the morning," I tell her.

"Okay, I love you," she says soothingly.

"I love you too," I say and hang up before I change my mind.

I've envisioned this conversation a million times in my head, trying to come up with the best way to tell him. But there's no way to ease him into this. To tell him that who he knows me as is a lie.

Taking a calm and shaky breath, I set my phone down and turn to face him.

"Let's go to my office, and I'll explain everything," I tell him, already leading the way.

He follows me down the hallway in silence and into my office, finding a seat on my couch. I opt for my desk chair to put some space between us.

"Promise me you'll listen until I'm finished, that you won't leave and that you'll try to understand," I beg him. "Please."

Meeting his eyes, I notice the fear in them and the way his posture sinks from my words.

He agrees, "I promise."

Blowing out a shaky breath, I stop my foot from tapping and force myself to be still, to try to calm my anxiety. "My name isn't Nikki Satinn."

He gulps. "What do you mean, it's not your name?"

I sit on my hands to stop them from quivering. "I mean that Nikki Satinn isn't a real person. I made her up. It was the only way I could escape."

I see the panic and the questions brewing in the constant adjustment of how he's sitting and in the rapid tapping of his foot.

"Escape what?" he quietly asks.

"Not what. *Who*," I breathe. "My ex-boyfriend, Trey, the one that I've told you about. I had to get away from him, and when the chance arose, I took it, and I ran. He was going to kill me even if he hadn't admitted it to himself yet. He was never going to let me go."

"If he thinks you're alive, he must still be looking for you … unless he thinks you're—"

"Dead. He thinks I'm dead," I state. "I made my parents bury a coffin that I wasn't in. I let everyone in my life believe that I died so I could get away from him and keep them safe. He had no reason to hurt them when he couldn't hurt me anymore." Images of him at dinner with my parents tighten my fists. "Do you know he takes them out for dinner, like they're a happy family? Like he isn't the reason why their daughter is dead."

"Nikk—I'm sorry."

"My real name is Morgan Dove," I tell him as I rub my finger over the tattoo on my wrist.

He whispers, "Little Dove."

"It was the one piece of myself that I kept—a reminder of who I am and why I'm here. If I stayed hidden, everyone in my life was safe, including you." The stream of tears continues to pour down my cheeks. "But now, he knows how to find me. I don't know for a fact if he's seen the article or your interview. But he will. And when he realizes I'm alive, he won't stop."

"I won't let him hurt you," Cam says. "I understand. I understand why you did what you did. But if you think for one second that I'm going to walk away and leave you to fend for yourself, you don't know me at all. Ask me what else I told that interviewer."

"What?" I ask, confused. "It doesn't matter what else you said, Cam. It's not your fault. I should have told you the truth sooner."

He stands, walks over to me, and grabs my hand, pulling me back to the couch with him.

He sits down and pulls me forward until I'm standing between his legs. "Morgan, ask me."

Morgan.

He said Morgan. Not Nikki, but my *real* name. I didn't think there would ever come a day that someone would call me that again. It's like waking up from years of dreaming and playing pretend.

What he said in the interview doesn't matter anymore. The damage is already done. None of it is his fault, of course. But there's nothing else I need to hear.

I expected him to be a little more upset that I'd been lying to him this whole time. But instead, he grabbed my hand and pulled me closer.

His hands hook behind my thighs, his thumbs stroking the fabric of my jeans, and I decide to let him tell me anyway. Nothing he could say would make me angry or sad or change what's already coming.

I whisper, "What else did you tell them?"

Looking deep into his eyes, I look for any hint of resentment or regret. But I find the complete opposite.

"That I love you, Little Dove," Cam blurts out.

My heart tumbles. "That you … what?"

He releases my thighs and grabs my face, pulling me closer to him. "That I love you. No matter what your name is, no matter where you came from or where you're going, I love you. I love you. I *fucking* love you. I don't care about any lies you had to tell me to survive. Only that you tell me the truth from now on. I'm here, I'm yours, and I'm not going anywhere."

I become weightless as I fall into his lap, straddling his legs, on a high of what he just said. He doesn't release my face as I cup his jaw and caress the stubble on his cheeks.

"I love you," I whisper. "I've wanted to tell you, but I couldn't until you knew who I really was. But I love you so much, Cam. Every moment with you is what I have always wanted. I didn't know that I could be loved like this, that I deserved a love like yours." My lip quivers. "Trey … he broke me. He controlled my body and eventually my thoughts. He made me think that I wasn't even good enough for him, that I wasn't good enough to make my own decisions, that I just wasn't enough. But I know that's not true."

"You are more than enough, Morgan. You always have been," Cam whispers as his lips brush against mine.

Is this what I've been missing out on my entire life? A love like this?

Trey has taken enough from me. He's not taking this. He can't. Our love is the one thing he can't break.

"I trust you," I say against his mouth. "I trust you *fearlessly*."

Sealing our lips together, I kiss him, long and slow, cherishing it.

His hands drift to my neck before skimming down to my shoulders and sliding onto my waist. Without breaking our kiss, he stands and lifts me up. I wrap my legs around his waist, and he carries me out of the office and to the stairwell to my loft.

His lips pull away from mine and find my jaw. With gentle and sweet kisses, he leaves a trail down my neck to my collarbone, following the path back up as he ascends the stairs with me in his arms.

Grabbing the door handle, I throw it open. Cam kicks it shut with his foot and carries me over to the bed, his mouth and tongue never leaving mine.

He lays me down and hovers over me, his hands on either side of my head. "I love you, Morgan."

"I love you too," I murmur as my fingers grab the bottom of his hoodie and lift, pulling it and the shirt beneath off of him.

I throw them to the floor, and his rough hands grasp my sweater, lifting it up and over my head. It quickly joins his clothes on the ground. My bra is next to go.

"You are so beautiful, every single inch of you," he says as his eyes explore me, burning a trail of desire on my body.

Sitting up, I reach for his pants, running my hand down the bulge that's trying to break free. I hook my fingers in the waistband and pull them down over his hips, surprised at how hard he already is as his massive erection springs free.

Grabbing my chin, he lifts my head up to meet his gaze and doesn't say a word. He doesn't need to. Words don't mean anything to people who were hurt by never-ending broken promises. His thumb swipes my bottom lip.

He nods his head, and I let him guide me to my feet. Holding my stare, he undoes my jeans and shimmies them down my legs, slowly bringing his fingers back up my now-bare skin to the lace of my panties. They are next to go. But first, he glides his fingers between my legs, finding how soaked I already am. He smirks and grabs the thin lace, pulling it down to my ankles in one smooth motion.

Every nerve in my body is alive and on edge, anxiously waiting for his touch.

Reaching out, I grab his dick, rubbing my thumb over the moist tip. He licks and bites his lip.

With a hand on my chest, he pushes me back to the bed, and I fall down on my elbows and shimmy my way closer to the pillows.

Cam stands at the end of the bed, just watching me. Smirking, he shakes his head, and his lips break into a full smile.

"I'm the luckiest man alive." He moans as he begins stroking himself, base to tip.

He follows me onto the bed and grabs my left leg, placing kisses from the top of my foot, up my calf, and up the inside of my thigh, each kiss more sensitive than the last. He repeats these steps with my right leg before lying down with his head between my legs.

His tongue runs up my soaked center, and I gasp, throwing my head back. He eases a finger inside me, circling it, over and over. Another finger joins in, stretching me slowly.

"So tight for me, baby," he whispers, adding a third finger.

His tongue latches on to me. As his fingers begin pumping faster and faster, his tongue matches the quick pace until I'm a mumbling and moaning mess on the verge of bliss.

"Fuck, that's it, baby," Cam praises me before his tongue finds the perfect spot again.

My breathing quickens, and—oh shit, here it comes. "Oh fuck! Cam!"

His fingers continue their delicious torture as he tears the top of a foil packet with his teeth that he seemed to pull out of thin air.

"You trust me?" he asks as he positions himself between my thighs.

"Yes," I whimper. "I trust you."

Fuck, I don't know how that's going to fit.

As if reading my mind, he says, "Don't worry, baby. You were made for me; you were made for this."

His tip slides in, and I gasp, feeling the tightness overwhelm every cell in my body. Thrusting in further, he stretches me, molding my body to his.

"Fuck," he growls as he grabs my thighs and lifts my hips up.

Reaching over me, he pushes in deeper and grabs a pillow, placing it under my hips and lower back, lining us up.

He pulls out just slightly and thrusts in harder and faster this time.

"Goddamn," I whimper and writhe as he begins pumping in and out of me, stronger with each thrust.

"You're doing so good," he says before pulling out to the tip and inching back in.

"Cam …" I beg him for more. "Please."

Pushing the tip in further, he teases me, "Please what?"

"Please," I whimper.

He pulls back out until just the tip remains. "Say it. What do you want?"

Cupping my breast, I meet his hungry, darkened stare. "I want you to *fuck* me."

"Are you going to take it all, Little Dove?" he begs.

"Yes," I moan, and his thumb circles my clit, making my hips buck.

He slams into me, and I moan and scream in pleasure, "Fuck!"

He pauses only for a second as I adjust to his size. I've never been so full.

He pulls out and thrusts back in, filling me more than before. "There you go, baby. Take every inch."

He grabs both of my ankles with one hand and bends my legs back toward me, sliding in and out of me deeper and deeper.

"You feel so fucking good." He cups my breast with his free hand.

Rolling his hips, he fucks me slowly, torturing me. I don't know how much more of this I can take.

"Harder, please," I whine.

Letting go of my ankles, he leans over me, pressing my knees into my chest, and smirks. "If you say so."

He pulls out and slams into me, over and over, tip to hilt. He fucks me without restraint, without any secrets between us. He fucks me with love and undying passion.

"Fuck, Morgan," he whispers harshly into my ear, and I lose it, hearing my real name on his lips.

"Cam! Cam, fuck!" I cry out his name over and over as a bolt of pleasure shoots through me.

He fucks me through my orgasm, not letting up in the slightest. "Give me one more, baby."

He picks up the pace, fucking me harder and harder with each thrust, moaning under his breath.

His thumb finds my most sensitive spot, circling it. My back arches off the bed as the sensations become too much.

"*Fuck* yes. What a good fucking girl you are, tightening around me, clenching my cock. Be greedy, baby. It's all yours," he grunts as he pumps into me, sending both of us into oblivion. "Fuck, Morgan."

My body lights up like a damn firework, exploding with pleasure.

He moans in my ear, and his hips roll as he comes, whispering my name—*my real name.*

MORGAN

"So, how was last night?" Chloe asks, looking over her mug.

Perfect. Amazing. Freeing.

"Mmhmm. Sure, keep all the good secrets to yourself," she adds before I have time to even open my mouth.

"It was better than good. It was the *best* sex I have ever had," I whisper to her across the table.

"Ooh … so, like, how big?" she asks, setting her mug down and guessing his size with her hands. "Bigger than *this*?"

I hear the door to my loft open and give Chloe the *don't say a fucking word* stare. She gives me an evil grin.

"Hi, sleepyhead," Chloe says as Cam walks over to us, wearing joggers and a hoodie.

Come to think of it, besides his hockey jersey, I don't know if I've seen him in a different outfit than these two things.

"Good morning," he says, his voice raspy from sleep. *Why is bedhead so sexy?*

He rubs his eyes and meets mine, and I'm helpless in fighting the blush that creeps onto my cheeks.

"Good morning, Cameron." I smile. "Sleep okay?"

He sits down beside me and grabs my chair, pulling it toward him. "Best sleep ever." He steals my water and takes a sip. "Why on earth are you guys up this early? It's barely six a.m."

He tips his head back and closes his eyes while I say, "I'm just used to it, I guess. I have to bake and get everything ready super early so it's done by the time we open."

"Are you guys opening today?" His head snaps up.

"No. Definitely not," I say. "I have enough to worry about without stressing about this place."

As I look around my empty shop, sadness crushes my chest. This has been my safe haven, and because of Trey, I can't open today and see my customers. But that day will come again.

"Let's go back to bed then. I'm *so* tired," Cam groans, drinking a third of my water.

"Did you want some of that?" I ask him, laughing.

"I'm sorry. I'll fill it back up for you," Cam says, attempting to contain his smile.

"You guys are adorable," she chimes. "I'm going to go get a couple of things done and grab lunch with my dad. Meet back up afterward?" She pauses, and I nod. "I really think you guys should come to my house. It's safer."

I twist my cup in my hand as swirling fear and anger slice into my chest from the thought of Cam or her not being safe and potentially getting hurt. Cam's fingers grab my thigh and press my foot down. I didn't realize I had been tapping it so aggressively.

"Cam should go. I don't want to be near you two when he shows up," I mumble, my voice shaky. "You don't know what he's capable of."

Cam's thumb caresses the top of my thigh. "I'm not going anywhere, Morgan."

Sighing, I take a drink of my almost-empty water. "Chloe, please, can you stay at your house after your lunch with your dad? I need to know you'll be safe."

"If you come with me," she argues.

When I say Trey won't stop until he finds me, I mean it. Chloe's guarded house won't change that. He's a cop. He's smart and patient. He'll wait as long as he has to. I can't keep Cam here forever, and knowing Trey, he would use Cam to draw me out. It would work too.

Which means that, very soon, I'll be seeing Trey again, face-to-face. A nightmare that I was hoping would never come true.

I don't know what will happen when we come together again. Will he kill me for leaving him? Will he touch me? Will he torture me? Will he see me and let me go?

The gun sitting next to me knows the answer to those questions. He wants to bring me back to his domain. He wants me to be his again. But I won't let that happen. I won't go back to him alive.

"Okay, *fine*. I'll meet you at your house after lunch," I lie to her.

She smiles. "Good. I'll see you then." She downs her coffee. "I love you."

"I love you too," I tell her as she walks to the door and leaves, locking up behind her and getting into the back of a black SUV.

I feel Cam's eyes on me.

He studies me for a moment before he asks, "You're not going over there, are you?"

"No," I answer flatly.

"Are you sure we shouldn't join her?" Cam asks hesitantly.

Leaning my head against his shoulder, I tell him, "I'm sure. But I meant what I said about you going."

He takes a deep breath and says, "Get it out of your head, Little Dove. You're stuck with me. Now, do you want to hang out down here or go upstairs?"

"Let me make a quick call, and we can go back up," I whisper to him as my heart jumps.

Cam chooses me every second of the day when it would be so much easier for him to run and forget about me. If I can't force him away to keep him safe, I'll have to find a way to keep him safe next to me.

The line rings twice before Bill picks up, and I speak before he can, setting the tone of our call immediately. "Don't say my name or let her know I'm on the phone."

"Good morning," he answers.

"You want to keep Chloe safe, right? That's your job?" I ask him, knowing what he'll say next.

"Yes, sir," Bill responds firmly.

Keeping my voice clear and concise, I tell him, "After lunch, she believes that I am coming over there. But I will not be doing that. My ex-boyfriend is coming here. He's a dangerous man, and there is no telling what he'll do to the people I love, if given the chance. After lunch, do not let her leave that house until you hear from me again. Do you understand?"

"Yes, sir," Bill responds, a slight inflection in his tone.

"She might die if she leaves that house. I swear to God, if she gets hurt because you couldn't keep her there—" My voice cracks, and Cam grabs my hand and places gentle kisses against my knuckles.

"I understand, sir. Thank you. You have nothing to worry about," he tells me, and I know that he means it.

As hard as Chloe fights, her security team won't let her leave.

Hanging up the phone, I'm rocked with the realization that if something happens to me, this morning might have been the last time I ever see her.

My best friend, her bright and bubbly face. The stranger who saved my life and gave me my new one. I can never repay her for what she has done for me. But I can make sure she is safe and untouchable from Trey.

"Are you okay?" Cam whispers, turning me toward him.

Nodding, I wipe away the tears building in my lower lashes. "I will be. When all of this is over."

The overwhelming feeling of dread pushes down on my chest and shoulders. It's a waiting game now. Going back to bed actually sounds amazing right now.

"Upstairs?" I lightly smile at him.

"Yes, please," he says, yawning.

Intertwining our fingers, he leads me back to my bed and crawls in next to me, pulling me into his arms with my head on his chest.

"We could fly back to New York. I could keep you safe there."

"What happens if a cop shows up and starts asking questions about me? Are they just going to force him away because I said so? He's a cop, Cam. You know that his words mean more than mine," I say, my voice muffled against his chest.

He sighs, and I know he's frustrated. He wants to find a way to fix this. But he, of all people, understands how different this situation is because Trey's a cop. Right now, it's his word versus mine, and Cam and I both know how much higher valued the voice of a law enforcement worker is.

"Okay, I'll do whatever you need me to do," he says, rubbing my back. "Don't want to go to New York? Fine, we'll stay here. But we need a plan for when he shows up. I'm guessing a stern conversation isn't going to send him walking? Should we try to involve the police? Or should I go out and buy a couple of shovels?"

I laugh. "The police? They are the ones protecting him. I can't tell you how many times I went to the doctor or the ER, covered in bruises, getting X-rays on my wrists or ribs. They all saw what he had done to me, and yet nothing ever happened."

If you think the first call I'd make when someone broke in is to the cops, you're wrong. I would call Chloe. She would have a team with her, breaking down the door, before the cops were even close.

"So, are we going with the shovel option?" Cam genuinely asks.

Before Trey, I wasn't sure I was capable of taking a human life—other than my own. He changed that in me. I know without a doubt that if Trey tried to harm me or Cam, I would put him down like the rabid dog he was.

"If it comes down to it, yes."

Waking up, I have a sinking feeling in every cell of my body. In the blink of an eye, reality slaps me, and I'm reminded of why I feel this way.

Peeling Cam's arm off of me, I roll over and check the time on my phone—12:42 p.m.

Holy shit, how in the hell did we sleep in this late?

I nudge Cam. "Hey, wake up. It's almost one o'clock."

"Five more minutes," Cam pleads.

Laughing, I tickle his side and watch all of his muscles contract as he laughs.

"Oh my God, don't do that. I hate being tickled."

Tickling him again, I giggle. "Well, we've got a problem then because this is way too much fun to never do again."

He rolls over and on top of me, pinning me to the bed. His hair falls down, framing his face as he stares at me.

"You are such a brat, Little Dove." He squints his eyes at me and lowers his hips down onto mine.

Biting my bottom lip, I whisper, "What are you going to do about it?"

His eyes darken as he hardens against me. "I have a lot of things I could do about that attitude, including a

326

really quick solution to get that pretty mouth to stop being so bratty."

"And what's that?" I challenge.

"Sliding my cock down your throat until gagging is the only sound you can make," he growls.

Sucking in a sharp breath, I wriggle beneath him, feeling his growing bulge press into me.

His stomach growls, breaking the silence between us.

Giggling, I ask him, "Hungry?"

He chuckles, showing off those pearly whites. "Yes, I'm starving."

Patting his chest, I say, "Come on. I'll make you breakfast."

We head downstairs, and I reheat a few muffins and brush them with melted butter.

"I hope blueberry muffins are okay," I say, sliding the plate toward him.

"Mmm-mmm-mmm," he hums. "Perfect."

While Cam stuffs down the first muffin, I decide to check the voice mails for my shop.

Two voice mails.

I click the first one and listen to a woman's voice.

"Hi. I was just wondering if you guys are open today. Give me a call back at …"

I click off since the voice mail is two days old. It would be almost rude to call back at this point.

I click the second voice mail and bring the phone back to my ear.

I hold my breath as a familiar voice on the other side says, "Hello, Honeybee. I've missed you. I'll see you soon. Then, I can finally bring you home."

Needles prick my body, and tears rapidly blur my vision.

My ears ring as my phone slips from my hand and crashes onto my floor.

"Hey, what's wrong?" Cam jumps off of the counter and is by my side in a second.

But nothing's working—not my mouth, my brain, or my body. I'm frozen in place as his words play over and over in my head.

Honeybee.

How do I know he's not outside right now, just waiting for me?

Cam rubs my shoulders. "Baby, what is it?"

I can't find my words, so I grab my phone off of the floor and hand it to him.

He presses play and holds it to his ear, listening to the voice of the man who abused me for years.

He sets my phone down on the counter and kisses my forehead. "What do you want to do? Do you want to stay here? I really think we need to go someplace else."

We need to not be in such a trapped space. The shop has two exits, but knowing Trey, he will block one somehow and corner us. I know just the place we're going to.

"Grab your stuff. We're going to the library," I tell him as I throw the phone back on its charger.

"I want to support whatever your plan is, but is reading *really* the answer right now?" he asks nervously as I take off for the stairs and he follows behind me.

I roll my eyes at him and timidly chuckle. "I'm not going to read. The library is closed today and tomorrow. We're going to camp out there. I know the ins and outs of that place like the back of my hand. If Trey doesn't show up by the end of day tomorrow, maybe we can go to Chloe's."

He nods, trusting me fully. "All right, let's do it."

Quickly, I throw some clothes into my bag along with my charger, my toothbrush, my hairbrush, snacks for a couple of days, and my box of ammo. You know, all the essentials.

Cam waits for me by the door with his duffel bag on his shoulder.

"Hey, can you grab those blankets, please?" I ask, pointing to the stack in the basket by the couch.

Tossing my bag down, I rush to grab something I forgot. Sliding my arms through the sleeves, I pull Cam's hoodie over my head and sigh at the happiness it brings me.

"Ready?" I say as I grab my bag and tuck my pistol into my hoodie in case we need it on the walk over.

Nodding, he opens the door for me, and I step outside first with my hand in my pocket. He shuts it, and I hastily secure a few of the locks behind me.

My ears listen for the smallest creak in a floorboard or a hinge opening on a door. But dead silence is all I hear.

I lead us down the stairs and out of the stairwell, walking on the balls of my feet across the sitting area of my shop.

Opening the front door, I throw my hood up and lock the door once Cam walks through.

"Take a breath for me, please," Cam whispers into my ear.

Forcing the air I was holding through my teeth, I slowly exhale. Scanning the streets, I look for anything out of place. But everything seems as it should be.

We make the short walk to the library and are approaching the doors when Cam says, "How are we getting in? Is there a hidden key or something?"

Digging my keys out of my pocket, I slide one into the door until it clicks and unlocks.

"About a year ago, Susan was really sick and couldn't run the library, so she asked me to watch over it while she was ill. I kept it in case I ever needed to get away or if she needed help again." I push the door open and relock it behind us.

Once we get to Susan's desk, I set my stuff down and turn to Cam. "Are you okay? With staying here, I mean."

He grabs my jaw with one hand, and I lean into his touch. "Yes. I'm here until this is all over. I'm not letting anything happen to you."

"But you have practice and a game coming up," I say as anxiety wraps around my throat. "You can't *not* go."

He grabs my waist and lifts me up, setting me on the counter. "I already texted Kos, Brett, and Coach, telling them I needed a few days for a family emergency." He grabs my face as my eyes well up with tears. "Get it through that beautiful, thick skull of yours." He kisses me. "I"—kiss—"am not"—kiss—"going"—kiss— "anywhere."

"Okay," I whisper. "Thank you."

"You are my family now, Morgan. We're in this together," he says against my lips. "No matter what."

We spend the next hour meandering around the library. I show him all the books I have read in here, all of them being in the Romance section. Then, we watch two movies on Netflix, and before I know it, it's six o'clock and pitch-black outside with no sign of Trey.

A sweet kiss presses onto my forehead before Cam whispers, "Hey. Sleep okay?"

Fluttering my eyes open, I take in my surroundings, staring up at the high shelves full of romance books that dream of what we have.

"I don't know how I slept at all," I grumble as I sit up from the hard ground.

"Because I'm here," Cam says before kissing my temple and standing up.

He reaches up and stretches, exposing the lines of scars that cover every part of his back and shoulders.

"Do you ever talk about what happened?" I ask him and set my hands in my crisscrossed legs.

"About my dad?" he asks and slips the tank top on.

I nod.

He sits down across from me and leans back against the bookshelf. "Not really. But if you have questions, please, ask them."

Grabbing my blanket, I pull it over my lap and lean back against the bookshelf behind me. "Was he always bad?"

Cam stares off, his mind going elsewhere. "He wasn't always *that* bad. He would raise his voice and shout, but he wasn't always physical." He pauses. "I have a few good memories with him. But I don't let myself think of them anymore. He deserves to be an evil man in my mind."

"I understand that," I tell him, feeling my heart ache for the pain he went through as a child.

He reaches up and pulls a book down from the shelf above him. *One Hundred and One Ways to Please Your Partner.*

Lowering the book, he raises an eyebrow at me, grinning. "I don't need to read a book to know how to please you."

"Oh, really? You're an awfully confident man," I tease him.

He sets the book down beside him. "I can show you one hundred and one ways I can make you come."

I wait for him to laugh, but he doesn't. He looks at me with a darkening stare.

Gulping, I ask, "What's one you haven't already done?"

Cam chuckles. "Little Dove, I could spend the rest of my life fucking you, and I would still find new things to try. There isn't a limit if you're imaginative enough."

"What would you do right now?" I ask softly.

Cam licks his lips and rises to his knees, saying, "I'll show you. Take your pants off."

Giggling, I ask, "What? Cam, we can't. There are cameras in here. No way am I making a sex tape with you for Susan to find one day."

"None point into this section. I already looked. Stop arguing and take your pants off, Little Dove," Cam orders.

I stand up, my cheeks flushing, and I unbutton my jeans as my stomach flutters. Pushing them to my ankles, I kick them off.

"Now, your sweatshirt," Cam says and runs his tongue across his bottom lip.

I take off my hoodie and shirt, leaving me naked, aside from my lacy bra and panties.

"Happy now?" I ask him sarcastically.

"Very," he groans. "Turn around."

Rolling my eyes, I turn around and face the bookshelf, waiting for his next move.

Warm breath sweeps across my bare ass, and I jump.

"Relax, baby," Cam whispers and presses his nose between my legs. "Fuck, you smell so good."

Grabbing my ankle, he lifts it up and places it a few shelves up from the ground, almost exposing me completely to him, sheer lace being the only barrier.

His rough thumb swipes my already-wet panties before pulling them to the side.

He doesn't hesitate and latches on to me, his tongue plunging inside. His fingers circle my clit, and then a finger slides in, quickly joined by a second.

"Ahh, fuck, baby," I moan, my hips bucking from the sensation.

Oh my God, I can't believe we are doing this inside of the library right now.

He pulls away from me, but I don't spin around. Instead, I rest my forehead against the books in front of me and try to calm my panting breaths.

"Do you think this is in that book?" Cam asks, standing at his full height behind me.

His cock slaps against my already-oversensitive center. I jump, and he does it again.

Oh my God, I need to feel him inside of me right now.

"No, probably not," I answer him, pushing my ass out, opening myself more for him.

He quickly puts on a condom and I get butterflies at what is to come. *Literally.*

He grabs my panties, and before I realize what he is doing, I hear the rip.

"You didn't need these anyway, right?"

"Cam!" I scold him and try to turn around, but his tip pushing into my entrance stops me in my tracks. "Fuck."

Will my body ever be used to taking him?

Thankfully, he unhooks my bra instead of shredding it, like he did with my thong.

"Do you think fucking a tight pussy against bookshelves is in that book?" He bends down and kisses the top of my head. "We should make a book of our own. *The Endless Ways Cam Can Make Morgan Come.* What do you think?"

He pushes into me more, and I moan, saying, "It sounds a little lengthy."

"That sounds fitting then." He chuckles and reaches down, cupping my breast. "Fuck, you feel so good, wrapped around my cock," Cam growls.

His control and patience snap, and he thrusts, sinking into me completely.

I cry out as he continues to thrust into me repeatedly, "Fuck!"

His hand shifts from my breast to my throat, but he doesn't push down. He lifts my head up and leans it against his chest so I'm staring up at him.

"Tell me something that is more beautiful than this," he says, rolling his hips and changing his rhythm, sending my eyes to the back of my head.

"Open your eyes, Little Dove. I want you looking at me when I make you come," he demands.

Opening my eyes, I look up at him, feeling my core clench as my body starts to tingle.

He smirks, knowing that I'm about to come.

"My pretty Little Dove," he hums.

My orgasm slams into me, but I keep my eyes locked on his as I cry out, "Cam! Fuck, Cam!"

He pumps into me furiously, faster and faster, until he goes still, twitching inside of me. "Perfection, baby. You are absolute perfection."

After we clean ourselves up and get dressed, I sit between his legs with his arms around me.

His raven tattoo catches my eye, and I let curiosity get the best of me. "Does your tattoo have a meaning?"

He lifts his arm up, showing it off. "When I got this tattoo, I was in a very dark place. I needed something to remind me to push forward. Ravens are often thought to be an omen of death, and I thought, in a way, that could be beautiful. Not in the sense that death is coming and you don't have a choice to escape it. But as a warning to either lie down and take it or fight to live. I figured my raven had been through a lot. It would have war wounds to show the times that I fought to live when death could have easily taken me. So, I thought this would be perfect—a one-eyed raven with missing feathers, emerging through the darkness."

I wipe my wet eyes and whisper to the strongest man I know, "I love you."

MORGAN

"Trey—"

He caught me by the throat and smacked my head against the wall.

"You let that man stare at you. Did you like it? Did you like him looking at you?" he snapped and squeezed tighter around my throat.

Excruciating pain crushed my windpipe.

I shook my head as much as I possibly could in his tight grasp. I hadn't let that guy look. I'd tried to stare him down and make him look away.

My body felt lighter, and stars appeared in my vision as he loosened his grasp slightly. I gasped for air, choking on my own spit. He tightened again and got in my face.

"Do it one more time, Honeybee. I dare you." Trey spit in my face before releasing me and storming out of the house, slamming the door behind him.

I dropped to the ground. The only support was the wall at my back. I grabbed my phone and called the only person who could help me.

She had suspected the truth of Trey's true nature when I ran into her a time or two and had the same excuse for new injuries. She told me of her ex, who had shared many of Trey's traits. I never fully admitted what Trey had or hadn't done. But she offered her name and number anyway and told me I should call her if I ever needed to leave without a trace. I'd just hoped I never had to make that call.

"I need"—I gasped—"your help. If the offer still stands." My voice was shaky.

"Well, my dear, you called at the perfect time. Meet me in an hour. I'll handle everything else," she told me.

"Wh-what is the plan?" I continued to huff and puff to catch my breath.

"It's better if you don't know the details. Just trust me and be at my building within the hour. Bring whatever you want to take with you. It will be the last time you are there."

The phone clicked off, and after a moment, I hustled, gathering some clothes, but nothing Trey would notice missing. I also grabbed a couple of snacks and the wad of cash that I kept hidden in case I ever needed it. I threw everything into a bag that I doubted Trey even knew existed.

With my hood up, I made my way to Abbott Funeral Home, sticking to the shadows of the streets. When I arrived, Nicole Abbott, owner of Abbott Funeral Home, ushered me inside and into the garage.

"Here are the keys to a car no one knows exists. It's older than shit, and it guzzles gas, but it will get you wherever you go. Here's a thousand dollars, some clothes I had, and some food for the road. Get rid of the car when you get there. Sell it, burn it—I don't care," she said, handing me bags full of food and a wallet with cash.

Tears streamed down my face as I took the bags from her.

Maybe I shouldn't do this. Maybe I should go back. What about my parents? What will they think?

Nicole studied my crying eyes before saying, "I have two options for you."

"And what are they?" I whispered.

She opened the SUV, took the bags from me, and threw them into the car before turning to look at me with worried eyes. "You run and don't say anything. Everyone will think you ran away, and no one will ever have a definitive answer."

"And option two?" I whispered.

She held the driver's door open and continued, "We fake your death."

"What? H-how?"

"I just need your answer," she demanded.

If I ran, he'd never stop looking for me. He would use my family to get to me. Either way, as a cop, he had resources that would make it easy for him.

But if I faked my death, that'd be it. I'd just be gone to anyone in my life. I'd force them to mourn and feel my death. Doing that to my parents? I didn't know if I could be responsible for that pain.

But what about the pain Trey would inflict on them if I didn't? He would think they knew something, that they had helped me get away. He could cover up their deaths, and everyone would pay as much attention to it as they did the abuse he'd inflicted on me.

The answer was easy really. There was only one option that would end Trey's grasp on me.

"Fake my death," I declared.

Nicole nodded and held her hand out. "Give me your jewelry, your shirt, and a chunk of your hair."

I had a sweatshirt over a tank top. I quickly removed the hoodie and handed it to her along with my necklace, earrings, and rings. Sliding the wedding band and engagement ring off of my finger felt like shackles being removed. Like the collar he had around my neck was gone. I wrapped my finger around a chunk of my hair on the back of my neck and yanked hard. I yelped at the sharp sting and handed the hair over to Nicole.

"What are you going to do?" I asked her. "You won't have my body."

"I have everything I need. I don't want you to know anything else. The less you know, the better. As far as anyone will know, you died tonight. Make a new name, a new identity. Find a place to start over. But you need to go."

"Okay, okay." I got in the driver's seat and started the car.

I didn't get to say good-bye to my parents. I racked my brain for the last thing we had spoken about, and when the memory came, my stomach twisted. They had told me how much they loved Trey and how they couldn't wait for us to have kids.

They wouldn't know the monster he was. I couldn't tell them. I couldn't say anything to them ever again. The weight on my chest threatened to suffocate me.

Before I could close the door, Nicole said, "Hold on." She ran away into another room and came back, holding a red wig and sunglasses. "Until you are far gone, wear these."

She threw her arms around my shoulders in the car, squeezing me gently, and whispered, "Be careful."

I nodded as tears ran down my cheeks. "I will. Thank you. Thank you so much."

Her eyes were watering when she pulled away. "I'm glad you called me. Don't thank me. Just take care of yourself. And have a good and quiet life, Morgan Dove."

She closed my door, and I slipped the wig and sunglasses on as she opened the garage door.

Pulling away, I was overcome with an abundance of feelings. Sadness for everything I was leaving behind. Peace for being rid of Trey. And hope for what was to come.

I needed a new name.

Glancing at the bags next to me, I saw red silk sticking out of the top. No, not silk. It was satin.

The name came to me, flashing in my mind. A name chosen because of the brave woman who had saved me.

Nikki Satinn.

Coldness creeps into my awareness as I begin to wake up. The warmth I was cuddling with is now gone.

"Shh, shh. Go back to sleep. I'm just going to go to the bathroom. Everything's okay," Cam whispers to me as I begin to sit up.

"O-okay," I say, my voice choppy from the dryness in my mouth.

I need water.

Cam walks down the hallway toward the restroom, and I reach over and grab my water, taking desperate sips.

"Ahh," I say, setting the bottle back down and grabbing my phone to check the time—11:33 a.m.

Cam is a bad influence on my sleep schedule.

Getting up, I fold our blankets, slip my shoes on, and grab two granola bars from my bag. I walk over to the table and take a seat to wait for Cam to get back.

But by the time I finish my granola bar, he's still not back.

I shoot him a quick text.

> Me: *Did you get lost?*

My heart starts to race as panic settles in. But then I hear his footsteps down the hallway and take a deep breath.

I text Chloe to give her an update.

> Me: *Good morning. I just woke up. How'd you sleep?*

When I set my phone down, my ears prick up at something familiar. But I can't quite place it. I freeze and listen.

All I hear is Cam walking down the hallway. Cool chills brush up my back. I don't know why I would have this reaction.

Taking a deep breath, I realize the reason why my body is responding this way to Cam's footsteps. Because they aren't Cam's at all.

"Hello, Honeybee," Trey hums, turning the corner with a pistol in his hand.

If I wasn't sitting at a table, I would have dropped to the ground at the sight of him after all this time.

My entire body quivers at the sound of his voice. I've practiced this a thousand times in my head. *React. Don't hesitate.* Yet, as his beady eyes stare at me, I can't move, and I can't breathe. It's like his hands are still wrapped around my throat.

As hard as I tried to prepare myself for a moment like this, I have failed. I didn't hop into action and make the first strike. I didn't protect anyone. I'm a coward.

"Did you miss me?" Trey asks as he takes another step toward me.

He looks different, thinner but more muscular. *Stronger.* His face has aged, lines streaking his forehead and the corners of his eyes.

But he's still exactly who I remember him being. The way he carries himself and speaks, like his words are the most important ones ever to be heard.

I've let him belittle me too many times in my life, convince me that I am less than. But I am not the same woman he hit and abused. I am confident in who I am and in who I love.

I love Chloe for everything she has given me when I have never asked. She has cared for me in ways I can never repay. She is my best friend in the whole world. For her, I won't cower.

I love Cam for showing me how I'm supposed to be loved. We have shown each other the darkest parts of ourselves, the pieces no one else gets to see. But instead of running from me, he embraced me and chose to love me. For Cam, I won't cower.

I love my parents, who don't even know the sacrifice they had to make for my safety and for their own. I love the childhood and life they gave me. They love me how every parent should love a child. For them, I won't cower.

For myself, I won't cower.

Despite the pain and wounds Trey had caused me, I started anew and healed myself. I found love in baking. I made friends with regular customers, proud of my work. I know that what Trey did to me was never okay, no matter how much I let him convince me of it back then.

I am Morgan Dove, and I will *not* cower.

"No," I snap. "I did not miss you."

Slowly, I stand up from the table and step behind my seat. I need to find a way to get to my bag and get my gun.

He laughs and swings the pistol in his hand like a toy. "Are you *sure*? You might want to be a little nicer to me if you know what's good for you."

"I know what's good for me. You are not it," I say with no inflection in my voice, no emotion.

"Where is Cam?" I ask.

He angrily chuckles. "Don't worry. He's a bit preoccupied."

Anger radiates from me as I demand to know, "What did you do to him?"

He takes another step closer to me. "Did you fuck him, Honeybee? Did you let him touch you?"

Before I can answer, he charges toward me, rounding the table, and jabs the barrel of the gun under my chin.

He drags his nose up my neck, sniffing me. "You smell like a cheap whore. Is this *his*?"

Grabbing the front of Cam's Nighthawks hoodie I'm wearing, he yanks me toward him and kicks my feet out until I'm on my knees in front of him with his gun pointed straight at me. He kneels down in front of me and brushes my hair to the side of my face with the cold barrel.

Ignoring his question, I ask mine again. "What did you do to him?"

He smiles proudly and pretends to shoot the gun, making a pew sound. "I made sure he can't come between us anymore."

I don't know if I should believe him or think he's bluffing. "I didn't hear a shot."

His smile widens when he hears the slight shake in my voice. "Who said I used a gun? I'm very skilled with a blade."

My stomach twists as images of Cam bleeding out fill my sight. *No, no, no. It's not true. This is just another tactic he's using to subdue you. Don't believe it until you see it.*

I focus on the gut feeling that I know he's still alive.

I know Trey has the capability to kill Cam. But he also craves power. He wants Cam to see him take me back. I've played Trey's games long enough to know his favorite moves.

Trey presses the gun into my stomach as his forehead touches mine. "How could you do that to me? Let me think that you were dead? Do you know the pain you caused me? The years of agony I can't get back?" His voice deepens with rage. "After all I did for you? Even now, when I tracked you down, you thank me by wearing his clothes and reeking of his scent?!"

He pulls back and slaps me across the face before gripping my jaw tightly in his grasp. Shaking slightly, he leans down.

His hand cups my breast through the hoodie, and he squeezes. I wish I could physically jump out of my skin.

His lips hover over mine, and I fight it as he squeezes harder and goes to kiss me.

But I'm no match for his strength. So, I let him kiss me. The second his lips touch mine, I thrust my mouth forward and bite his lip as hard as I can, and the metallic taste of blood explodes in my mouth.

"You bitch!" Trey rears back and stands up, backhanding me with his gun.

Warmth pools down my cheek as he grabs a fist of my hair.

"We will talk about this when we get home. I'm done dealing with this tantrum of yours."

He leans down once more, but instead of trying to kiss me, he stares at my hair. "You dyed it."

Gulping, I nod and smile at him. "I like it like this."

His fist pulls my hair back, tearing pieces from my scalp. "I know you did it just to piss me off. We'll dye it right away. This doesn't suit you."

He pulls me by my hair, lifting me to my feet, and walks us over to my bag. With his grip locking me at arm's length, he digs in my bag and finds my gun. He pops the clip out and fires the gun toward the ground in case one was in the chamber. He throws the clip across the room, and it lands between some shelves.

"I knew you would have something. You're not stupid," he says.

He continues to drag me through the library, and I decide to stop fighting. Not because I'm giving up, but because I'm saving my energy. When we get outside, I will suck up to him, play into his needs. And then I'll make a run for it to Susan's. If I can get to her, I can get her gun and end this once and for all.

The entire walk to the front, I check for Cam, for any sight of what happened to him. But I don't see anything, and worst of all, I don't hear anything.

He kicks the door open, and I see two tools sticking out of the lock on the door.

He picked it.

His pickup is parked out front, and memories crash into me as fear takes over. I will die before I get into that truck. I won't let him take me.

"I'm sorry," I cry out as I step into the wet snow, feeling it soak into my tennis shoes.

He yanks my head back, grimacing. "You're sorry?"

Tears stream down my face. "Yes, I'm sorry that I ran. I'm sorry that I lied to you."

Victory twinkles in his eyes. "Continue."

"I love you. You're the only one who protects me and keeps me safe. I have been lost without you." My words are toxic in my mouth.

His grasp loosens and loosens more. He cups my cheek with one hand and pushes the gun against my other cheek, holding my head in place. "I have been waiting for you to say that. I know it's not your fault that you were resisting me in there. That boy brainwashed you. He made you think you hated me."

I nod, and he crashes his lips onto mine, kissing me. My stomach churns at the contact.

And I make my move. Pulling my knee back, I plunge it into his groin as hard as I possibly can. He screams and falls to the ground, cupping himself.

I turn and run without looking back. I take off through the snow.

Turning the corner of the library, I see Susan's house across the frozen lake, and I make a decision before I even allow myself to question it. I'm going across the lake, not around it. I don't have time.

Trey's feet pound behind me, and I dig in harder, no longer having feeling in my toes and up to my ankles.

The ice is slick, but there's enough fallen snow for me to maintain balance as I fly across the pond.

"Come here!" Trey screams behind me.

Without looking back, I continue to race to Susan's house. I'm halfway across the ice. *Almost there.*

Trey tackles me, and we slide across the ice together. He wraps his hand around my throat and squeezes. I fight him, slapping and scratching his hands, arms, face, any part of him that I can reach.

"Why couldn't you just be *good?*" Trey spits at me.

My vision flickers as my ears ring from a gut-wrenching sound. The ice cracks around us, and in a split second, we crash through the ice and are completely enveloped by bone-chilling water.

Our hands clash as we try to grab on to one another, desperate to get out of this dangerously cold water. We

351

thrash, trying to hit each other anyplace we can as the surface seems to drift farther and farther out of reach.

Holding my breath, I force my eyes open in the dark abyss. Trey does the same, and I reach for his throat, but I move slower than anticipated under the water. He catches my hand and tightens his hold on the gun. He lifts it up, and I know what's coming. An odd sense of serenity calms my body—or maybe it's the hypothermia setting in.

Picturing the pieces of happiness in my life, I think of Chloe and her laugh, of my parents and the love they share, and of Cam, who I love so dearly. His perfectly messy brown hair and those stunning blue eyes stole my fucking heart. I'm so lucky to have been loved by him for the short time we had.

Had.

I don't want it to be over. I don't want everything to change to the past tense. I don't want people to say, *She was kind. She was …*

I don't want my life to end by his hand. I strike, and for once in my life, I don't hesitate. As he lifts the gun higher, I reach for it and grab the top of the barrel with my right hand and his wrist with my left.

I pinch his wrist. His grip loosens, and I pull the pistol free.

My tears mix with the water as my air runs out. I turn the gun on Trey as my chest feels like it's going to cave in on itself, and as I meet Trey's now-fearful stare, I fire the gun until it won't fire anymore.

He tries to say something, but nothing leaves his parted lips. I hold his gaze, watching the animation fade from his eyes before he sinks, deeper and deeper below.

My lungs are *burning*. I look up and see a spot in the ice where it looks brighter than the surrounding area, and I swim toward it. My body is completely numb. I can't even feel the cold anymore as I near the ice.

Breaking the surface of the water, I gasp for air and throw my arms onto the snowy ice.

How in the hell am I going to get out of here?

When I brace my weight on my arms, the ice breaks more, plunging me back into the cold.

Shit.

Looking around, I see Susan's house and remember a story she once told me. How she got out of the broken ice when she was younger. Closing my eyes, I calm my mind and my breathing, trying not to panic. And I follow the same steps she did.

Placing my arms on the ice, I fill my lungs and lift my legs up until I'm almost horizontal with the ice. With all of my remaining energy, I kick with my legs in short and fast movements. Propelling myself further onto the ice, I kick harder until my knees are out of the water.

Taking a deep breath, I hold it and carefully roll away toward Susan's until I'm a good ten feet away from the hole. Gently, I rise to my feet and take light steps, carefully making my way toward her house.

My hands and body are shaking so horribly. I didn't even realize it until right now. My steps slow, and my legs quiver as I near the edge of the lake.

Almost there.

But as my foot takes my next step, my knee buckles, and I fall to the solid ice, my eyes fluttering shut. I'm exhausted. I just need to rest for a second before continuing. Then, I can get to her house, and she'll get help.

But when my head touches down on the ice, everything goes black.

25

CAM

My head is pounding as I come to. Touching the back of my head, I wince as my fingers smear something wet. Pulling my hand back, I see blood.

What happen—

Trey.

I need to find Morgan.

Pushing myself up, I slam my eyes shut as blood rushes to my head, and excruciating pain squeezes my skull. That piece of shit must've knocked me out, hit me with something.

Bracing myself on the door outside of the restroom, I shout, "Morgan!"

My ears are ringing, but I shout again, "Morgan!"

No answer.

I race to where our camp was set up, but no one's here.

No. Fuck. Please don't tell me she's gone. That he got her. That I couldn't save her, save someone I love—again.

Flying down the hall, I race to the front doors and see a red pickup parked out front. That must be his. Which means they are still here. The door is ajar, but no one's in sight.

Pushing the door open, I spot the footsteps leading to the truck and the area where she must have fought to not get inside—snow is matted down all over.

"Where are you, Little Dove?" I whisper as my heart pounds against my rib cage.

Little footsteps lead away from the truck. I follow them, taking off as fast as I can. They wrap around the building. When I turn the corner, my chest cracks wide open.

Across a frozen lake, I spot that light-pink hair on the ground.

Little Dove.

I take off running, numb to the cold air, snow falling down on me.

I can't lose her. Fuck, I can't fucking lose her.

My throat tightens, and my breaths quicken as I continue to race across the ice.

Please be okay. Please be okay.

I didn't fall in love to have her ripped from me. I didn't let her in, just to be torn apart. I didn't tell her that I would keep her safe, only to fail her now.

The hole in the ice slows my steps, and I realize it might not be as thick as I thought. My pace remains fast, but my steps are gentle, almost gliding instead of running.

My baby, my Little Dove, is the best thing that has ever come into my life, ever happened to me. I used to think that was an odd phrase, that it sounded off, because people don't happen to someone else. But I just didn't understand it before.

Morgan happened to me. I didn't just meet her and decide to love her, and that was that. No. She slammed into my life and changed absolutely everything. The way I looked at the sport I'd always loved, at the pain of my past, and at how I saw myself. The time I'd spent without her in my life seemed dull in comparison to life with her.

There is no way I can go back to life *without* her.

Closing the distance to her, I gently place my hand on her chest and focus. Holding my breath, I wait to see hers. The second I feel her inhale, I scoop her up and run as fast as I can to the house by the lake. I would go back to the library, but it's too far. She needs to get warm as soon as possible. She is soaking wet and stone cold in my arms.

"Morgan? Baby?" I cry out to her as tears run down my cheeks. "Wake up, baby. Wake up. I've got you."

Racing to the little house, I fly up the porch, brace Morgan's weight on one arm, and pound on the door.

"Help us! Please! Open the door! Please!" I cry out louder and louder. "Hello!"

Someone runs to the door and throws it open.

Susan.

"Oh my Lord, what happened?" Susan shouts as she ushers us inside.

My breaths are choppy and ragged as I try to explain, "We were staying at the library. Her ex showed up. He knocked me out. I came to and found her soaked on the ice. Please help her." My voice cracks. "I can't lose her."

"It's okay. She's still breathing. But we need to warm her up," Susan tells me, helping me lay Morgan on the rug in her living room.

"We need to get these wet clothes off of her. Go to the kitchen and grab the scissors in my knife block," she orders.

Nodding, I rush to the kitchen and find the scissors. I return to her side as fast as possible and hand Susan the scissors as she talks to someone on the phone.

"Hi. A girl fell through the ice on the lake near my house. We need an ambulance right away." Susan gives them her address, and they assure her that help is on the way.

She cuts the bottom of my hoodie all the way to the neck and peels it off of Morgan's delicate frame. She is so lifeless as Susan cuts through her leggings and strips the pieces off of her.

"Grab those blankets," Susan says, pointing to the stack of blankets on the couch.

Reaching over, I grab the blankets and follow what she's doing. Draping them over Morgan, layering them, and covering every inch of her, aside from her face.

"We need to slowly raise her temperature. If we go too fast, it can be deadly."

Deadly.

As she lays the final blanket over her, I rock back onto my ass and wrap my arms around my knees as cries burst from my chest. "Morgan, please don't leave me. Please. I'm sorry. I'm so sorry."

Susan pats my knee. "She would be dead right now if it wasn't for you, Cam. You saved her life. She is alive, she is breathing, and help is on the way."

Clenching my teeth, I groan, and tears continue to stream down my face. Sirens wail in the distance, growing louder by the minute, and I do my best to calm my uneven breathing.

Lying down next to my Little Dove, I kiss her forehead and whisper, "I love you so much. Don't leave me, Little Dove. I wouldn't be able to bear it."

She is so strong and resilient. And funny. And beautiful. And everything I was scared of in life. I was scared to love because love was a constant risk of pain. But I didn't stand a chance when she kissed me. I was already too far gone. Maybe deep down, I loved her even then.

The door opens, and cops and EMTs file in and begin asking a bunch of questions, all of which Susan answers for me. Telling them how Morgan's ex showed up, how he must've fallen through the ice, too, and how he either never got out or ran for it.

They load Morgan onto a gurney and wheel her to the ambulance.

I follow them out, and a cop stops me.

"Sir, we're going to need to speak with you. Can you tell us what happened here?"

Looking down at his worried stare, I say, "Ask me at the hospital or afterward. I'll tell you everything. But my only concern right now is her."

He nods. "We will meet you there."

I hop into the ambulance, the doors are shut, and we pull away to the hospital.

I have felt fear a lot of times in my life. Every time I came home, every time my dad was mad, every time I made a mistake and knew what punishment was coming. When I came home and found my mom. I couldn't save her. I couldn't stop that monster from taking her life. But I could put him away by facing those fears and telling the cops everything he had done. By showing them my scars and fresh wounds and the whips he kept in the house. By being on display at the trial for the jury to see and feel pity for.

Fear has never felt as painful as the thought of losing *her*.

"Can you sit up for me?" the EMT asks, and I oblige. "I'm going to check you over. What happened to your head?"

"I got hit. I don't know what hit me. I was out for a few minutes, I think," I tell him as he shines a light in my eyes. "Can we do this later? Focus on her."

"We can do this now or when we get to the hospital," he states.

"Make it fast," I tell her, grabbing Morgan's hand.

He finishes looking me over and says I might have a concussion, and he gives me the rundown on concussion aftercare. I don't remember a single word. I can't think of anything other than Morgan.

I wish I could give her my warmth and give her the air in my lungs. I wish I could've taken Trey down. I hope he is lying dead in that water. If he's alive and out there somewhere, I will hunt him down.

When we get to the hospital and they rush her inside, and I drag myself away from her and walk to the waiting room.

The cops walk in shortly after I take a seat in the waiting room, coming over to me immediately. They ask my name and my statement of what happened. I tell them everything. How Trey stalked her and broke into the library, knocked me out, clearly tried to kidnap her, and that I don't know what happened after that. That I came to and found her and rushed her to Susan's.

"We found three sets of footprints on the ice, but only two leading to the hole on the ice. With a thermal drone, we detected an abnormality in the water and will do a proper search of the water as soon as possible. What do you know about this ex? Name?" the cop asks.

That's my girl. She did it. She won. Pride bursts across my skin like fireworks of happiness.

He's dead and never coming back.

"I only know his first name. It's Trey. I'm sorry. But her best friend might his last name. Chloe…" *shit, what's her last name?* "Du-"

"Chloe DuPont?" the cops asks, clearly knowing exactly who Chloe is.

"Yeah. I don't know his name. But I know he used to hurt her really bad, but she ended up getting away. She came here and was safe for a while. But he found her again," I tell them as a mix of rage and relief floods me that this is finally over for her.

One of them steps away and makes a phone call out of earshot.

"We will need to get her statement as soon as she wakes up." He hands me his card. "Call us when that happens."

"You got it," I tell him before he walks over to the other cop.

After I pace for what feels like hours, someone comes out and gets me.

"She is stable and awake. And asking for you."

"Can I see her?" I gasp.

"Right this way," she informs me, and I follow her with my heart in my hands, ready to completely hand it over to Morgan.

She leads me down never-ending hallways before stopping at a door and knocking. She pushes it open slightly, and I burst through it.

"Morgan?"

Seeing her awake and sitting up in her bed is the best thing I have ever seen.

"Oh, thank God," I whisper and throw my arms around her.

Tears rush down my face as I rub my hands on her back.

My Little Dove. My Morgan. My fucking everything.

"Are you crying?" she whispers, pulling back enough to see my face.

Nodding, I gently cup her face and press my lips on hers. "I love you."

Her eyes well up with tears. "I love you too."

"Are you okay? Pain? Are they taking good care of you? Do you need any—"

"Shh. I'm okay, Cam. You saved me," she whispers, caressing my jaw with both hands.

Our tears fall between us.

"I should've been there. I should've seen him coming."

Her thumbs stroke my cheeks. "Trey is gone, and I am safe and alive. I would be dead right now if it wasn't for you. Don't you understand that? *You* saved my life."

Nodding, I stare into her eyes—those perfect blue eyes. Ones I want to look into forever.

Sitting down in the chair next to her, I take her hand in mine. "The cops want to talk to you whenever you're up for it."

The door swings open, and we expect a nurse or doctor. But an angry Chloe Dupont bursts through the door.

Her anger fades immediately when she spots Morgan. "Oh my God. Are you okay?"

She rushes to the other side of the bed and leans over her, lightly squeezing her in a hug.

"I'm okay. Better now that Trey's gone," Morgan says, smiling.

"What happened?" Chloe asks.

My brave, strong girl takes a deep breath. "We were at the library, and Cam went to the bathroom, so I got up and went to sit at the table next to us to wait for him. But when it seemed like he'd been gone for too long, I kind of started freaking out. But then I heard his footsteps coming back and relaxed." She takes a deep, shaky breath. "But it wasn't Cam. It was Trey."

"I'm so sorry." Chloe takes Morgan's other hand in hers.

I caress her still-cold fingers in mine as she continues, "H-he dragged me outside to his pickup. When I saw that truck again, it made me sick. I couldn't get inside it." Her eyes well up with tears. "I kicked him as hard as I could in his balls, and I ran as fast as my legs would take me to Susan's house. But he caught up to me when we were on the lake, and when he tackled me, we fell through the ice. It was so cold. I felt like we were down there forever. We fought under the water, and I somehow got the gun from him. And I shot him. And I didn't stop shooting until it stopped firing."

She looks at me with fear, and I don't know what she's scared of right now. If it's of judgment from me, she won't find any here.

Nodding at her, I show her my support with my smile and kiss her hand.

"When he went still, I waited to see if he would move. I swear I saw the moment when he died. In his eyes, I mean."

I wish she hadn't had to see that. The way her eyes are glazed over right now, I know she's back there, watching it all over again.

"I was able to get out of the water and onto the ice, but when I was walking back, I must've passed out. Next thing I knew, I was here," she says.

"I'm so proud of you," I whisper to her.

Reaching out, I wipe her tears away from her cheeks.

"Thank you," she whispers back with sad eyes.

"It's over now, thank God. Cam messaged me, and I rushed over here," Chloe says, grabbing her attention. "I guess I won't scold you for having me locked up by my own staff." She smirks.

Morgan grimaces. "I'm sorry about that. But I knew your crazy ass would try to be a hero. If I could have, I would have had your team take this one too," she says, looking at me.

I laugh. "They could have tried. Nothing was keeping me from you."

Morgan stares at me with adoration and asks, "Do you want to let the cops know I'm awake? I want to get that over with already."

"Are you sure you don't want to rest? They can wait, baby," I tell her.

She needs to take care of herself and relax. But I know she won't fully breathe until all of this is done and gone.

"Call them, please," she says as a knock sounds at the door.

A nurse enters and says, "There are some police here who want to speak with you. But I can make them come back if you're not up for it right now."

Well, with that response time, they must have a mind reader on the force.

"It's fine. Let them in," Morgan tells the nurse.

She nods and leaves the room, appearing shortly after with … definitely not cops, but agents of the

Federal Bureau of Investigation—clear from the jackets they are both wearing.

"Morgan Dove?" the male agent asks, walking into the room.

"Yes?"

"My name is John. May we ask you a few questions about what happened today?"

"Yeah," she answers. "Can I ask why you're here and not the police?"

The female agent introduces herself. "Hi, Morgan. My name is Elle. We were brought in because the man who attacked you crossed state lines to do so. The second he did that, it became a federal case."

"That makes sense," Morgan mumbles.

"How did you know the man who attacked you tonight?" John asks her.

Morgan tells them about the past she had with Trey. She continues to answer nonstop questions from the agents, who take down every detail.

When they finish questioning Morgan, they do the same to me. I explain that Trey hit me in the head, and when I woke up, I went looking for Morgan and found her on the ice.

They thank us for our time and say that if we remember anything, we should give them a call, and they will reach out if they need anything else.

Deciding to give Chloe and Morgan a few minutes of their own, I offer to grab them dinner. I also need to let the team know I might be gone for a few more days.

After getting Morgan's request for KFC, I give Kos a call to fill him in on why I haven't responded to his texts or calls the last few hours.

"Hey, man. What's going on?" Kos asks, sounding concerned.

"Mor—Nikki was attacked by her ex-boyfriend. The cops are here; the Feds are here. It's a long story. But she's okay. I'm okay. I just might be gone a few more days," I tell him.

"Holy shit, Cam. That's insane. Did they catch the guy at least?" Kos asks, and I hear Brett in the background, telling him to put the phone on speaker.

"Well, kind of. He's dead now. They have to fish his body out of a lake."

"Oh my God, you killed him? Do you need me to send a lawyer? Money?" Kos asks, jumping into dad mode.

I laugh. "No. The piece of shit came up behind me and hit me in the back of the head. Long story short, Nikki took off from him, but he caught her, and they fell into the frozen pond. She managed to shoot him and get out. That's when I found her, passed out on the ice. She was so cold. I don't know how she's alive. She felt … dead." My voice cracks on the last word.

368

I almost lost her. In a matter of minutes, she could have never woken up. Terror racks my body at the thought.

"I'm so sorry, man. She's okay now though?" Brett asks.

"Yeah. She's awake. I went and grabbed food for them, and her best friend is there with her now," I tell them, my voice returning to normal.

"Take as much time as you need. I'll let Coach know. But you might want to shoot him a text or something too," Kos says.

"I just need to make sure she stays awake and alert. I wish I could bring her back with me," I say, feeling my chest tighten at the thought of leaving her here.

"Do it!" Brett shouts excitedly.

Sighing, I say, "She's got her business here. It's not that easy."

"You guys will figure it out," Kos says, sounding so sure.

"Yeah," I say, tucking the bag in my coat and walking into the hospital. "I'm just getting back. I'll update you in a bit."

"All right, man. Tell her hi for us," Kos says, and Brett says, "Bye, Costy."

Hanging up, I walk back to her room, and when I walk in, her face lights up.

Kos was right. I could bring her back with me. But that's a conversation we need to have later. Although I'm exhausted and in emotional overdrive, I've never thought so clearly about her. I love Morgan with everything I have, and I'm never letting her go.

26

MORGAN

"Are you sure you're ready?" Cam asks me again as my thumb hovers over my mom's phone number.

With a trembling breath, I answer, "Yes, I'm sure."

I never thought this day would come. I hope they aren't mad at what I had to do, that I lied to them and made them think I was dead. But I think, more than anything, they'll be happy that I'm actually alive.

When I press the Call button, my stomach flutters as the most intense nerves quiver through my body.

Oh my God, what if I'm not ready?

When I look at Cam, my heart feels like it's going to beat right out of my chest.

You got this, he mouths to me.

The second ring sounds ten times louder than the last. I wipe my sweaty hand on my blanket.

He's right. I've got this.

"Hello?" my mom's voice sings through my phone.

Breathtaking sobs tear through me. Trying to catch my breath, I hear her gasp.

"Baby? *Morgan*, is that you?" Her voice is barely a whisper.

Blowing out a few short breaths, I whisper, "Mom, it's me. Please don't be mad."

I can picture her face right now—her eyes shut with a downturned smile.

She cries out, "How is this possible? Is it really you?"

"Yeah. I'm so sorry. I'll explain everything, I promise," I say as guilt slices through me at the pain in her voice.

"Dave! Get in here! It's Morgan." She pauses. "Yes, our Morgan," I hear her say away from the phone.

"Morgan?" my dad asks with anguish.

The sound of my dad's voice absolutely wrecks me.

"Dad?"

Tears roll down my neck, soaking the front of my gown. My dad is the best dad in the whole wide world. Hearing the pure panic in his voice is painful.

"Sweetie? What's going on?" he begs. "Where are you?"

Gulping, I take a deep breath. "I'm in Minnesota. St. Luke's Hospital, to be exact."

"We're coming to you right now, baby," my dad declares with the ferocity I remember in him.

He is a passionate man in everything in life. He loves my mom in a way I always hoped to find. He can't help but put his all into whatever he does. When he says he's coming, he will be here as fast as humanly possible. By flight, train, car, or walking, he will get here.

"Okay," I whisper. "I can't wait to see you both."

"We need to call Trey and let him know you're alive!" my mom shouts, and I interrupt whatever she's about to say.

"You won't be able to reach him. He's dead. And he's the reason you thought I was. I promise I'll explain what happened when you get here," I say, knowing this is another shock on top of them finding out I'm even alive.

"You got it. We found a flight that leaves in an hour and a half. We'll be with you as soon as we can. Should we meet you at the hospital?" my mom asks.

"I get out this afternoon. I'll send you my address. Meet me there. I love you guys so much. I'm sorry."

My mom hugs me with her words. "We know you well enough to know that you had no choice, baby. Take a deep breath. You explain when you're ready. I love you, sweet girl."

"I love you," my dad snivels.

"I love you too, Dad," I whisper before hanging the phone up.

Setting the phone down, I look at Cam through blurry eyes. "They're coming here."

He smiles. "That's good, right? That's what you wanted?"

Nodding, I say, "Yeah."

He looks quizzically at me. "Why do you seem so sad?"

Biting my bottom lip in an attempt to stop the continuing flow of tears and cries, I mumble, "You should have heard them. The pain in their voices. I did that to them."

He grabs my face and makes me look at him. "No, you didn't. You didn't flee without absolute necessity. You had no choice. They will understand that. I guarantee it." He leans down and kisses my forehead. "Scoot forward."

I do, and he hops on the bed behind me, placing his legs on either side of me. He pulls me back against him and wraps his arms around me.

"You are the strongest person I have ever met, Morgan," he says in my ear before kissing it. "I'll be with you the whole time. Unless you order me away, I'm not leaving your side. I've got you, Little Dove, for now and always."

Pacing in the front area of the shop, I shove my hands into my hoodie pocket, anxiously waiting for my parents to arrive.

Chloe and Cam are sitting at a table, staring at me. I don't think they've stopped staring since the accident. Like they're afraid if they look away, I'll vanish. But I'm not going anywhere.

I'm done running. I'm done hiding.

"Don't panic," Chloe says, and my eyes fly to the windows.

A white car pulls up in front of the shop, parking on the street. The front doors are thrown open from the inside, and I swear time actually slows down.

It's a crazy phenomenon. That your brain can live so intensely in a moment, taking in every *single* detail, not a fleck going unnoticed. Like the look in my parents' eyes when they see it's really me through the glass, the relief that simultaneously passes between them. The feel of goose bumps breaking over my skin as the shop door is opened and a gust of cold air sweeps over me. The sound of their feet stomping across the tiles as they rush toward me. The way I can see the tears streaming down their already-reddened faces, the way I can feel mine mirroring theirs.

The way my mom's voice feels like a blanket wrapping around my shoulders as she cries out, "My baby!"

They barrel into me, completely encasing me in their arms. Their scent invades my nose, and I feel my lungs expand further than they have in years.

They smell like *home.*

With our heads and bodies pressed into each other, we hold on for dear life. I don't feel like a twenty-two-year-old. I feel like a child in her parents' arms.

We stand there for minutes, holding each other and crying as one before we finally pull apart and take a step back.

"You're alive," my mom whispers as she holds my head, studying my face. "What happened here?"

She's looking at the bruises and gashes on my cheeks from Trey.

"Trey happened," I say. "Why don't you guys have a seat?"

They sit down at the same table as Chloe and Cam. I sit between them and take Cam's hand in mine for support.

"This is Chloe. She's my best friend, and she's helped me in more ways than I can explain. She gave me a place to live, a means for income. She took me in when I had nowhere to go," I say. I turn to her watery gaze and smile.

"This is Cam. He's my boyfriend, and he saved my life," I tell them, nervous of the probably overwhelming information.

But we're just getting started, so they'd better buckle in.

He stretches his hand out to my dad. "Cam Costello. Nice to meet you, sir."

A light bulb goes off behind my dad's eyes as he shakes his hand. "Costello? What do you do for a living, Cam?"

Cam smiles at my dad's telling gaze. "I play hockey for the New York Nighthawks."

My dad grins, and I can't help but smile with him. He's aged since I last saw him. His hair is mostly gray, and his wrinkles don't fade after a smile quite like they used to.

"We will have to chat about that later." My dad winks at Cam.

They are going to be the best of friends—I just know it.

Taking a deep breath, I make myself focus on telling them the truth about what happened. About my story. I keep to the details they need to know, the ones that will make them understand. But I keep the worst ones to myself. They have been through enough. I'm not letting what Trey did to me hurt them too.

I tell them about the incident with the coffee table. I would have left that one out, but they will see the scars eventually. I tell them of Nicole from the funeral home, who got me out of town and helped me fake my death. I tell them that Trey found us at the library, attacked Cam, stalked me, and tried to kill me when I wouldn't go with him. I don't know how Trey found me at the library. But he knew I used to like to read, so I'm guessing he took a chance. Honestly, now that it's over, I don't really care. That mystery can die with him.

My parents are devastated that they didn't see it, that they didn't help. But I assure them that no part of what happened was their fault. With each word I say, I feel the walls around myself lift away. By the time I finish, I finally feel *free*.

My parents console me as best as they can and offer their apologies for not seeing Trey's true nature. I of course, assure them that none of this was their fault.

I yawn and my mom smiles at me with such love and pride.

"Can we come over in the morning?" my mom asks me.

"Of course. I'll call you as soon as I wake up," I assure her.

I can't imagine what they feel right now, leaving to go to their hotel.

"I promise I will be here tomorrow. I'm not going anywhere, not anymore," I tell them both before pulling them into a hug. "I love you."

They tell me they love me, too, and walk outside, leaving Cam, Chloe, and me inside the shop.

"I'm going to head out too. I'll come over in the morning, just text me when, okay?" She grabs me and hugs me tightly.

"I will." I hug her back, and she leaves, locking the door behind her.

Cam walks behind me and bends down. He wraps his arms around my shoulders. "Are you ready for bed?"

In the last few days, I have felt the highest highs and lowest lows. I have hugged my parents—something I thought was never going to happen again.

I am free. To live. To love. To do whatever I please.

And right now, I am exhausted to the core and can't wait to go to sleep. But there is one thing I want to do first.

I nod, and Cam releases my shoulders, only to grab on to my hand and slide his fingers in mine. He leads me to my room in a calm and liberating silence.

Opening my door, I spin around and grab his face. Gently pulling his lips to mine, I kiss him softly. I do it again and again. Every kiss becomes rougher and needier. Our hands dance over each other bodies, eager to touch every inch.

I trust Cam fearlessly, but now, I can love him fearlessly too. There is no danger or threat lurking in the shadows. There's nothing stopping me or holding me back anymore.

The gentleness and hesitation we had before fades as a primal desire for each other takes over completely. It thrums between us.

He kicks the door shut and slides his tongue into my mouth while grabbing the bottom of my sweatshirt.

He strips it off of me. My bra, pants, and panties quickly follow. When I'm completely naked, he groans as he walks me backward to the bed and lightly pushes me onto it.

When I sit down, my hands grip his pants, pulling them down as fast as possible.

I need to feel him. I need to feel his need for me.

He lifts his shirt up as I slip his boxers past his already-massive erection.

Wasting no time, I take him in my mouth—as much as I can fit. I suck and lick him as his moans make my core pulse.

Without a word, he pulls his dick out of my mouth and adjusts me on the bed with my back against the comforter and my head hanging slightly off of the end.

Cupping his balls and grabbing his shaft, I shove it into my upside-down mouth, feeling it slide down my throat.

"Keep going. Don't stop," he orders and leans over me.

His rough hands grab my inner thighs and push my legs apart as wide as they will go. "Such a pretty pussy."

He slides a finger through my wetness and pumps slowly. He adds a second finger, and I gasp as his tongue flicks across my clit.

I stop sucking him and moan, "Cam."

He freezes with his fingers still in me. "Ah, ah, ah. If you stop, I stop, baby."

I take his rock-hard dick back down my throat, and he continues to finger- and tongue-fuck me until I come, moaning against his dick.

He pulls out of my mouth and lifts my shoulders. As I turn around to face him, he sucks his fingers clean, smiling at me.

"You are so *delicious*, Little Dove," he groans. "Now, get on all fours for me."

Wiping the drool from my chin, I do what he said and get on my hands and knees with my ass facing him.

He walks away for a second and returns. His tongue runs up my center and continues to glide higher, lapping against a hole he will never enter. But I'm turned on even more from the tingles that one pass of his tongue gave me.

He tosses a now-empty condom wrapper onto the bed next to me and says, "Please get on birth control soon. I need to fuck you without a barrier between us. I need to feel every pulse your perfect pussy makes."

Nodding, I agree. But right now, I'm sure I'd agree to almost anything he asks of me.

He pushes into me, his fat tip stretching my entrance. "*Fuck.*"

He runs his fingers down my spine, zigzagging across every bump.

His cock twitches, which is the only warning I get before he fills me to the brim, slamming into me.

"Ahh!" I gasp from the pleasure and slight pinch of pain.

He pulls out and reenters slowly. "Is that okay?"

Fuck yes, dear God.

"Yes," I whimper.

He continues to fuck me slowly. Circling my hips, I push back against him and hear him groan.

"You want it faster than this?" he asks deeply.

Pushing my hips back into him again, I nod. "Fuck yes, please," I whine.

His fingers trail across my back, circling lower to my ass. Lightly, he slaps my cheek, and I arch my back, taking his dick deeper inside of me.

Fuck, that felt so good.

"Put your hands and arms straight out in front of you on the bed," he demands.

Stretching forward, I lie down on the bed, my head lying on its side with my arms in front of me. He sinks even deeper.

His callous fingers trail up my sides, shooting tingles across my body.

He grabs my hips, pulls out, and thrusts mercilessly into me. "Yes, baby. Ugh, fuck." He pounds into me harder and harder. "I wish you could see your pussy taking me so well."

His hips push and pull, and I meet his thrusts in a perfect rhythm.

His hand slaps the top of my ass, and as the contact makes my core pulse, I shout, "Fuck!"

He slaps my other cheek and switches back and forth, and I feel myself getting ready to come. Who knew a little pain could feel so good?

"There you go, baby. You've still got to come again for me tonight," he groans.

What?

His thumb finds my clit and sends me completely over the edge. My back bows as I come with his dick's continued relentlessness.

"You're not allowed to come until I do this time," he says. "Tighten your core and focus. You can do it. I know you can."

I laugh, and he slams into me repeatedly, over and over, somehow faster and harder than before.

"*What the fuck?*" I mumble, not meaning to say it out loud.

He slows down and kisses my shoulder blade, saying, "What, you thought *that* was all I could give you? Little Dove, I am just getting started with you."

He thrusts back into me, finding that faster pace again. I'm not going to last another thirty seconds like this.

"Fuck, Cam," I whine into the mattress. "I'm going to—"

"Wait for me. Tighten your core," he instructs, and I listen, tensing my ab muscles.

It doesn't ease the overwhelming sensations, but it slows down the inevitable orgasm.

He pulls out, flips me over, and picks me up, wrapping my legs around his waist. He slides back into me and bounces me against his cock, his hands finding my hips as my arms wrap around his neck and shoulders.

I hold on tight as he plunges into me over and over, slamming my hips down onto his.

"Fuck, baby, open your eyes," he demands.

I didn't even realize that they had drifted shut. Opening them, I clench around his dick, feeling hopeless in trying not to finish.

The look of unadulterated desire and love shining in his eyes sends me right to the edge, and with his breathy plea, "Come on my cock again, Little Dove," I explode with body-shaking pleasure.

"Fuck, fuck, fuck!" Cam growls as he slams my hips down once more.

I am the luckiest girl in the world for many reasons. But being fucked by Cam has got to be on top of that list.

MORGAN
SIX MONTHS LATER

"Have a good day, Morgan!" my boss shouts to me as I smile and wave and walk out.

I thought working at Starbucks would at least fill the coffee-shop void of moving to New York. But I was so wrong. It's mass chaos, always.

After the case with Trey was put to rest, Chloe and I decided we needed a change. She confessed that she had only stayed in Minnesota for me and was happy to move anywhere else. It wasn't hard for me to pick a place, considering where a certain hockey player lives.

It was also a plus for Chloe because her dad's business partner also lives in New York. Now, they can see each other more often. They are still sneaking around and haven't told her dad yet, which is bound to blow up in their faces if he finds out.

I let Chloe take charge of finding a place. After all, it was her account that would be primarily funding the new place. And I like to think I won't be living there forever.

We sold the shop, and I gave Chloe every penny. I built a little savings nest egg from running the shop, and that will carry me for the time being.

We moved into this beautiful four-bedroom and three-bathroom home. I insisted it was way too large, but Chloe, the businesswoman, said that she'd turn it into a rental when we eventually moved out.

I have spent one night there in the five months we've been here. I would stay there more, but Cam holds me hostage every night at his place. I don't really have a choice in the matter, although I don't put up much of a fight.

It's been amazing, practically living with Cam.

After moving here, I didn't miss a game. I'd sit ice-side, cheering him on at every game. But now that they are in the off-season, there are no games for me to go to, although I have stopped in for a practice or two.

I usually sit with Jack and Laura. Watching Alec skate over to Jack whenever he can melts my heart. It makes me want a little Costello to bring to the games.

Alec and Laura's wedding is tomorrow, and I just know it is going to make me cry. The love they have for one another is so pure, and you can *see* what they mean to each other. I hope people think the same thing when they look at Cam and me.

My heart flutters when I see Cam leaning against his car with red roses in his hand.

"Good afternoon, beautiful. How was work?" he asks, handing me the flowers.

I happily take them. "As fun as it always is. How was practice?"

"Eh. Come on. I've got a surprise for you," he says, tapping his fingers on the hood of his car.

He opens my door for me, and I get in, swooning at the sweetheart Cam is. I'm going to marry that man.

He gets in and pulls off to wherever our destination is.

"Now, don't freak out. I know it's kind of a lot. But I also know how much you miss Nikki's Coffee back in Minnesota," he says, pointing out the window as we pull to a stop at the curb.

"What do you mea—"

Oh my God.

"You deserve it. You deserve all of it. I'll spend the rest of my life proving that to you," he says before kissing my cheek. "Welcome to Little Dove, your new coffee shop."

"Cam," I whimper. "It's beautiful. I don't know what to say. *Thank you* doesn't feel like enough."

My eyes well up with tears as I stare at the circle logo on the brick building. *Little Dove.* It's perfect.

"It's exactly one-point-one mile from the arena," he says proudly.

I'm in shock, frozen in my seat. I want to run into the building and explore it. But I also want to jump into Cam's lap.

I figure I'll start with the latter.

Throwing my arms around Cam's neck, I pull him in for a kiss. "I love you."

He smiles against my lips. "I love you too, baby. Come on. I'll show you around."

I rush outside and follow him like a puppy to the double-door entrance. He unlocks it with a key already on his key ring, and I wonder how long that has been on there. Have I touched it before, not even knowing that it would unlock *this*?

After he opens the mirror glass doors, I step inside and find the place is completely decked out with furniture—rustic tables and chairs, countertops that will become my workstations, and registers.

The Little Dove logo is burned into the backs of the chairs. No detail goes unnoticed. We wander to the counters that are empty and begging to be filled with equipment.

"How long have you been planning this?" I ask him in shock.

He rubs the back of his neck. "Since you said you were moving here."

My head snaps to him. "You've been keeping this a secret for over five months?"

"I wanted to tell you so badly. But this reaction is everything I was working toward. I didn't want to ruin it for myself or for you. You moved here for me. The least I could do was bring your shop to life here."

Hooking my arms around his neck, I pull him down to me. "*I love you* will never feel like enough to describe what you mean to me."

He kisses me, deepening it instantly. His tongue delves into my mouth, tangling with mine as his fingers run between my legs.

Pulling away, I ask him, "Can we come here anytime?"

He nods and kisses me again with more fervor. "Yes. It's ours completely. Why?"

Looking into his eyes, I grab his dick through his sweats. "Because I want you to take me home and fuck me right now."

He picks me up and sets me on the countertop of my new coffee shop, and my body reddens at the thought of what he's doing.

"I can't wait until we get home," he growls and strips my leggings and panties down my legs.

He pulls me off of the counter, spins me around, and leans down until his lips press against my ear. "Bend over the counter, Little Dove," he whispers.

I gulp as a spike of adrenaline soars through my body, and I obey, leaning across the cold countertop.

He groans, "Fucking perfection."

I peek at him as he pushes his pants and boxers to his ankles, and his already-hard cock springs free.

He meets my stare right before sliding two fingers into me. He bites his lip and smirks.

"Already soaked for this cock, aren't you?" he groans. "I should make a habit of fucking you in here. Then, every day, you'll remember me bending you over this counter and fucking you senseless as you hand someone their drink."

His fingers pump in and out of me, and I nod, unable to form a single word because of the sensations pulsing through me.

"What a good fucking girl you are," he praises and slides a third finger in while his other hand finds my clit.

He pumps me and rubs my clit as I feel my core start to tighten. But instead of letting me finish, he stops and pulls his fingers out.

Missing the feeling already, I whimper, "Why'd you stop?"

"Because the only way I want you to come right now is with you wrapped around my cock," he says, pressing his fat tip against my soaked entrance.

That's the only warning I get before he sinks into me completely.

"Ahh! Fuck!" I scream.

He grabs my hips and fucks me relentlessly against the counter of my new shop.

"Such a good fucking girl you are, taking this cock," Cam growls, pounding into me intensely. "I'm going to fill this sweet pussy up."

I become a puddle of pleasure as he continues to rock into me. He smacks my ass, growing harder with each hit. A firework of sparks shoots to my core with each contact.

Incoherently, I moan and whine with each thrust and smack.

He never pushes me without my acceptance first, and he always makes sure I'm comfortable with whatever we are trying.

But sometimes, I like to be caught off guard with him, like a slap on my ass or when he lightly grabs my throat or switches positions without warning.

He moans and pants, pulling out to the tip and slamming back into me. When he picks his pace back up, my legs start quivering as my orgasm nears.

"Fuck, baby, hold on, not yet," Cam orders, and I feel him harden inside of me, about to come.

"I can't hold on any longer. I'm going to—" My words are cut short as an earthquake rocks my body, pleasure bursting across every cell inside of me.

Cam groans and comes inside me, breathing heavily.

He slides out, leaving me feeling full from the cum left behind.

"Fuck, watching my cum drip out of you is a sight I will never get over seeing, Little Dove."

Hearing him talk to me like that is something I will never get used to. Cam loves me, all of me—the great parts, the absolute worst parts, and the parts I haven't even learned yet. He protects me and cherishes me. He assures me when I need to hear it. He loves me, broken and bruised or glowing and healed.

Trey taught me what love wasn't; he taught me what possession was.

Cam helped me find my worth and what I deserve, and he never lets me settle for less.

CAM

"I present to you for the first time, Mr. and Mrs. Kostelecky!" the announcer shouts into the speaker as Kos and Laura—or Mrs. Kos—burst into the ballroom.

"Woo!" I scream along with the rest of the room.

After what feels like forever, I can finally get Morgan on the dance floor for the first time tonight. Pushing my sleeves up, I stand up and stretch my hand out to hers. "Dance with me?"

Her eyes glisten. "Of course, Cam. I would love to dance with you."

She places her hand in mine, and I lead her to the dance floor. Hooking my hands around her waist, I stare down at those stunning blue eyes that still captivate my heart. Her pink hair is pulled up in a braided updo, completely exposing her neck. One that I am having a hard time resisting kissing.

"I have a surprise for you, and I can't keep it to myself anymore. Can I tell you?" she asks me with pleading eyes.

Swaying to the music, I chuckle. I knew something had been up with her these last few days. She's been secretive and sneaky with her phone.

"Tell me, baby," I answer her with a smirk.

She grabs her phone from the inside of my coat pocket. "I hope you like the present. It's for your birthday."

She must find what she's looking for because she pulls the phone to her chest with the biggest smile on her face.

"You can name her," she says, turning the phone around and showing me a picture of a fluffy German shepherd puppy.

"Morgan," I whisper in shock as my love for her pulses in my body. "She's so cute."

"I know. I have videos of her too. We will pick her up next Friday. Happy early birthday, Blue Eyes," she says, leaning up and kissing me.

We sway, and I spin her all the way through a Taylor Swift song until my heart feels like it's about to explode for what I feel for her.

"Come on. I have something to show you," I whisper into her ear and take her hand in mine.

She giggles and follows along, whispering, "Where are we going?"

I drag her out to the hallway and unbutton my sleeve, rolling it up over the wrap on my forearm, above my raven.

"What is that?" she asks quietly.

Smiling, I say, "My new tattoo."

When it's revealed fully, she gasps and covers her mouth.

Meeting Morgan completely changed my life. I hadn't known it, but I was lost before her. She is the happiness in my life and the future I look forward to. I knew I loved her before finding her on the ice. But the earth-shattering fear of potentially losing her reset my soul. I knew then that I didn't want a day without her. I didn't want to go to sleep without her in my arms. I didn't want to love if I wasn't loving her.

She stares at the new black ink on my forearm. Placed above my raven is a one-eyed dove with missing feathers, coming out of dark smoke.

"Do you like it?" I ask her nervously.

Without words, she grabs my face and kisses me deeply. "I love it, and I love you."

Somehow, we escaped the darkness of our own lives and found each other. At different points in our lives, we saw death knocking, but we refused to answer. Every day, we choose to live and choose each other, and I'm going to continue to choose her for the rest of our lives.

Kissing her, I brush my finger against the most recent scar on her cheek and whisper, "I love you too, Little Dove."

ACKNOWLEDGMENTS

There are countless people that helped this book come to life. I can never truly put into words how thankful I am for the support and love that I had while writing this book.

Thank you, reader, from the bottom of my heart for loving the Nighthawks. Your passion for these hockey players means more than you know. Seeing your love for Alec and Laura in Find Me in the Rain melted my heart and I hope you share the same love for Cam and Morgan after reading this book. I can never thank you enough for supporting me and the stories I write. I live my dream every day because of you.

Nicole, thank you for being exactly who you are. Thank you for lifting me up every time I doubt my writing and myself. You keep me sane, and I would truly be lost on this journey without you by my side. Thank you for helping me fine tune my characters and my stories.

Thank you for hyping me up on all of my down days. Thank you for believing in Cam and Morgan's story and for being Cam's biggest fan. You are the absolute best friend in the entire world and I love you so much.

Dante, thank you for putting up with my late-night writing and chaos that comes every time I near the end of a story. And thank you for reading me and knowing me so well. For knowing when I needed to spend countless hours writing and editing, completely lost in my cave. For knowing when I was needing a break and asking to watch a movie with me. You are the most thoughtful man and the best life partner. You inspire me everyday to continue to write great love stories because I get to live the greatest with you. Thank you for supporting me endlessly. I couldn't do this without you, my love.

Mom and Dad, thank you for being the greatest parents in the world. I would not be where I am today without you and your support. You inspire me every single day to keep chasing my dreams. Mom, you are the most resilient person I know, and I am so proud of you. Thank you for always teaching me to fight for what I want in life. Dad, thank you for being so interested and invested in my writing, but please don't read any of my books. I can never fully express the love I have for you both. You are not only my parents, but my best friends. Spending countless weekends at hockey games with you and Dante have become some of my favorite memories. I love you both so much.

My grandparents, thank you for always being there for me in any way I need. You have shown me my entire life what unconditional love means. I cherish every single second we spend together, and it will never be enough. You guys have always supported me and believed in me every step of the way. Thank you for lifting me up and pushing me to pursue my dreams. I love you all.

Billy, Savanna, Tommy, and Lil Millz, thank you for being my cheer team and always hyping me up. You guys never stop encouraging me, and it means the world to me. I love you.

Jovana, thank you never quite feels like enough. But thank you for taking the mess of my writing and turning it into a book. You are the best editor in the world and a dear friend. I am so eternally grateful for you.

Amber, thank you for always checking in on me when I go silent for a while and get lost in my writing. Thank you for always helping with anything and everything I need. You are the sweetest soul.

Murphy Rae, thank you for creating the absolute perfect covers to hold the Nighthawks' stories. Your talent is unmatched.

To my Tree, thank you for being my cheerleader behind the scenes and for supporting me. It means so much to me.

To the wine and snacks that were consumed during the creation of this book, your sacrifice is greatly appreciated.

About the Author

Pru Schuyler is an Amazon best-selling author, known for her Nighthawks hockey romance series.

She lives in North Dakota with her adored furbabies and fiancé. She writes characters and stories that her readers can truly empathize with. At the heart, her books focus on undying love.

When she isn't getting lost in her writing, she is at hockey games, watching really shitty movies that make her laugh, and reading a good book, and spending time with her family.

OTHER BOOKS BY PRU SCHUYLER

THE WICKED TRILOGY

The Wicked Truth
The Wicked Love
The Wicked Ending—Coming Spring 2023

NIGHTHAWKS SERIES
(INTERCONNECTED STAND-ALONES)

Find Me in the Rain
Find Me on the Ice

FIREBORN TRILOGY
(NEW ADULT FANTASY)

Book One—Coming Fall 2023

MRS. CLAUS DUET
(INTERCONNECTED STAND-ALONES)

Stealing Mrs. Claus
Becoming Mrs. Claus—Coming December 2023